JUST WHAT THE DOCTOR ORDERED

Rayna Michaels may be a veterinarian, but she knows a little something about the human heart—especially when it comes to worried pet owners. Law enforcement's bonds with their K9 partners are legendary, and Derek Hansen is a perfect example—he's had his dog Axle in more times than she can count in the last few months. And Derek's sculpted muscles and heart-stopping smile would be truly irresistible, if only he wasn't an officer of the law . . .

Derek can't get Rayna's stunning face and no-nonsense smarts out of his mind. Any excuse to see her will do, until he works up the nerve to ask her out. He's not sure where her resistance to cops comes from, though he's more than willing to prove he's one of the good ones. But when casual dating turns into explosive lovemaking, Derek knows he has to come clean about his past before the woman he loves finds out what he's been hiding and turns tail to run . . .

Visit us at www.kensingtonbooks.com

Books by Dorothy F. Shaw

Arizona K9
Avoiding the Badge

Published by Kensington Publishing Corporation

Avoiding the Badge

Arizona K9

Dorothy F. Shaw

LYRICAL PRESS
Kensington Publishing Corp.
www.kensingtonbooks.com

Lyrical Press books are published by
Kensington Publishing Corp. 119 West 40th Street New York, NY 10018

First Electronic Edition: September 2018
eISBN-13: 978-1-5161-0676-9
eISBN-10: 1-5161-0676-8

First Print Edition: September 2018
ISBN-13: 978-1-5161-0679-0
ISBN-10: 1-5161-0679-2

Printed in the United States of America

For Kelly Langford and author Liz Iavorshi-Braun
May you both rest in peace

Acknowledgments

A big shout out and thank you to the following awesome men in law enforcement for their dedication and service to the community. And their help with info on my book. Officer Matthew Warbington, Sheriff's officer Andy Tramundanas, and finally my wonderful adopted Dad, retired Connecticut state trooper, Sargent Robert Gawe.

Special thanks to Dr. Jaimie Schmidt, an awesome vet and owner of Life Care Animal Hospital for his medical consultation.

Sidda Lee Rain...as always, love you dearly, my friend. I hope I always know you.

And last but not least, to my Facebook, Night Writers group. To those that wrote with me night after night, thank you. You rock!

Chapter 1

"Ahem... Heeeee's heeeere."

At her head vet tech's declaration, Doctor Rayna Michaels looked up from the lab report she was reading in the back of the main treatment area and furrowed her brow. "I'm sorry. Who is 'he'?"

Andrea leaned her hip against the counter and dipped her chin. "Seriously?"

"Always." Careful to keep her expression blank, Rayna stared at the woman.

Andrea sighed and rolled her eyes. "*He* as in the hottest pet owner we have." Even as Rayna returned her focus to the lab report in her hands, Andrea continued. "Come on, really? *He* as in 'the cop' who's so freaking hot we could fry an egg on his unbelievable abs. We haven't seen the abs, but we all know he's got them. In spades. The same *he* who's so totally into you—so into you that the rest of us are green with envy."

He was not and they were not. Rayna sighed and set the report back on the counter. Yes, she knew *exactly* who Andrea was talking about, but no way was Rayna going to let her vet tech know that.

And yes, Officer Derek Hansen was handsome—very handsome in fact. The kind of handsome every hot-blooded woman, self-assured man, or more specifically a gay man—her receptionist Billy had pointed out last time Officer Hansen had been in—on the planet took notice of. If they didn't, they were likely dead, because *very* handsome was not only accurate, it was also an incredible understatement.

Dark, close-cropped hair, just a little longer on top. Dark, straight brows. Green eyes. Full lips. Always clean-shaven, but Rayna bet he looked good with a five o'clock shadow, too. His nose wasn't perfect, but it fit his face perfectly. And then there was his body...

Rayna sighed. Great. The mere thought of how good-looking Hansen was had heat spilling through her system like warm syrup. If she hadn't put the report down, she could've used it as a fan—though that would've been way too obvious. "I'm sorry, but you're going to have to be a bit more specific."

"I swear, Doctor Michaels. Sometimes I don't even know what to do with you." She threw her hands up in the air with a harsh sigh, then let them flop back down at her sides. "Fine. Officer Derek Hansen is here with Axle for yet *another* 'checkup.' Specific enough?" Andrea smirked.

"Well then, let's hope Axle is okay. I know Officer Hansen has been a tad...cautious, possibly overly so, since his canine partner was injured. But honestly, as you know, there is *nothing* wrong with taking good care of your animal. Especially one as important as Axle." She smiled, knowing her statement was only going to annoy Andrea further. Which served as a fantastic distraction from the heat rising in her body. Rayna cleared her throat. "What room is he in?"

Andrea let out an exasperated groan and grabbed a file off the counter. "Exam room four. And not for anything, but he's been in twice already this month. This makes visit number three. I think it's a sign." Andrea grinned and started to turn away, but then stopped. "All professionalism aside, enjoy the view for the rest of us, please? You know we're all going to want a full report when you're done in there." After a wink, she headed for the short hallway leading to the front of the office.

Rayna watched her go before picking up the lab report and reading it over once more. Deep breaths, in and out. In and out. In and—

It wasn't working. Desperate for some relief, she fanned herself with the lab report.

Around six months ago, Officer Derek Hansen's canine partner, Axle, had been injured in the line of duty. Apparently, her clinic had been the closest place to where the injury happened, and when he'd burst in the front door, of course she'd immediately treated the animal.

The injury hadn't been anything too serious, thank goodness. Axle had needed a small laceration stitched up, but the animal had also popped his kneecap out of joint on his left hind leg. Leg injuries could lead to hip issues with many big dogs, but shepherds especially. Ensuring Axle was healed properly was essential for his career as a police dog, but more importantly, the animal's overall well-being and quality of life.

However, after the dog had healed, Officer Hansen continued to bring Axle into the clinic—to the tune of every three weeks, give or take, for what he called "regular checkups." It didn't mean anything more than that the man was caring for his animal. Rather typical for an officer and their canine partner. Those teams never left each other's side.

Besides, who was she to turn away a patient?

Hansen wasn't a man of many words, but he was always polite, respectful. And, of course, considering Rayna was counted as a red-blooded woman, she'd also noticed he was gorgeous. How could she not? She had a pulse, after all.

Still, checking out her patients' owners wasn't something she made a habit of, or ever did, so she made sure to keep their dealings strictly business. It would be unprofessional and highly inappropriate for her to act in any other way.

Every time he'd been in the office, Rayna tried for all she was worth to *not* focus on how beautiful he was or how incredibly well built his body was, but with each visit, she failed. Plus, whenever she was in one of the exam rooms alone with him, her skin got warm all over, and without a doubt her face was the shade of a fire truck, her spray of freckles becoming little red spotlights.

Worse, each visit, she emerged with the effects he had on her nervous system on display for all to see. As if she were having some sort of allergic reaction, the skin covering her sternum and neck was completely flushed and blotchy. Her entire office staff would not let her forget it.

Frankly, not noticing the officer wasn't possible. After all, how could anyone with a set of functioning eyes *not* notice a well over six-foot-tall, hard-muscled, incredibly gorgeous cop?

The answer was plain and simple: they couldn't.

Rayna grabbed her mini medical bag filled with doggie treats and moved to exam room four's entrance. With another deep breath to cleanse her mind and hopefully cool down her body, she pressed her palm to the metal panel of the door.

As she was about to push it open, Andrea sauntered back into view, a stack of files in her arms. "Good luck! He looks really, *really* good today," she whispered.

Rayna's eyes went wide. She was going to kill Andrea if Officer Hansen heard the woman's comment. "Are you done yet?"

Andrea grinned from ear to ear. "Nope. I have to get these files updated in the system."

Reining in the nervous tension crawling up her spine, Rayna switched topics. "How many more appointments are on the schedule for today?"

"Lucky you, none. He's your last one. You get to take *all* the time you need." Andrea placed the files on the counter and sat in front of the computer.

"Great." What on earth did luck have to do with it? And wait, he looked good *today*? How was that different from any other day? The man *always* looked good. Like when he crossed his thickly muscled arms over his very broad chest, the veins in his forearms stood out in harsh relief against his tanned skin.

A flash fantasy of running her tongue along all those perfect veins made—oh dear, she hoped like hell the heat rising from her stomach to her chest like a wildfire would settle enough for her to do her job.

And do it without her face glowing bright as the Arizona sun.

* * * *

"Oh yeah, that's right, Axle. I heard her, too. She's coming." With nervous energy pumping through his system, Officer Derek Hansen took a seat on the small bench in the vet clinic exam room and did his best to appear calm, cool, and collected.

His five-year-old black- and rust-colored shepherd glanced over at him and licked his chops before going back to pacing around the tiny room.

Doc Michaels was right on the other side of the door. Derek would know her voice anywhere. Not that he'd been paying attention or anything. It was merely one of those things a person picked up in his line of work.

At least that was the story he was going to keep telling himself. Derek extended his legs, crossing them at the ankle, and focused on Axle again. "You should probably sit down, too. Seriously, try not to look so eager, dude."

Axle gave a small huff, followed by a whine, before resting on his haunches and facing the entry door to the exam room.

Derek let out his own whine, not audibly of course—at least he thought so until Axle jerked his big head Derek's way. Okay, fine. His partner heard it, thanks to his keen canine hearing. Whatever, as long as the doc didn't hear him, Derek was good.

The door shifted open a crack. "Andrea, would you call the Bensons and let them know the tests were all negative for Caspian, please?"

Derek straightened, ready to hop to his feet, then stopped himself, remembering he was supposed to be going for calm and cool. Oh yeah, and collected, too. Damn.

The door opened the rest of the way, and after she walked in, she set her little baby-blue medical bag down on the counter as she smiled down at Axle. "Hello there, big boy!"

Axle's ears dropped, flopping all puppy-dog style. Derek rolled his eyes and smothered a grin. His partner was such a ham.

She squatted down in front of the dog, scratching his ears. "Aren't you so handsome in your uniform?" She moved her hands over his head, and Axle's ass started wiggling. "You certainly are."

"You keep talking to my partner like that, Doc, and you're gonna give him an ego." Unable to sustain his calm presentation any longer, Derek got to his feet.

Doc Rayna smoothed her palm down Axle's back and glanced up at Derek. "I think he's far too humble to fall into such a trap." She grinned, stood and held out her hand. "Officer Hansen. How've you been?"

He took her soft palm in his own and tried like hell not to revel in how petite it was in his larger one. "Please, call me Derek."

She ducked her head before sliding her hand free. "Sorry, I know you've said that before. I tend to forget when you're in uniform."

"Understandable." Derek watched as she moved her small medical bag to the side and pulled the stethoscope from around her neck. "Yeah, so I know we were just here, but he's had a couple chases and takedowns this week, so I figured, best bring him in."

"He's a busy boy." She gave Derek a small smile and knelt in front of Axle again. With ease of movement, she pressed the round disk to the dog's chest. "Is he eating, drinking okay?"

"His appetite seems fine. Plus, he's drinking water whenever I do during shifts."

She glanced up and nodded as she slid the stethoscope disk to the other side of Axle's rib cage. Derek's breath caught in his throat. Jesus, her blue eyes were brighter than an Arizona summer sky. From the first time he saw her, Doc's eyes captivated him. He'd never seen eyes as beautiful in all his life.

Her eyes were nothing compared to her smile though. Doctor Rayna Michaels had a smile that made Derek's insides melt. Those precious lips, the bottom fuller than the top, did things to him that were not normal—maybe normal for other guys—but in no way normal for him.

The crazy part was she also had a banging body. Like, seriously fucking hot. All petite but with curves in all the right places, and a head full of long, obviously natural red hair he was dying to run his fingers through. Plus, she had a whole "pretty without any makeup" thing going on, with freckles for days, too. Amazing.

But the smile...

God help him, her smile got him in the gut and made him want to get on his knees and worship at the Altar of Doc Rayna. True story.

What made the urge crazy was Derek was not the kind of man who got on his knees for any woman. It was always the opposite. He was a dominant guy; he preferred to be the one in charge. Call the shots, give directions, and control the situation. In addition, he enjoyed a bit more of the rougher play, too. A little bondage, a little pain play, but only with the right partner.

The doc didn't strike him as a woman who'd head down the BDSM trail. Derek was okay with that. Though he'd be a bald-faced liar if he said he hadn't thought about how unbelievably hot she'd look on her knees before him. Hands cuffed or bound behind her back, while he played with her nipples until she squirmed... Derek stifled a groan.

Still, if rougher play wasn't her thing, he'd handle it. He'd respect it and accept it, because the woman aroused a whole other side of Derek he hadn't even realized existed. One which had nothing to do with sex. The physical attraction was there for sure, but it went far above and beyond carnal desires.

She rose and swung the stethoscope around her neck. "Everything looks good to me."

Derek shoved his hands in his pockets. "That's great. Yeah, he earned his pay this week for sure. Chased down the bad guys. But the suspect last night struggled more than usual when Axle got hold of him. I figured, after this week, plus the tussle last night, it's always best to have him checked over, you know? Make sure the knee is still good." In combination with a shrug, Derek nodded to the side once, hoping he didn't sound like a complete moron. Or worse, like he was full of shit.

The story was true...for the most part. Axle *had* taken down a perp the night before and a few others earlier in the week, but the dog was fine. Regardless, it was a "plausible" reason to see the gorgeous doctor. Far be it from him to not take advantage of the opportunity.

Sadly, Derek knew he was running out of excuses to see her. What he wanted to do was ask the woman out, though from what he could tell, she didn't appear to know he even existed.

"Oh?" With her brow furrowed, she glanced at Axle again, watching him sniff around the floor in the exam room. "He doesn't appear to be favoring it. I think... Hmm...let me have another look." She bent again and palpated Axle's back haunches, then moved down to the knee the dog had injured originally. "Have you noticed any signs that he's having pain?"

Doc was the consummate professional. Polite, of course. She smiled, she made chitchat between professional conversation regarding Axle, but that was it. No more, no less. Derek definitely wanted to take her out on a date, get her out of her natural environment and see if she'd drop the professional persona. But whenever he thought to ask, mustered up enough nerve, he couldn't seem to get the damn question out of his mouth.

Lack of balls, anyone? Please...that was not a label that had ever been attached to Derek. However, with the doc, he turned into a tongue-tied, pimply-faced, sweaty-palmed teenage boy with not a damn bit of game whatsoever.

Because what if she wasn't interested in him?

Though some women from his past might disagree, Derek didn't consider himself to be an egotistical asshole. Not *all* women were attracted to him, obviously. But man, if he got turned down by this particular woman, he wasn't sure his ego could take that kind of hit.

Realizing he hadn't answered her question, he got his mind back on track. "No, you're right. He doesn't seem to be favoring it at all, but you know, I just wanted to be sure."

"Honestly, I think he's fine." She stood again and retrieved a small dog biscuit from her medical bag. "But if you're really concerned, we can do some X-rays. Or just keep an eye on him for now. Whichever you prefer."

Axle, knowing what was coming, sat, ears at attention, eyes locked on his doctor. Not begging, but definitely ready for the treat. Doc Rayna smiled down at the animal, tenderness clear in her expression. Bending at the waist, she smoothed her small palm over the dog's head before feeding him the biscuit. "Here you go, good boy."

Once again, everything inside Derek went soft as things south of his belt attempted to go rock-hard. He tamped the urge down quick. The last thing he needed was to be waving that flag at her. "I think I'll just keep an eye, for now."

Jesus, the expression in her eyes when she looked at his partner made Derek want to pull her against his body and never let her go. Her heart was pure sweetness, and he could see it in everything she did.

He wanted to know if everything else about her was pure sweetness, too.

* * * *

"Sounds good!" Rayna turned away from Officer Hanse—Derek's—gaze and closed up her little treat carrier.

He'd started calling her "Doc" sometime after the first month he'd been visiting her practice. Now, it'd become a sort of nickname for her. Regardless, something about the way he said it, the tone in his voice, always had hot lava pulsing through her veins.

As a result, every inch of her skin was prickling with heat. And she was quite positive her neck was flushed red to the point it looked like she'd been lying out in the sun for way too long.

"Thanks so much for taking the time with him, Doc. He really likes you."

Swallowing hard, then silently blowing out a breath, she grabbed the blue medical treat bag and turned partially toward him, making sure to avoid his gaze.

With a small smile she couldn't keep from arching her lips, she directed her attention to the dog. "Well, he's a likable boy." Rayna bent and smoothed her palm over Axle's head again. "How can you not love that sweet face and those big dark eyes?"

The dog sat, ears flopped down, tongue hanging out and tail wagging side to side so fast he was giving the tile a buff job. Considering the animal was a force to be reckoned with when he was on patrol with his handler, capable of taking down criminals of any size, Axle definitely turned into a big softie when he was near her.

Rayna glanced up at Officer H—she pressed her lips together—Derek. *Okay, that's just...* She couldn't bring herself to call him by his first name. It felt like doing so would wipe away some imaginary line she'd drawn between them.

Even so, curiosity tickled the back of her mind. Was the man as big of a softie as his canine partner? Judging by the expression he wore in that moment, he likely was. Officer Derek—*okay, a compromise*—was looking at her as if she was some sort of superhero or...good grief, she wasn't even sure what, but whatever it was, it was definitely in a way she'd never have expected from a hardened, good-looking man like him.

Clearing her throat, she straightened and extended her hand. "Be safe out there, okay?"

His lips split into a shy smile. "Always, Doc. Axle has my back, and I have his." He grasped Rayna's palm, his big hand dwarfing hers as he wrapped his fingers around in a firm though not painful grip.

Tingles spread from Rayna's hand, zipping up her arm. Heat flared like a fire blast through her body, and her stomach got tight. She almost fanned herself, but since he was still holding onto her, essentially, he saved her from embarrassing herself. Oh dear. *Wrap it up, Rayna!*

Any minute now she was going to spontaneously combust. Especially if he didn't let go of her hand. Rayna forced a smile. "You make a great team." "Definitely." Eyes going soft, his smile relaxed into a far too sexy smirk. He nodded. "A perfect match."

Was the room getting smaller? Another moment passed and he'd yet to let go of her, which was awkward, but in a sweet sort of way. A nervous giggle she was trying to contain escaped, and she glanced down at their still-linked hands.

He pulled his palm away like he'd been burned. "Oh, wow! I'm sorry. That was weird. Sorry."

"It's okay." She laughed as relief blasted through her, and she moved to the door. "Have a good day."

"You, too. Thanks again, Doc."

She glanced back as she opened her way into the back area. He'd shoved his hands in his pockets and was still watching her. His expression carried a small hint of embarrassment, but he was still smiling, so maybe he didn't care. Her cheeks, however, burned hot as fire, and Rayna couldn't help but smile back.

When the door closed behind her, she pressed her back against it and blew out a breath. "Good grief."

Andrea strolled by, either the same or a new stack of patient files in her arms. "You need a cold shower?"

Rayna groaned and held out her hand. "Pass me one of those files."

Andrea furrowed her brow as if confused, but then did as Rayna asked.

Rayna took the file and fanned herself with it as she stepped away from the door and past the woman. "Not a word, Andrea. Telling you right now, not a word."

"Yes, Doctor." Andrea laughed.

Rayna continued into her small office and closed herself in. The space was about half the size of her twelve-by-twelve exam rooms, and yet there was way more oxygen to breathe in there than in the room with Officer Derek. Hansen. Derek. Ugh...whatever.

Rayna took a seat in her small desk chair and crossed her legs. Whoa! The rub of her wet panties sent a shockwave of lust ricocheting through her. With a hard swallow, she closed her eyes, willing the ache to settle.

She didn't spend much of her time, if any, fantasizing about men, much less dampening her panties over them. Yet here she was, drowning in a puddle of arousal. Literally.

Ugh...with her eyes still closed, she fanned herself with the file. Immediately, an image of him appeared in her mind. His dark, close-cropped hair. His tanned skin. Eventually he'd go back to his PD's contracted vet, right? He had to. Didn't he?

Good grief, what if he didn't?

Chapter 2

"I'll take a Devil's Ale, please?" Derek settled on a barstool and scanned the happy hour menu.

"Hello there." His best friend and fellow officer, Jeff Pearl, smiled at the bartender as he scooted his stool forward. "I'm gonna go crazy and get the Epicenter today."

"Perfect choice."

"I know what I like." Jeff winked and gave the bartender one of his famous panty-dropping grins.

Derek shook his head and smothered a chuckle. Jeff was a huge flirt.

After letting out a giggle, the bartender looked from Jeff to Derek as she motioned to the menu. "You need a couple minutes for food?"

"Definitely. G'head and grab the brews while I decide. Cool?"

"You got it." With a pretty smile, she stepped away...adding a generous sway in her hips.

Derek looked at his friend and nudged his arm. "Go easy, now."

"What?" Jeff glanced over from staring at the waitress.

"Dude, she can't be more than twenty-three. You know there isn't a damn thing you have in common with that child."

Jeff gasped. "How dare you! She's a woman." He laughed. "In common? Oh, you mean, besides what it feels like to be naked with her? You might be right."

"You're such a slut."

"Nah, I'm just kidding. I haven't been naked with her—" The bartender came back and served them their beers, and when she moved to another customer, Jeff continued, "—yet."

Derek almost choked on his first sip. Laughing, he set the glass down and wiped his mouth. "Ass."

"Slut? Ass? Honey, I didn't know you cared so much." Jeff laughed and clinked his glass against Derek's. "Here's to a long future together, baby." Derek picked up his beer again. "You know you're the only one for me." "Thank God for that!" Jeff pulled the menu his way. "Okay, I think I want onion rings."

"No way. Get the pretzel bites with beer cheese. Like heaven."

"Pretzels it is, so we can pay homage to our Lord and Savior." With a chuckle, Jeff set the menu down.

Derek motioned to the bartender. After he'd ordered and taken another sip of his beer, he glanced up at the big flat screens above the bar to check the scores of the various games on. Did the doc like sports?

God, wouldn't that be like hitting the relationship lottery. Animal lover, sports fan, beautiful, sexy, *and* smart? For the Powerball win, she'd be killer in bed, too. Talk about a dream woman...

"You still taking Axle to that chick vet?"

Yanked from his gazillion-dollar fantasy, he glanced over at Jeff. He'd barely talked about Doc, but his best friend must've been paying attention the few times he had. Damn cops and their ability to retain *every* minute detail. "Yeah. Why? You looking for someone for Rio?"

"Nope. Just wondered if you tapped it yet."

Annoyance shot through Derek, and he jerked his head back, scowling. "Whoa, dude, seriously. Go easy. Not cool."

Jeff looked at Derek like he had two heads, but then his expression changed to one that screamed, *Really?* "Wait a second. Are you going all caveman on me?"

Derek did his best to reel himself in because, yeah, it wasn't like he had a right to go all alpha male, especially on his best friend. The woman wasn't even his, maybe never would be his. Still, it was *not* sitting right with him that anyone, even Jeff, would be talking about his Doc with any sort of disrespect.

His Doc?

Oh man, Derek was already in deep and they hadn't even gone on a date. *Shit.* Derek shook his head and took a swig of his beer. "It's all good. Not trying to come off like a caveman. Just saying, she's Axle's vet. No way I'm gonna sleep with my partner's vet. It's like a conflict of interest or some shit."

Jeff frowned, his dark brows lowering over his eyes. "Uh-huh."

"What?"

The waitress brought the pretzels and smiled at Jeff. "Can I get you anything else?"

"Not right now, darlin'. Maybe in a bit though, 'kay?" Jeff pursed his lips as he jerked his chin up at her, and she stepped away, again rocking the sway in her hips.

Derek scrubbed his palm over the top of his hair. "Listen, just because you're banging anything with two legs and a heartbeat doesn't mean I am."

His best friend rested his forearms on the bar's edge and looked at Derek. "Let me remind you, Shirley, that on occasion you have. So let's not pretend about that. But if you're not banging the vet and you're getting all upset at me because I asked if you were, that only means one thing."

Fuuuuuck...was it *that* obvious? Knowing Jeff was about to call him out on the whole deal, Derek cringed. In preparation for the lecture he was about to endure, Derek took a swig of his beer and then picked up a pretzel bite, dipped it in the cheese and popped it in his mouth. After he chewed and swallowed, he took another sip of beer. "Go ahead, I know you're dying to say it."

Jeff grinned. "You like her. It's okay. I get it."

Derek glanced up at the various televisions again. One had a NASCAR race on it. Maybe the doc liked racing, too? For fuck's sake. He sighed. "Okay, yeah. I like her."

"Called it." Jeff took a swig of his beer.

"Yeah, yeah. Doesn't matter. The woman doesn't even know I exist."

"That's impossible."

"No, I'm telling you. She's not interested."

"Derek, any woman not interested in you is crazy. Listen, you're totally my man crush. You're built, you're good-looking, and you're a cop. You got a clean house, a badass truck, plus an even more badass canine for a partner. Should I go on?"

"I'm still trying to get past the man crush part."

Jeff laughed. "I'm being serious."

"Yeah, I know. That's why I'm scared." Derek put his hand on Jeff's shoulder and tried to look all serious and sensitive. "I'm flattered, sweetheart, really, and I'm going to let you down easy. Sorry, but I only see you as a friend and—" Derek busted up laughing.

"All right, Shirley. Break my heart, go ahead." Jeff laughed and shoved Derek's hand off his shoulder. "My point is, you're a great guy. So if she doesn't see that, it's her loss."

Derek shrugged. "I don't know. I'm not *that* great of a guy...although, I'm not a slut like you, so I guess there's hope for me."

Jeff placed his palm on his heart and gasped. "You wound me. So cruel." He sniffled and wiped a nonexistent tear from his cheek. "For serious, ask her out."

"I don't know." Derek raised his glass. "Did you just say 'for serious'?" Jeff rolled his eyes. "*Juuuust* ask her."

"Maybe." Derek swallowed the last of his beer and signaled the bartender. He didn't know if he *could* ask Doc Michaels out. As it had always been with her, the fear of rejection was huge. Which was crazy because he could go on a date at any time, typically...or at least he had been until his Doc came into his life six months ago.

Once Derek met Rayna, he hadn't been the least bit interested in dating anyone else. No one had even remotely piqued his interest like she had. In addition, he'd deleted all his online dating accounts too. It wasn't like him at all, but nonetheless, that's what had gone down.

For the past six months, Doctor Rayna Michaels had Derek wrapped around her pinky finger... Crazy part was, the woman had no damn clue. Though, it was also possible she didn't even care.

Damn...he was in deep.

* * * *

"So what's new with you and...Joe? Shoot. John? Yeah, John?" Rayna glanced over at her best friend, Tish, in the seat beside her.

"Jerry. His name is Jerry." Tish laughed and pushed her dark hair over her shoulders.

Rayna cringed. "Sorry. At least I got the first letter right, right?"

"I'm not giving you points for that." Tish laughed again.

"Okay fine. But in my defense, I've been a little preoccupied lately. So, how's it going?"

"P.S., you're always preoccupied. Anyway, I don't know how it's going. I mean we're just sort of..." Tish looked up from the magazine on her lap, as if the wall across from them held the words she needed to explain her relationship. "Existing? Does that make sense?"

Rayna frowned. "Uh, no. Existing doesn't make sense to me. Why stay with someone if he's not making you happy?" She glanced down as the pedicurist placed Rayna's foot back in the water and reached for the other, pulling it out of the bubbling warm water to begin trimming Rayna's toenails.

Rayna loved her best friend, and she wanted Tish to be happy. Shoot, everyone deserved to be happy. Then again, Rayna really shouldn't worry. Joe, or John...or Jerry, whoever he was, wouldn't last much longer. Her best friend was beyond gorgeous, and funny and smart, and went through guys like a medical professional went through sterile gloves.

"Well, you're right, existing doesn't make sense. We're supposed to go out tonight, but I think I should cancel." Tish's head fell back, and she let out a sigh as her pedicurist began rubbing her feet. "It's not going anywhere, so there's no point in continuing."

"Well, at least you're not upset. I mean, you don't seem upset. Or are you and I'm just not seeing it?

"Nope. I'm good. Which goes to show you that poor Jerry's just not the one for me. The one is out there. I know he is. Just gotta find him. Kiss a few toads, so to speak." Tish glanced over, her full, nearly puffy lips arching into a devious grin. "But if you want, I can pretend I'm upset and we can go out on the town tonight."

Rayna frowned. "But it's Thursday."

"And?" Tish scrunched her brows together.

Rayna shook her head and laughed. "*And* I have work in the morning. So do you, for that matter."

"What? Are you eighty or something? Geez, Grandma, can't we go out for a little while on a school night?"

Rayna laughed, but then groaned as the pedicurist starting scrubbing her heels with a pumice stone. "That always tickles a little."

"I know." Tish flipped a page in the magazine she was looking through. "Anyway, there's a cute spot in Chandler we can hit up. It's ladies' night."

"Which place?"

"The Whiskey Barrel."

"I don't think I've been there." Rayna leaned back and closed her eyes as her tech began her foot and calf massage.

"Why does that not surprise me? In case you haven't noticed, Ray, you don't get out much."

Rayna cracked one eye, but then closed it again. "That's not fair. I'm busy with the clinic. And it's not like I have a partner helping me. You know that." Frowning, she refused to open her eyes again and let Tish distract her from the relaxation zone she was shooting for.

"I know. You're right. But you need to hire someone. Anyway, I've been down there a bunch of times. A few times with Jerry, and also Jimmy— not getting into that one so don't even go there. What a pain in the ass he turned out to be. Anyway, it's a really fun place."

Rayna jerked her head up and looked at her best friend. "See! I knew there was more than one guy that started with the letter *J*. I was close!"

Tish laughed. "Fair enough. So, what do you say? You want to go check it out? Dust off your cowgirl boots?"

Rayna's eyes went wide. "It's a country bar?"

"Yep, and there's a live band and even country dancing happening. I know a few guys who'd take you for a turn around the dance floor." Tish winked.

Ugh, it was completely unfair that Tish was baiting her with the lure of country music and dancing. Rayna was a huge anything country fan and loved to dance, but it'd been so long since she'd two-stepped her way anywhere near a dance floor, she wasn't sure she even knew how anymore. She bit her bottom lip, torn on what to do.

"I can see on your face how bad you want to go now. It's stamped all over your freckles."

"Leave my freckles out of this! Brat." Rayna laughed. "Yes, you're right, I do want to go. But seriously, I'm exhausted. And I didn't even get to tell you what happened today. Plus, I've got a completely full schedule tomorrow. If I promise I won't back out, can we do it next week?"

Tish frowned, but then rolled her eyes. "Okay, fine. It's a date. Don't even think about backing out. Because, honestly, Rayna? You need to get out more. You need to have some fun. You need to meet people—more importantly, you need to meet a guy. You need—"

Rayna raised her palm in the air, knowing what was coming next. "Don't say it!"

"—to get laid." Tish stuck out her tongue. "Too late. I said it anyway."

"Totally a brat." Rayna frowned and glanced down at the technician massaging her.

The woman was grinning because, regardless of whether or not she was Asian, she sure as hell understood English clearly enough. Rayna cringed as she felt the heat of embarrassment rise from her chest up her throat. Blowing out a sigh, she glanced back at Tish. "Can you please *not* broadcast my sex life to the world?"

"Oh, come on. She doesn't care." Tish motioned to Rayna's nail tech and then to her own. "She doesn't, either. Do you?" she asked both ladies, and they giggled in unison, with grins far too wide as they shook their heads. "See? No one cares. Except you."

"Good grief." Rayna covered her face with her hands. "Lord, spare me the embarrassment."

"All right, enough with the theatrics. Tell me what happened today. Did you have to put some poor sweet fur-baby to sleep? I honestly don't know how you do that." Tish took a sip of her water bottle. "It's just so damn sad."

Rayna gave Tish a comforting look. "Yes, it is always sad, and part of the job unfortunately. But no, that's not it."

"Oh? Okay, good. Then what?" With a smile, Tish wiggled her toes after the nail tech got them prepped and ready for polish.

"That cop came in again. You remember the one I told you about?"

Tish sat up straight. "The hunky K9 one?"

Rayna tipped her chin down. "I don't recall using those words...but yes, him."

"Right. Those were the words Billy used. He's adorable by the way, as well as hilarious. Perfect fit to be your front receptionist."

"Agreed. Anyway, yes, Officer Hansen came in today."

"Did his dog get injured again?"

Rayna ran her fingers through her hair at the scalp. "No. His police dog is fine. It's just..."

"Before I turn old and gray, spit it out." Tish placed her elbow on the armrest and rested her chin on her fist.

Rayna bit her bottom lip and folded her hands on her lap. The mere thought of the cop had heat rising in her chest and spreading through her limbs. "He's been in three times already this month."

Tish's brows drew together. "But the dog is fine?"

"So far, yes." Rayna blew out a breath, grabbed a magazine and started fanning herself with it. Were hot flashes even a thing in a woman's early thirties? *I wish.* Rayna rolled her eyes. Only if they were inspired by a totally sexy hot guy.

"Okay, wait, let me get this straight. The dog is fine, and he's been in three times already this month? Was it back-to-back visits, or are they spaced out?"

Rayna glanced at her friend, knowing the expression on her face could be read as "Well, do the math." Rayna tapped a fingertip to her bottom lip. "It's the end of the third week of this month, so I guess we can just average it to once a week. Either way...today was his third visit."

"Ah. Got it." Tish shook her head. "Let me guess? You can't figure out why he's coming in so much, right?" Tish laughed, but then stifled it, and did her best to make her expression a serious one. It wasn't working though.

"Pshhaw. Of course I know why." *I have no idea why.*

"Yeah, you definitely need to get out more."

"Stop it, I do know why." Rayna frowned, knowing she sounded as clueless as she truly was.

"Honey, this is a slam dunk. *And* a no-brainer. He's either a crazy closet stalker or the hunky officer of the law has it *bad* for you. My guess is the latter."

Rayna sat forward, shock and denial flooding her brain. "He's not a stalker! That's crazy. And there's no way he has it bad for me."

Tish laughed and sat back, closing her eyes. "Like I said, the latter. And yes, honey. He does have it bad for you."

Hansen had it *bad* for her? Good grief, what did that even mean exactly? If it meant what she thought it did, Rayna was going to be in a world of trouble. She'd made a point of not noticing cops. Ever. Frustration spilled through her veins. She wasn't attracted to cops. She certainly didn't date them. "It doesn't matter. You know my rule. No reason to break it just because he's good-looking."

"Rules are meant to be broken, my friend." Tish chuckled and looked back at her magazine.

"Not in my world." Rayna closed her eyes and tried to quiet the thoughts buzzing around her brain.

So much for a relaxing pedicure. Thanks to her childhood, Rayna wanted *nothing* to do with any kind of officer of the law. Plain and simply put: Rayna didn't do cops. She sure as heck didn't "get it bad" for them.

As her father used to say: end of discussion.

But good grief, if she were honest with herself at least, she'd be hard-pressed to deny that she maybe, kinda, a little bit, sorta wanted to make an exception and break her rule for the ultrasexy Officer Derek Hansen.

Not good. Not good at all.

What the heck was Rayna going to do now?

Chapter 3

"Well, well, well. What an unexpected but exciting surprise!" Billy, the receptionist at the vet clinic, leaned forward, a broad smile on his face as he rested his chin on his fist and gazed up at Derek. "How can I help you, Officer?"

With a grin, Derek shook his head. "It's good to see you, too, Billy. So, listen..." Derek leaned forward, and Billy leaned closer. Derek stifled a chuckle. The receptionist had to know Derek wasn't gay, but that didn't mean the guy wasn't going to flirt.

Though some guys might take issue with being hit on by a gay man, it didn't bother Derek at all. Live and let live as far as he was concerned. Just don't break the law while living it. "I know I don't have an appointment, but is she free? You think you can squeeze me in?"

Billy's lips split into an even bigger smile. "For you? I'll see what I can do." With a wink, he shifted back from the counter, focused on his computer and started typing on the keyboard. "Kitten at one. Doberman at one thirty...hmmm." Billy glanced over his shoulder before looking at his computer again.

Derek held his breath, nervous energy bouncing through him, as he waited to see what the answer would be.

Billy pursed his lips and tipped his head to the side. "Yep, like I thought. She *just* finished eating her lunch. Which means..." Billy winked. "You just lucked out. She'll be free in less than ten minutes."

Excitement sped through Derek like a rocket. "Awesome! Should I wait here?"

"Ummm..." Billy looked from side to side. "Go into exam room four again."

"Thanks." Derek nodded and set off for the exam room.

"Wait. Officer Hansen, aren't you missing someone?"

Derek stopped and looked back. "Excuse me?"

Billy smiled again. "Axle. Aren't you missing Axle?"

"Right, well. I had something I needed to ask the doc, and I was in the neighborhood, so yeah. I figured I'd just stop in quick."

"'Bout time is all I'm sayin'..." Billy smirked and focused on his computer screen again.

Derek chuckled. "Can I ask you a question?"

Billy glanced up and batted his lashes. "*Anything.*"

"Is she single?"

"I can't say. It's not my place really." He drew little designs on the countertop with his fingertip. "But you know, Derek. Can I call you Derek?" He pursed his lips and continued before Derek could say yes. "Anyway... Derek, take me for instance? I don't get out much, you know? So busy with work and all. Plus, there's no prospects knocking on my door. It's sad." Billy frowned and let out a melancholy sounding sigh. "Honestly, I haven't been on a date in...well, I just don't even know how long." His gaze trailed off to the side, as if looking wistfully at some beautiful mountainside or sunset. Then he smiled and focused on Derek again. "You know, Doctor and I are just so much alike. We're practically twinsies. I swear it. Except she's sweeter. Better hair, too. I like to think I'm as sweet as she is. But who knows. Isn't she sweet? She is, huh?"

Derek smiled as he watched Billy's performance and his chosen way of telling Derek exactly what he needed to know. The doc was single, which meant the light just turned green. "Sweet is only one of the amazing things about Doctor Michaels, Billy. Thanks."

"Anytime. Now scoot. Room four is waiting."

Derek turned and hightailed it into the exam room. Which had started to become "his" room, as far as he was concerned. God knew he'd been in it too many times that month already.

Call it coincidence that his fourth visit landed him back in room four, or maybe it was luck. Either way, fourth time's a charm maybe? Yeah, now he was being lame, but so what.

Derek took a seat on the small bench and ran his palms down his denim-covered thighs. Nervous tension crawled over his skin, tightening every muscle. Unable to sit still, he stood and paced the small space.

He both hated and loved how she always managed to have him in knots like this, and still, he was sure the woman had no clue.

It'd been exactly a week since he'd seen her last, and he had no idea what he was going to say. Derek knew he'd figure out the right words, because it was time. He had to ask her. Christ, he *had* to do *something*. Besides, if he didn't ask her out, Jeff was never going to let him live it down. His best friend would probably come up with a new shot of liquor and name it after Derek if he didn't go for it. Something stupid like No Balls or Fucknut Coward. Derek groaned—

The exam room door opened. Doc Michaels came in, her focus on a file in her hand. "Officer Hansen, I didn't expect—"

"Please, call me Derek."

She jerked her head up, her gaze connecting right with his. Her chest rose fast, as if she'd just caught her breath in a rush. He knew exactly how that felt, because he was trying to catch his breath too.

Her hair was pulled up in a ponytail. She wore no makeup and was clad in a set of green hospital scrubs. As if she'd just done a surgery or something. God, she made those green scrubs look like the hottest thing he'd ever seen, plus the fact that she'd probably just saved some sick animal's life made his heart go soft in ways he couldn't predict.

Enough already. No more waiting, wondering, wanting... Without another thought, Derek stepped toward her. "Can I ask you a personal question?"

With her gaze still locked with his, a quiet but electrically charged moment passed between them before she answered, hesitation clear in her tone. "Um... Sure..."

"Are you single?" He knew she was, thanks to Billy. But he wanted to hear it from her.

"Oh! Uh. Yes, well, that *is* a very personal question." She swallowed.

"Sorry, I just—"

"No, no. It's fine. I..." She glanced away, pursed her lips and then returned her eyes to his. "Yes. I'm single."

"Perfect." He smiled and stepped as close to her as he could without touching.

She tilted her head back to not break eye contact. He wanted to touch her, wanted to trace every one of her freckles and memorize how they framed the perfect angles of her face. He didn't dare though. Not yet. But soon. Soon.

He'd wasted two months; he wasn't wasting any more time.

* * * *

"Why do you ask?" Rayna couldn't tear her gaze away from his as she ignored how breathy her question sounded.

She swallowed. Holy cow, was he going to kiss her? Did she want him to kiss her? Nervous anticipation boomeranged through her system, hitting every nerve ending beneath her skin along its journey, and her palms began to sweat.

He raised his hand, as if he was about to touch her, but then dropped it. "I realize you're Axle's vet, and I also know you're a consummate professional. I respect that. Completely. Totally. Fully. But..." His lips curved into a meek smile. "Do you think we can go off the professional trail for just a moment?"

I really don't think that's a good idea, Officer Hansen. "I think the minute you stepped so close to me that our bodies were almost touching we got off the professional trail."

Where the heck had that answer come from? And why did it come out sounding even more breathy than when she asked him why? Rayna blinked and had to stop herself from stepping even closer so that their bodies actually *were* touching.

Good grief, she wanted to put her hands on him. And that was so wrong, so very, very wrong. She couldn't want this. But, oh dear, she did. She really did.

"Fair enough." His meek smile broadened to a more confident one, and a low chuckle came out of him. "There's something between us. An energy of sorts. At least, I feel it, and I want to know if you feel it, too."

I'm sorry, but I have no idea what you mean. "Yes...I feel it." Rayna suppressed a groan. What was going on with her? And again, more with the breathlessness? Was she seriously breathless right now? Worse, her brain and her mouth seemed to have completely disconnected from each other, and what she intended to say was definitely *not* what was coming out of her mouth.

Heat bloomed across her chest, spreading up her neck. *What* is *wrong with me?* Cop or not, it was as if she'd lost all need or desire to steer clear of him.

"I knew it." He let out what sounded like a relieved sigh. "Can I take you out on a date? Dinner, lunch, coffee...anything. Just please, can we go out and talk when we're not in uniform?"

She allowed herself a quick glance down his body. He wore a pale blue T-shirt, which clung in a mouthwatering way over his broad chest, the sleeves stretched tight over his thick biceps, as if the seams were barely hanging on by a thread. Dark blue jeans covered his long, muscular legs. A pair of gray Chuck Taylors on his feet. A leather bracelet on his right wrist.

Rayna let her gaze roam back up his perfect body. "It looks like you're out of uniform right now."

Was she trying to be coy? Cute? What? *Oh dear, no...* Flirting? She didn't even know how to flirt. Good grief, she must sound like an awkward idiot. Derek chuckled. "Yes, I'm definitely out of uniform. But you're not. So, what do you say? Are you willing to get out of uniform for me?"

Rayna's legs went weak, and she almost moaned. *Right now, I'd let you remove my uniform.* She drew in a deep breath and tried to cool her now boiling blood to a reasonable simmer. Without a doubt, her chest, neck and face had to be beet red. "I think I'd like that. Please know, I haven't done this in a really long time, but yes. Sure."

"Great!" Derek smiled so big Rayna wanted to kiss him. "How's Thursday night? I know it's a weeknight, but I'm off and also free. Will that work?"

"I think so, yes." She smiled as a different kind of heat pooled in her stomach, but then it was as if someone pulled the plug and all her nervous excitement spilled right out of her. *Crap!* "Wait, no. That won't work. I forgot that I promised my best friend I'd go out with her Thursday night. I'm sorry."

"Oh." His face fell, and along with it, a block of ice filled Rayna's stomach.

Without thinking, she reached for his hand. As usual when her skin made contact with his, a thousand tingles shot up her arm and the ice in her stomach melted into a heated puddle. "Well, wait. What if you met me there?"—*Holy cow, what'm I doing?*—"I mean, maybe you won't want to, but it might be...I don't know, fun?"

Once more, he smiled. "That could work. Where are you going?"

"Some place called the Whiskey Barrel? It's a country bar, so it might not be your speed."

"Perfect. I've been there before. How about this, is your friend single?"

Rayna smiled, knowing Tish might kill her for this. "She is, yes."

"Fantastic! I can bring my best friend and then...maybe, since you said you haven't done this in a while, it'll take the pressure off. How does that sound?"

"Please don't take this wrong, but actually, yes, less pressure sounds perfect."

"I promise to go easy on you." Derek reached for her other hand and clasped it in his.

A bolt of electric lust shot up her arm. Her stomach tightened, and she had to fight the urge to clench her thighs together. "There it is..." Rayna glanced down at their linked hands and then back up to his eyes. "The energy."

"Yes. Chemistry. Connection." He drew in a breath. "I really want to kiss you right now, Doc."

Doc...

Everything inside Rayna went soft as liquefied lust spilled through her nervous system. More than anything she wanted him to kiss her. Which was completely contrary to what her logical mind was screaming at her to remember.

With anticipation pulsing through her veins, her breaths grew shallow and she licked her lips. Derek's eyes darted to her mouth then back to her eyes. All at once, Rayna couldn't recall why she shouldn't want him. "What's stopping you?"

Derek dipped his head, his lips hovering a bare breath away from hers. "Just the anticipation, Doc. It's too good, almost as delicious as I bet you taste."

"Oh." Heat engulfed Rayna's entire body, and as her shallow breaths quickened, she swore she felt a trickle of wetness in her panties.

"I'll see you Thursday." He pulled back and let go of her hands. Although she wasn't expecting him to move away from her, the loss of his heat and touch did nothing to diminish the fire burning inside her.

"Thursday." The word came out of her as a bare whisper as she tried to remember how to breathe.

Rayna was doing this. She was going on a date. With a cop. At that moment, she could no longer remember why that should be a big deal. At that moment, all she really wanted was to feel his lips on hers and feel his hard body cradled around her.

Oh dear.

* * * *

Kiss her...

As Derek stepped away from the doc, and then turned and walked toward the exam room door that led to the lobby, the voice in his head got louder. *Kiss her, you ass! Kiss! Her!*

Fuck it. In one motion, Derek pivoted and took two strides back to her, wrapped an arm around her waist, bent forward to meet her much shorter height and took her sweet lips in a kiss.

At first she stiffened, but then a low moan came out of her and she softened against him. Lust erupted in his system, sending bolts of desire down his spine and through all of his limbs. In an instant, his cock was stone-hard behind his zipper.

Tilting his head to the side, he slid his tongue along the seam of her lips. She opened for him, and he felt the tip of her tongue touch his...and that's when everything changed.

Derek picked his Doc up, turned her and pressed her back against the wall of the exam room. With a firm grip on her ass—which he now knew was perfect—their tongues collided, tangled and wrapped around each other. She gripped at his shoulders, clenching the fabric of his T-shirt in her hands. Derek rolled his hips. She moaned and rocked her pelvis against him, confirming the solid ridge of his cock, through his jeans, struck its mark between her parted thighs.

As she kissed him, his sweet Doc rode him. God, she was perfect, and she was giving him more than he'd ever dared to hope, and only dreamed he'd ever get from her.

Goddamn, he'd needed this. So much more than he'd even allowed himself to think.

Fucking, yes! Derek had just found heaven.

Chapter 4

Rayna stood in front of the bathroom mirror, staring at her reflection in complete and total fear.

Make no mistake, this wasn't any sort of real fear, meaning the kind where she was concerned for her safety. No, it was more the kind of fear where self-doubt called the shots. No matter how much she'd tried, Rayna couldn't understand what a man like Derek Hansen could or would ever see in her.

Her chest and face were in what she was starting to think was a permanent state of splotchy pink. Definitely not the pretty kind of flush and shine a person got from being out in the sun or among nature on a hike. No, Rayna's was the kind that looked like she was one allergy attack away from needing a massive dose of Benadryl.

Mouth gone dry. Nervous tension centered in her palms, making her hands sweat. She kept clenching and unclenching her fists, trying to relieve the ache, but it wasn't working. Her stomach was in a knot. And her heart beat so hard she could hear it in her ears.

Totally ridiculous. Rayna leaned closer to the mirror. *What does he see in me?* She'd always been told that she was pretty, and Rayna didn't entirely disagree. More that she felt her looks fell on the plain, low-maintenance side of the female populace. Unlike her best friend and many other women, Rayna rarely wore makeup, though she'd planned to put on a little for her date tonight.

Regardless, Derek was the type of good-looking she would expect to be paired with some exotically gorgeous, super-fit, athletic woman...with long, flowing blond hair, maybe, and a perfect body.

Definitely not freckles, red hair, a fairly decent figure—meaning a little too soft in places that wouldn't be so soft if there were time in her life for the gym—nothing special for sure.

But good grief, he'd kissed her and touched her like she was the hottest thing on the planet. It was crazy, and Rayna could not make heads or tails of it! So, for the past three days, she'd been a train wreck of anxiety.

To make matters worse, the kiss—or rather, the out-of-this-world kiss, which turned into an out-of-this-galaxy make-out session—had left her in a state of the most intense sexual arousal she'd ever experienced in her life, a craving she'd been unable to satisfy on her own, either.

After their dry-humping marathon against the exam room wall had gone down, and she'd gone home, Rayna had brought herself to orgasm at least three times, maybe even four, in bed that night. God help her, she'd masturbated every night since.

But considering she hadn't heard from him the rest of the week, Rayna was convinced he'd changed his mind. And why wouldn't he? Except then he'd called the office this morning, requesting she call him back.

When she did, she was so rattled with nervous anticipation her hands were shaking and she had to dial his number a few times before she finally got it right. He asked for her cell number and told her he couldn't wait to see her.

So, there it was.

He still wanted to see her.

He still wanted to take her out on a date.

Rayna thought he was freaking nuts.

However, the one thing that trumped all of that was the fact that she was breaking a vow she'd made to herself as a child. At the tender age of ten, thanks to her father, who was now a retired police officer, Rayna had vowed she'd never, ever, no matter what, date or be with a cop.

Her father had excelled in his career with a badge but had failed miserably, thanks to that badge, at being a husband. And here she was breaking the very rule she'd sworn to heaven and hell she'd never break.

With a sigh, she pulled open the top drawer in the sink vanity and pulled out the copper eyeliner Tish had made her buy a few months ago but Rayna had yet to wear. Leaning forward and doing her best to steady her hand, she drew a line on the top lids of her eyes, then another along the lash lines on the bottom.

She blinked and swallowed. Not too bad. Next up was mascara. After coating both the upper and lower lashes, making them look twice as long as they looked naturally, she tossed the tube aside. After adding just a hint of blush to her cheeks, she closed things up and studied her reflection again. With a curt nod, Rayna decided this was as good as it was going to get.

But maybe it wasn't so bad.

"Hey— Wow, you look fucking amazing!"

A scream punched out of Rayna as every muscle in her body jumped to high-alert attention. With wide eyes she clamped a palm over her mouth and gripped the bathroom counter with her other hand to keep herself from falling on her butt.

"Shit! Sorry, I called for you when I came in through the laundry room—" Tish reached for Rayna and rubbed her upper arms. "I guess you didn't hear me."

With her hand still clamped over her mouth, Rayna shook her head side to side.

Tish raised both brows. "Do you need to sit down?"

Rayna sucked in a breath through her nose and finally pulled her hand away. "No. I'm okay." She patted her chest. "Sorry, you just really scared me." She turned and faced the mirror again. "And it's not like I didn't know you were coming. I'm just nervous, and I was too busy thinking of the million reasons why I should *not* be going tonight and then a million more reasons why this man should not be interested in me."

"What? Why would you think he shouldn't be interested in you?"

Rayna reached for the flat iron. "Because, have you seen him? Oh, wait, you haven't." With a frown, she smoothed the iron through a section of hair. "He's good-looking, like really good-looking. Billy wasn't exaggerating."

Tish sat on the edge of the large soaking tub. "So?"

"Ugh, so? What do you mean, so? Have you seen me lately?" Rayna pulled another section of hair through the flat iron. "I'm way too conservative. Makeup is a chore, so I don't bother. Plus, I'm more comfortable in a set of scrubs or jeans than tight skirts or low-cut tops. You know that. A guy like Derek doesn't go out with women who don't wear makeup or show cleavage."

"When did you become psychic?" Tish stood and moved to the counter. She bent close to the mirror and examined her face.

"I'm being serious, Tish."

"Believe me, I know you are. But so'm I." Tish grabbed a Q-tip and dabbed the eyeliner at her lower lash line. "So, answer the question. Because if you're psychic, then I have a lot of other questions to ask you, all about my future, of course."

Rayna let out an exasperated sigh and ran another section of hair through the straightener. "No. I'm not psychic."

"Damn, I was really hoping." Tish rolled her eyes. "So, then how is it you know what kind of women Derek goes out with? I mean, if I'm not mistaken, he did ask *you* out, didn't he? Plus, the guy's been stalking you, in all the best ways, for the past six months—the whole time you've been in your 'no makeup and conservative dress code.' He's hot, and oh—" Tish gave Rayna a devious grin. "Guess I need to remind you that he pushed every single one of your sexual buttons on Monday. Plus a few you didn't even know you had." Her friend wagged her brows then gave her long dark hair a fluff job with her fingers. "It would appear as though you are definitely his type."

Rayna put the flat iron on the counter and grabbed the hair spray. "Sometimes I hate you."

"Translation: you love me." Tish leaned over and kissed Rayna on the cheek.

"I do love you. Now please tell me you have some cover-up or powder or contouring stuff I can't even begin to figure out in your bag, because I'm really blotchy and I don't own a drop of foundation."

"Stay here, I have something better."

Rayna turned back to the mirror and finished up with the hairspray. After she put it away under the sink, she checked her mascara again, and then for the hundredth time, cursed her complexion.

Blowing out an exasperated breath, she took a few steps back and smoothed her palms down her thin sleeveless sweater, which was blousy on top but narrow in the waist. It created a slimming effect is what the saleswoman had told her in the store today. Good news was, it appeared to be working. So at least she had that in her favor. Plus, it made her boobs look a lot more...ample than her scrubs did, that was for sure.

"Here is your something better." Tish held out a shot glass full of clear liquid.

"Oh dear. What's that?"

"Tequila." Tish smiled. "Bottoms up, buttercup."

Rayna eyed the glass. "I don't know if that's a good idea."

"It's not a good idea; it's a fantastic idea." Tish nodded, grinning from ear to ear. "Besides, it's just one. All it's gonna do is take the edge off."

"Aren't you at all nervous to meet his friend? What if you two don't get along?" Rayna took the shot glass from her friend. "What if he's the biggest jerk on the planet?"

"That's why I downed two shots in the kitchen."

Rayna frowned, jerking her head back. "Seriously?"

Tish laughed. "No. Just one shot. But look, I'm taking one for the team. If the guy is a jerk, I can deal for a few hours. No biggie."

"Thank you." With a sigh, Rayna eyed the clear fluid and tossed it back. The taste, then the familiar burn, hit, sliding down her throat and into her stomach. "Whew." Rayna licked her lips and handed the glass back to Tish. "You sure I look okay?"

"Honey, you look amazing. And that man is gonna die when he sees you. Now let's go. I'm calling us a Lyft."

"Okay." Drawing in another deep breath, Rayna was tempted to stop by the kitchen and have another shot for the road.

If one was good, two was better, right? Then again, she was a bit of a lightweight, and considering how nervous she was, the booze would probably hit harder than normal. And being the sloppy, slurring drunk girl on a date was definitely not on her agenda.

Bypassing the kitchen, she grabbed her small clutch bag from the entryway table and followed Tish out the door. No turning back now. This was happening. She was going on a date—okay, technically a double date, but that still counted—with a cop. A very hot, sexy, muscular cop. But a cop, just the same.

Dad would be so proud. *Ugh.*

* * * *

"Did she say what her friend looks like?" Jeff nudged Derek's arm.

Derek refused to take his eyes off the entrance to the bar for even a second. "Nope. Just that her name is Tish."

"Tish? Huh. Sounds snobby. Christ, if she's snobby, I hope she's at least hot. And if not hot, I hope she's not snobby and at least interesting. Hot and interesting, minus the snob, would be preferable. But still. I'll take hot over just interesting, any day. But snobby and me don't get along. Just saying."

Derek shook his head then took a swig of his beer. "I swear to God, you are the most shallow guy I know."

"That's not true. Did you meet that new guy on swing shift yet? Rob Pacheco or something? Anyway, that bastard is shallow. Not even kidding, he's married and already earning a rep."

"Haven't met him. But I'll take your word for it, because as you know I hate that shit."

"Noted. I'll be sure to never invite him for beers."

Derek looked at his best friend. "Seriously, Jeff?"

Jeff laughed. "Nah, kidding. But I got you to look away from the door."

Derek frowned and pointed his finger at Jeff. "Someday this is going to happen to you. When it does, I'm gonna give you so much shit you're not gonna know which end is up."

"What's gonna happen to me?"

"You're gonna meet a woman and be all caught up in her." Derek picked up his beer.

"Never gonna happen, Shirley."

"It will. Be warned becau— Shit, heads up, she just walked in." Derek slid back from the table and stood. At the sight of her, his throat got tight and heat spread from his chest outward to his limbs. Wow, she looked amazing.

"A real ginger?"

Derek couldn't help the smile that spread across his face. "Yep."

"Holy shit... Wait!" Jeff grabbed Derek's arm. "Please tell me that the brunette behind her is Tish?"

"No clue. Stay here." Derek stepped away from the table and migrated through the crowd toward Rayna.

She'd stopped and turned away, because apparently the brunette *was* Tish, and Tish was saying hi to a table full of guys. Now she was introducing those guys to Rayna.

Uh, no.

Hell no!

A coil of rope, braided with undiluted caveman possessiveness, unfurled in Derek's stomach. He forced himself to slow his steps and draw in several deep breaths before he acted on every alpha male instinct screaming through his veins for him to pull her away from the table of testosterone and make sure every swinging dick in the building knew she was his.

A mere two feet away from her and closing in fast, Rayna turned and collided with him.

She let out a little squeak when her face made contact with his chest, and Derek clasped his hands on her arms. "It's okay, Doc. I got you."

Her head tipped back, and she looked up at him. "I guess you do."

Unable to speak, all Derek could do was get lost into her sky-blue eyes. The world slowed to a crawl, and as it did, he let his gaze roam over her features. The perfect skin of her face, and the freckles that marked nearly every inch of it.

She looked a little different tonight, and it definitely caught his attention—though she'd had his full attention from damn near the first time he'd laid eyes on her. This was the first time he'd ever seen her with makeup on, and although he'd always found her beautiful without it, seeing her with the little bit on her face blew every one of his brain cells.

Tonight, she'd added a bit of eyeliner and mascara to her already captivating almond-shaped eyes and just a touch of gloss to her full lips, giving her already perfect features a boost.

Her mouth curved into a small smile, and she glanced down, blinking once before looking back up at him. "You okay, Derek?"

He rubbed his hands up her soft arms. "You're wearing makeup."

She raised a hand and touched her lips. A small frown drew her brows together, and Derek could see clearly it was inspired by doubt.

Shit, he didn't mean it like she was taking it. "Wait, what I mea—"

"Well..." She shrugged. "Surprise! I'm a girl."

She's a girl? Uh, yeah, he was well aware. But... Without letting her go, and because he hadn't been able to yet, Derek shifted back only a little and looked down her body and then back to her eyes. "Nope. Not a girl. A woman. A very beautiful and sexy woman."

A blush appeared on her cheeks, and she closed her eyes. After a moment, she drew in a breath and then once again gave him her eyes. "Thank you."

Goddamn, he wanted his mouth on her. Every sexy centimeter of her. Derek closed the distance between them and bent to her ear. "I want to kiss you."

She placed her hands on his chest and smoothed her palms down his sides. "What's stopping you?"

Holy Christ, this woman. Heat sped through his veins, and his dick thickened behind his zipper. She set every inch of him on fire. Derek ran his nose along the shell of her ear. "Patience, Doc. Anticipation, remember?"

She let out a little moan and gripped the sides of his shirt. "Yes, I remember."

Derek moved one hand down to the small of her back and pulled her tighter against him. "Haven't stopped thinking about you all week."

"Me either." She moved her hands up his sides and around to his back. "Can I ask you something?"

"Anything."

"How tall are you?"

Derek grinned and grazed her ear with his lips. "Six four."

"Wow, that's tall."

"Does that work for you?"

She dug her fingers into his back, holding him tighter. "Mmhm, yes."

The feel of her touching him sent tingling bolts of lust down his spine and every bolt was a direct hit to his dick.

Goddamn, he wanted this woman.

* * * *

"*Sooooo*, hi there. I'm Tish. As much as I hate to break up this little hug fest, I'm gonna take a *wild* guess that based on the way you got a hold on my girl, you're Derek. And if you're not Derek, then brace, dude, because I'm going to have to take you down to your knees. The old-fashioned way. Catch my drift?"

Rayna buried her face in Derek's shoulder and giggled like a fool. Then she spoke, even though she knew only he'd be able to hear her. "That's Tish. Best take a small step back and say hi before she goes all pit bull on you."

"Wow, Jeff is going to fucking love you." He didn't take a step back, but as he laughed, Derek released the arm he still had hold of her with, (though he kept the other pressed tight to her lower back, which kept her pressed tight to his hard, perfect body, which was fine with her because he felt really, *really* good!) and Rayna assumed he extended it to Tish. "I'm Derek Hansen. Pleasure to meet you, Tish."

"Pleasure to finally meet you, too. Let me guess, Jeff is your bestie?"

"Damn straight, I'm the bestie. Jeff Pearl. You're Tish, I assume."

Rayna raised her head and peeked over at Jeff as he extended his hand to Tish. Well, now, he was rather good-looking, too.

Tish took his hand and shook it. A smirk on her lips. "You assume correct, Jeff."

He let go of her hand and raised his palm up. "Wait a second. I'm the bestie, and you're the bestie?" He pointed at Tish. "Then we already have something in common. Of all the luck!"

"Oh, Christ." Derek shook his head and looked at Rayna. "This is going to be interesting, isn't it?"

"I'm thinking so. But scary versus interesting isn't off the options list yet. Could go either way." Rayna laughed again, loving how at ease she suddenly felt with him. She may as well go with it and see if at least she had a little fun. Which was exactly what Tish wanted her to be doing. "We might want to sell tickets. Maybe some popcorn, too."

He smiled down at her, his eyes dancing and full of humor and excitement. "Can't wait!" He bent and pressed a kiss to her cheek, then took her hand. "Come on, let's get you two a drink."

"Lead the way." Rayna glanced back at Tish, who was still tossing shit for shit with Jeff. *Okay then!* Apparently Tish would catch up, no doubt with Jeff in tow. Or vice versa.

She returned her focus to Derek. Good grief, the man looked good tonight. He wore a pale blue, short-sleeve button-up shirt, and a pair of dark, almost black jeans. And his backside, or what she could see of it beneath the hem of the shirt, made for an outstanding view.

After navigating the crowd, Derek brought her around to a four-person high-top table and pulled out the chair for her. "Doc, please have a seat." She took her small purse off her arm and set it on the table. "Thank you."

He moved to her right, but instead of sitting, he scooted the seat over and stood between it and Rayna. "What would you like to drink?"

She sighed and focused on his green eyes. "Considering Tish gave me a shot of tequila before we left my house, maybe I should stick with that?"

"Tequila, huh? Who knew you were such a wild woman." He covered her hand with his and stroked the side of her wrist with his thumb. "You want a shot or a mixed drink with tequila?"

Tingles spread up her arm from where he was touching her. Rayna drew in a breath. "Definitely not a wild woman, but I can hold my own...on occasion." She winked. "Mixed drink. Actually, a margarita would be wonderful."

"You got it. I'll be right back." He lifted her hand and kissed her knuckles, but then threaded his fingers with hers. "On second thought, I'm going to wait for the waitress. I suddenly don't want to be anywhere but near you."

"I'm good with that." Yes, totally going for it. She leaned just a little bit more in his direction as he raised her fingers to his lips once again.

Good grief, she was going to spontaneously combust. The heated desire rising inside her was surely making her chest, and likely her face, all flushed, but for the first time since she'd met him, Rayna could not be bothered to care.

Either Derek really *was* into her, or he was one hell of an actor and just wanted to lay his canine's veterinarian. Which would be just...weird.

Then again, cop, right? Who knew what made those guys do the stuff they did. Rayna frowned at the negative direction her thoughts immediately went. She didn't want to think about it—the fact that Derek was a cop. The way many of them conducted themselves.

Right then, he was just a guy. A very hot guy, who happened to be very interested in her. And that's what she needed to focus on.

His pretty green eyes bore into her, and Rayna felt them like a physical touch. Her nipples got hard, and she had to cross her legs and squeeze her thighs together. Her clit was pulsing, aching, nearly begging to be touched. Good Lord... This was bad.

Rayna was attracted to him so much more than she'd even thought.

And yes, the anticipation. She liked that.

She liked him.

So far, she liked a lot of things.

Oh dear.

"What can I get you two?" A petite, very girl-next-door-looking waitress set a drink menu down on their table.

"Hey, girl!" Tish came up from behind and the waitress turned to face her.

"*Hiii, Tish!*" The girl practically jumped into Tish's arms. "You look gorgeous, as always!"

"You are an angel, I swear. Where's that man of yours? Things still good? I want to meet him."

The waitress blushed, but her smile was bright as the sun. "Rig is awesome. He's working over at Deuce's, but he's getting off early tonight, so maybe you'll get your chance."

"Yay! I'm so happy for you two."

"Man of my dreams. *We're in lovvvvve!*" The waitress giggled.

"Rayna, this is Bethany. She's the best damn waitress in this place. Bethany, this is Rayna, my best friend. And this is her...uh..." Tish smiled. "Her friend Derek."

"Yep, already know this guy." Bethany gave Derek a quick hug, then with a big smile, held her hand out to Rayna. "It's nice to meet you!"

"Yeah, you do." Derek smiled, more like smirked.

A smirk Rayna had seen a few times already. *Awesome, he's famous and apparently a flirt with every pretty lady that crosses his path.* Sheesh, was he going to flirt with Tish, too? It wouldn't surprise Rayna if he did. Tish was beautiful in a way that made people stop in their tracks. Most people, male and female alike, flirted with her without even knowing it.

Ugh. Rayna was not going to be able to do this. Served her right. After all, she should've known better. Her stomach rolled over on itself and then clenched into a tight knot. She swallowed past the lump in her throat, took the waitress's hand and forced a smile. "Nice to meet you, too."

The waitress let go of Rayna's hand and turned to Derek. "You want a refill?"

He nodded. "Sure do."

Jeff leaned over and grabbed his empty glass. "Me too, sweet Bethany."

"Well now, everyone just knows everyone, huh? Apparently the three of us get around." Tish gave a little eye roll and smiled. "Gotta say though, I don't recall seeing either of you here before. But then again, I'm not always paying attention." She stepped up to the table, positioning herself to Rayna's left. "Bethany, can I get a margarita for my girl and I'll have a Shilling tonight."

"You got it. Do you want salt?" Bethany looked directly at Rayna.

Rayna swallowed again, forcing the knot in her throat as far down as she could manage. "Sure."

"Perfect! Back in a jif." Bethany turned on her booted foot and walked away.

Derek bent close to Rayna's ear. "I was going to order that for you."

Rayna shrugged. "No big deal."

Jeff stepped beside Tish and bumped her hip with his own. "I've seen you here before."

Tish pursed her full lips and crossed her arms. "Have you?"

"Sure have." He rested his forearms on the table.

Tish mimicked his pose. "And?"

"Just saying." He grinned.

Once more, Derek leaned close to Rayna's ear, but this time placed his palm on her lower back. "You okay?"

Nope. Definitely not okay. Electricity pulsed up her spine from where he was touching her. Geez, her body automatically responded to him. And how insane was it that she was still reacting to him physically, even though she was feeling like she should just end this right here, right now and go home. She managed the barest of smiles. "Yes, totally fine, but I think I'm going to run to the ladies' room."

He nodded. "It's right over there"—he pointed toward the back of the bar—"to the left of the stage and down the hall."

"Thank you. Be right back." Rayna looped her small purse on her shoulder.

"You want me to go with you?" Tish asked.

"No need. Stay and have fun." She smiled and headed away from the table.

If Rayna was lucky, there was a backdoor she could sneak out. When she got down the hall, she found the ladies' room easy enough, but looking around, she found no other options that didn't look like they'd set an alarm off somewhere.

Probably best she didn't have an escape route. Not very dignified to just walk out on a date, unless of course the guy was a complete lunatic. Which Derek wasn't. He was likely a total and complete man-whore instead.

A really good-looking one, but that didn't matter. Not anymore. The blinders—constructed by sweet lust—had come off. And Rayna had no intention of putting them back on. Finding the bathroom, she turned the handle and pushed the door open.

One room, all to herself. Good, she could lock the door at least and try to figure out what she was go—

As Rayna tried to close the door, it was shoved open, and Tish stuck her head into the opening. "Uh, what are you doing?"

I'm losing my mind. What do you think? "Going to the bathroom. Why?"

Tish opened the door wider but stayed where she was, essentially blocking the way out. "Yeah, right. You look like someone just killed your dog."

"Nice. For the record, I really hate it when you use that reference." Rayna crossed her arms, but Tish just stared at her, as if waiting for Rayna to confess. *Ugh!* "Oh geez, come in already and lock the door, please?"

Tish did as Rayna asked, and Rayna turned to face the mirror. Bracing herself on the sink, she looked up and caught Tish's reflection in the mirror. "I can't do it. I can't, Tish. Did you see how he smiled at that waitress? Do you think he's been with her?"

"With Bethany?"

"Yes."

Tish frowned. "Seriously, Rayna, Bethany is all of twenty-four. Plus, I know for a fact the girl has never messed with the guys in this bar—they're all too old." Tish smirked. "With the exception of her boyfriend, Rig, who she met here and is her age, but that story doesn't matter right now. Short answer is no. I bet a million bucks he's never laid a hand on Bethany."

Relief blasted through Rayna like a hurricane. "Okay..." She blew out a breath. "Okay." Rayna washed her hands and tried once more to get the rational side of her brain online. "I know I'm being stupid. But I can't help it."

Tish tipped her head to the side. "Not stupid, just a bit panicky or paranoid? Yeah, paranoid sounds right."

Rayna groaned. "You're not helping."

"Look, I get it. You're doing this thing you swore you'd never do. But just because your dad was the douche of all douches does *not* mean that Derek is a douche, too. Or any other cop, for that matter."

"Don't go there. Many of them are. You know that. As far as Derek goes, it's...ugh...you don't understand, Tish." Rayna stepped away from the sink, grabbed a couple of paper towels, and wiped her hands. "He's so deadly sexy, I mean I'm sure the notches in his belt are endless."

"Wow, so, if he's had a lot of partners then that means you're not interested? Isn't that like reverse feminism or something? I mean, I've had a lot of partners, a few I don't even remember the names of, so does that mean you're not going to be friends with me anymore?"

"No!" Rayna pressed the damp paper towel to her cheek. "Good grief, don't be ridiculous. And fine, that didn't come out right, but you know what I meant."

Tish set her palm on the counter and leaned on it. "No, I'm not sure I know what you meant, *or* mean, for that matter. Who cares how many women he's been with before you? And I'm just going to remind you, it's kind of shitty to assume that he's slept with a bunch of women just because he's good-looking. Or because he happens to know one or several. You're freaking gorgeous as hell, and I doubt you've had enough partners to even count on one hand."

"Wow... When you say it like that..." An ache bloomed in Rayna's chest, and she looked down at her feet. "God, I'm a terrible person."

Tish sighed. "Look, first of all, you're not a terrible person. You're the kindest person I know. Second, I'm sorry I was harsh, but you really need to get your head straight. Give the poor guy a chance, won't you?" Tish rubbed Rayna's arm.

"Okay. You're right, I need to give him a chance." Rayna blew out another relieved breath. Sheesh, she was a complete freak. And yes, paranoid. And also, a total drama queen.

Rayna closed her eyes and let all the fear go. Pushed it all out of her mind. She could do this.

She needed to do this.

Heck, she deserved this, him. Whatever he had to give her. "Okay. Let's go."

"All right then." Tish opened the bathroom door.

"All right." With a nod, Rayna tossed the used paper towels in the trash can and stepped out into the corridor. She was going to have a fantastic date with Derek.

And she was going to have fun, dammit!

Chapter 5

"Gonna hit the head, too. Stay with the drinks, Jeff?" Derek nodded at his best friend and made his way through the crowd to the men's room.

After finishing his business, he headed back toward the bar. Just as he passed the ladies' room, Rayna and Tish emerged.

Tish smiled and continued on down the hall, but Rayna stopped and faced him. "Fancy meeting you here."

He stepped closer. "Hell, I think I just won the lottery."

She smiled and raised her gaze to meet his. "How so?"

Derek took another step, so close their bodies were touching. Jesus, without even knowing it, the woman held him in the palm of her hand. Before realizing what he was doing, her took her chin between his thumb and forefinger and tilted her head back. "Fuck, I want to kiss you."

"What's stopping you?"

"Not a damn thing." Derek bent forward, closing the gap in their height difference, and took her mouth.

She had to be just under five foot six, which meant he was nearly a foot taller, and yet she fit against him perfectly. Rayna rose on tiptoe, wrapped her arms around his neck and moaned into his mouth. Her firm breasts pressed to his chest, and the urge to explore them rode him as hard as his dick was quickly getting.

God help him, she was heaven. Her taste was sweeter than the finest honey, her scent more intoxicating than any flower. The chemistry between them exploded, something he was coming to realize could always be there. He hoped it would.

The heat burning through him was way more than the typical "new person, new excitement" kind of fire two people felt when they were attracted to each other. It was a fire he'd never experienced with anyone prior. She moaned again, and reluctantly, Derek broke the kiss. Sucking in a breath, he pressed his forehead to hers. "I gotta confess, I want you. Badly."

Her lips curved into a meek smile, and she let out a little giggle. "I can feel how badly."

"Yeah well, you've cast a spell on me, Doc. It can't be helped."

Her smile got bigger. "A spell, huh?"

"Yes." He brushed his lips over hers. "For months now. All I can think about is you." He tipped his face back so he could see her clearly and also look into her eyes. "If it's too soon for me to say that, I'm sorry. But it's true."

"Whether or not it's too soon doesn't really matter..." She licked her lips. "I like knowing it."

He smiled as warmth spilled through his body. Feelings were growing within his heart and mind, taking root in ways he knew would be permanent. He should be scared. It should be too soon, but it didn't matter because all he wanted was her.

There was no stopping what was building—had been building for months. He wanted more of her, he wanted to make her smile, hear her laugh. He wanted to make her coffee, find out if she even liked coffee, or what her favorite food was, her favorite color.

Of course, Derek wanted to know what she sounded like when she orgasmed. Also wanted to see her in the morning, with her hair all a tangle of red waves, voice and eyes heavy with sleep... He wanted to know what her favorite position was when sleeping *and* when fucking.

The list was never-ending, and he had no issue with all it contained. But he knew he couldn't tell her all that yet. That much information would spook anyone. The last thing he wanted to do was blow his shot with her.

Instead of blurting every single dream and desire he had for her, and them, Derek took her mouth in a soft, tender kiss, and then as he left her lips, he let her slide down his body, reveling in how good she felt against him. "How about we go enjoy our drinks?"

Her eyes were a bit glazed, her lips swollen, and then they spread into a sexy-as-hell grin. "I'd like that."

"Me, too." He took her hand, turned and led her down the hall and out to the main bar area.

The cover band was just starting their set, and a few people were already on the small dance floor. When he got them to the table, Jeff was standing close to Tish, and it appeared they were...arm wrestling? Oh, hell, really?

Derek looked at Rayna. "Do you see this?"

She blurted a laugh and covered her mouth. Shaking her head, she reached for her margarita, snaked her tongue along the edge of the glass to gather some salt, and then sucked a healthy sip through the straw. After she swallowed and licked her lips, (God help him) she set the glass down. "Should we wager who wins?"

Derek was no longer focused on Tish and Jeff, since obviously the two were happily playing out their own version of foreplay. Instead, Derek focused on the fact that he just watched his woman lick the edge of her glass, the sight of her tongue a temptation he wasn't sure he'd survive much longer.

He drew in a slow breath, and after he let it out, he bent to her ear. "When you do stuff like that it only serves to shore up the spell."

"Huh? Stuff like wha—" Her eyes went wide, then narrowed. "*Ohhh*, the salt?"

He raised one brow and smirked. Snaking an arm around her, he squeezed her side. "*Ohhh*, the salt, *yes*."

"Should I do it again?"

"You enjoy torturing defenseless creatures?"

"What? No!" She laughed and swatted at his chest. "You're in no way defenseless, Officer Hansen!" She laughed again and picked up her glass. "Just for that..." With a devilish glint in her eye, she swiped her tongue along the edge of the glass again, and then wrapped her sweet lips around the straw.

Derek let out a groan and ran his palm over his short hair. "Doc, you keep doing that, and we're not going to be in public much longer."

She raised her brows. "Oh no? Where would we be?"

He bent to her ear. "Any place where we can be alone. That way, if you want to use that sweet tongue of yours, you can do it freely where the only one watching is me."

It was her turn to groan, but hers carried a bit of a whimper to it. It was a tempting preview of what she might sound like if he was able to touch her in all the ways he was aching to. Derek ran the tip of his nose along the shell of her petite ear. "I like the sound you just made."

"I think it's you who's doing the torturing now." She ran her palm down his stomach, then gripped his shirt.

"Nah, just building it."

"Building what?"

"The anticipation." He nipped her earlobe, then pulled away. Though only so he could straighten and take a swig of his beer.

She gazed up at him but didn't say anything more. He didn't need her to, though. Derek knew she was feeling every spark igniting between them as much as he was.

At that moment, they were in total sync, and that just made the fireworks dancing between them even hotter.

* * * *

Anticipation might just be the death of Rayna. Her mouth had gone dry as the Mojave Desert in the dead of summer, but her panties were a completely different story.

As it had been from the first time he touched her earlier that week, Derek was hitting every sexual button she had, and some she didn't even know existed. It was, if she allowed herself to think about it too much, a bit disturbing.

She wasn't a prude, by any stretch, but she definitely had never had her panties soaked through in public before. Come to think of it, she wasn't sure she'd ever been this turned on in private, either.

Her libido was working on overtime, making her want to do things like take him out back and lick salt off his body from head to toe—an idea that, in her entire life, had never crossed her mind but was completely appealing now, and in every way.

Derek placed his palm on the small of her back as he talked with Jeff over the music. A shot of heated tingles pulsed up and down her spine and then arrowed straight for the spot between her thighs where it counted most.

She took a healthy sip of her drink, swallowing the groan that she couldn't suppress, and prayed Derek didn't hear over the band. The group finished their song, and most of the bar applauded.

Sheesh, Rayna had always heard that women hit their sexual prime in their thirties, so maybe this was it for her? Maybe her body was going to take over logical thought and reason and go all Uninhibited Lolita with an officer of the law.

Derek gave her a smile and caressed her lower back, and Rayna wondered if it was possible to keel over from sensory overload...or pass out due to spontaneous orgasm? Was that a thing? Oh, wait...spontaneous orgasm actually was a thing. A serious medical condition. She remembered a few people making a bet in veterinary school about it.

Chuckling at the memory, Rayna took another sip and glanced over at the band. A female had joined the gang of men on the small stage, and the beat of the next song began. Ooh, Rayna knew this song! A new one by Lady Antebellum called "You Look Good." Rayna shifted her hips ever so slightly to the beat as she watched a handful of pairs take to the dance floor.

"Looks like we found our song."

She glanced at Derek. "Our song?"

"Yep. *Ours* as in you and me, Doc." He held out his palm. "May I have this dance?"

Rayna's eyes went wide as she shifted her gaze from his eyes to his palm. "Really?"

He winked. "Yes, really. You're not gonna break my heart, are ya?"

Heat spread up her chest to her face, and Rayna couldn't stop the smile that bloomed across her lips. She put her hand in his. "Not on purpose."

"Good to know." Derek turned and led her onto the small dance floor.

Rayna absolutely could not believe this was happening. Of all the guys she could've but never went on dates with over the years, she'd picked this one. And he knew how to dance, too. Well, maybe he did...

When he reached the center, he pulled her around him, and before she'd even gotten her left hand on his shoulder, he'd hooked his right hand under her left arm, on her upper back, and started them moving.

Good grief, yes, there was no maybe about it. Derek Hansen knew how to dance.

Rayna gazed up at him as he two-stepped them in time with the beat, then pushed her out to spin her, crossed her back in front of him and spun her again, before promptly tucking her back in.

Oh dear, yes indeed, he knew how...more than how.

And she was definitely liking him. A lot. A whole lot.

Quick quick, slow...quick quick, slow...turn—Rayna smiled as Derek spun her once more, then took both of her hands, raised them up, and then came under her arm, around to her left and into a cuddle move—their hands still linked as they rocked side by side.

Her smile got bigger, and a giggle escaped.

Derek came around, rotating her so she was once again facing him. He grinned. "She's smiling. I like it."

"Is there anything you can't do?"

He pushed her out for another turn; this time she rotated twice and then came back around to pick up the step. Derek kept them moving. "Oh, I'm sure there's lots I can't do."

"Now you're just being modest." As he turned and dipped her, she giggle-squealed.

Derek pulled her up and resumed his hold. "I like the giggling, too. You should see your face right now, it's—"

"Oh dear, I'm probably flaming red."

He moved them around the edge of the dance floor. "I was going to say beautiful."

At a loss for words, Rayna felt her face get hotter. Coming around him for another turn, she took his other hand as he ducked under her arm then pivoted in front of her, once more picking up the step, then dipping her one last time as the song ended.

After he righted her, he pressed her against his body, his lips close to her ear. "Beautiful *and* unbelievably sexy."

Rayna ran her palm up the back of his close-cropped hair, the softness tickling her fingers. "I could say the same of you."

He nuzzled the spot just below her ear. "*Are* you saying the same?"

"Yes." Rayna glanced out over the crowd as the next song began. No one was watching them, except...Tish and Jeff. Both sporting grins the size of the Grand Canyon.

She felt his fingers press into her lower back, holding her tight to him. And Rayna suddenly wanted to know what it would feel like to be skin to skin, completely naked against him. Her soft curves molding themselves to his ridges of hard muscle.

She drew in a slow breath as he started an easy sway with her to the next song. "How late did you want to stay out tonight?"

He shifted against her. "As long as you want."

As long as she wanted...and boy, she certainly *wanted*. "Good to know. But what if I want to go home sooner rather than later?"

His brow creased. "Sure. I mean, whatever you want, Doc."

Rayna wanted a whole lot of things. One of those things was to go home sooner rather than later...but to bring him with her.

Head tilted to the side, she traced his lips with her fingertip. "Don't frown. I'll be needing you to give me a ride. Are you willing?"

As Derek's frown disappeared, one of his eyebrows twitched, and then his lips curved into a lust-filled grin. "You can have a ride anytime, anywhere, whenever you want, Doc."

Gazing into his eyes, heat swirled low in Rayna's tummy and lust pulsed through her veins. She dragged her teeth over her bottom lip.

A ride was exactly what she wanted.

Chapter 6

"Later, Jeff. Nice to meet you, Tish." Derek nodded to both friends before he and Rayna walked away from their table toward the exit of the bar.

He had a grip on Rayna's hand...because no way he'd take any chance of losing her in the crowd—or losing her, period. Derek would give the woman damn near anything she wanted. Her request? An escort home. He could do that. Absofuckinglutely!

Even if he only dropped her off at her front door, and she didn't invite him inside, he'd still get some significant alone time with her. Of course, if she *did* invite him inside, he'd count himself the luckiest son of a bitch on the planet. But either way, he'd be happy.

He glanced over at her and squeezed her hand. "I'm right down this way."

"Okay." She gave him a small smile.

They crossed the back alley behind the bar and traversed the many parked cars in the gravel parking lot. When Derek reached his black, four-door Dodge pickup near the back, he went directly to the passenger door and hit the unlock button on the fob. "Your chariot awaits."

She let out a small giggle.

After opening the door, he turned to her. "Let me help you in, you know, since..."

"Since I'm short?" She grinned.

"I was going to say petite." Stepping close, he placed his hands on her hips and pivoted them around. Gazing into her blue eyes, he walked her backward to the opening of the cab and after he lifted her onto the seat, he took her lips in a kiss.

Rayna parted her thighs, and Derek slid between them. She moaned. The heady sound of it sent shockwaves whipping through Derek's nervous system, and his cock went rock-hard. With her arms around his neck, she tugged at the back of his shirt with one hand, and with the other, gripped the back of his head.

Fuck, her tongue was the sweetest treat he'd ever tasted. As he stroked over it with his own, he let his hands roam her body. Derek smoothed his palms down her slender waist, to the flare of her hips, and then continued over her thighs before reversing direction and running them up her tummy and finding her breasts.

Rayna tilted her head in the opposite direction, whimpering into his mouth as she wrapped her legs around his waist and pulled him tighter to her center. Goddamn, he needed more of this...he needed—

Fuuuuck!

She rolled her pelvis, rubbing against his hard shaft, and his arousal shot off the charts with such speed, Derek thought he might come in his jeans. In return, he slid a hand beneath her fantastic ass, gripped it tight and rocked his hips forward...giving it back to her. "Feel what you do to me."

She broke the kiss on a gasp. "*Mmmgod...*" Sucking in a breath, she gripped the back of his neck. "I feel you."

Eyes locked on hers, Derek did it again. Her head fell back, and she moaned. He bent and ran his lips along her jaw, to her ear, and then nipped and sucked at her neck. God help him, the way she felt, the way she tasted and the sounds coming from her sweet mouth overwhelmed him in a way that made his whole body throb.

Every part of her seeped into him, pooling beneath his skin and leaving him with a craving he *had* to sate. "You feel so fucking good, Doc."

He rolled his hips again, and she let out a little squeak before dragging her blunt nails down his back. "Please..."

Please...

One word.

That was all it took.

The trigger was pulled—and Derek knew, at a bone-deep level, she was giving him everything. Maybe she didn't realize it, but either way, it was more than he dared to dream he'd get from her.

Please...

Derek framed her jaw in his palm and gazed into her eyes. "So fucking hot. So goddamn sexy." He licked at her upper lip. "Is your cunt wet for me?"

Her body jerked in his hold, though not away from him or in a negative way, more as if he'd shocked her. Rayna blinked, and a flush came over her face. Then she sucked her bottom lip into her mouth, dragging her teeth over it as she let it go.

Derek grinned, wanting to nibble that lip for her. "Tell me."

Her cheeks grew more flushed, and she broke his gaze and nodded. Yeah, she was definitely a little shocked, but he had a feeling it was more shyness than anything else.

"Ah, I see now." He rubbed his nose over hers. "Your eyes, please." Almost immediately, she focused on him again, and he continued. "Anyone ever talk like that to you before?"

"No." She worried her bottom lip with her teeth once again.

"Did you like it just now, what I said?"

Her brow creased. "I..." She bit her bottom lip again.

Derek straightened a little, giving her some breathing room. The last thing he wanted to do was push her too far. It was too soon. He ran his gaze over her face. "You can tell me anything. I promise." He shrugged. "I'm a dominant guy, and I really dig talking dirty. But if you don't like that sort of thing, that's okay. If you do like it, then that's great. But I hope at least you feel comfortable enough to let me know which way to go."

Rayna stared at him for what felt like forever before, finally, she leaned forward and kissed him. It was unexpected, but completely welcome. There was nothing timid or hesitant about the way she took his mouth either. Rayna drove her tongue between his lips and held onto his shoulders as if she were drowning.

She sucked and licked at his tongue, tangled hers with it, and tightened her legs around his waist as she rocked against him.

Derek did not want to break from her mouth, in no way wanted to end the moment that had turned frenzied and heavy with lust...nor did he want to pull away from the heat of her cunt that he could feel right through their jeans as she rubbed herself against him.

But he needed her to answer him.

Derek ran a hand up her back and into her hair. Gripping the strands close to her scalp, he gently pulled and tipped her head back. "Rayna, I need an answer."

She licked her lips, her lids heavy, her hold on him still tight. "I answered."

The corner of his lips twitched in a grin. "With words. And without looking away from my eyes."

She drew in a breath and cleared her throat. "It's obvious you're a dominant guy. I get that. But the dirty talk? I liked it. A lot. Honestly, I never thought I'd care for such a thing. If you haven't noticed, I'm not a person who swears often, if ever." She blinked and drew in another breath. "But when you said what you did? Every inch of my body lit on fire, and I just..." She dropped her gaze.

"Eyes, Doc." He gave the spot just beneath her chin a little nudge and brushed his lips over hers. "You just what?"

She closed her eyes, then after a moment, opened them and looked right into his soul. "I wanted more of it. A lot more. But also, and this is crazy... but I *needed* you to feel how very, very wet I was...am, how much I want you. I knew, like I know my name, that it would please you." She shook her head. "And I've never said anything like that to anyone ever, in my life."

Everything inside Derek went still. A deep calm came over him, and he knew—he knew he'd found her.

He'd found the one.

* * * *

Had that just come out of Rayna's mouth? Good grief, had she seriously just told the man she *needed* to please him? Holy cow. And what on earth did that even mean in the real world?

Rayna held her breath, praying that she hadn't gone too far as she watched the expression on Derek's face go through a series of changes. Nervous energy broke over her skin, making her tremble. She'd lost her mind saying all that stuff to him, no matter what he'd said to her before that.

Panic took root deep in her gut. Wanting nothing more than to go bury her head in the sand, Rayna tried to pull from his embrace, but considering the position they were in—her perched on the edge of the passenger seat of his truck, him pressed between her legs—there wasn't really anywhere for her to go.

But for Pete's sake, the way he was looking at her now, she needed to do something, say anything. She pressed her palms against his chest. "I shouldn't have said all of that. I'm sorr—"

Derek's mouth was on hers faster than she was able to process anything happening. His divine lips and tongue, his taste, his hands, his big body, his scent...every bit of him overwhelmed Rayna to the point of delicious sensory overload.

Moreover, considering what she'd confessed, the way he was taking control now made her crave things—things she'd heard about, read about, but never thought she'd ever experience in real life, let alone be aroused by. More aroused than she'd ever been before.

As Derek devoured her mouth, she felt his hand spear into her hair, grip the strands at her scalp tight before yanking her head back. She moaned as the stinging pleasure raced through her body.

Derek growled, and Rayna's world spun on its axis.

Without warning, he jerked away from her entirely. "In. Now."

Rayna blinked, trying to register what he was saying. "I'm sorry?" She brushed her hair away from her face and drew in a breath.

"Rayna. Get in the truck now."

"Oh. Um, okay." Still dazed, but clear on his direction now, she twisted on the seat and tucked her legs in the cab of the truck.

Derek closed the door for her and a few seconds later, he opened the driver's door and hopped in behind the wheel. With his jawline hard, his face a serious mask, he cranked the ignition, and the engine started with a rumble. Not another word was said as he put the truck in gear and got them moving out of the parking lot and onto the main road.

Insecurity itched along Rayna's skin, and she twisted her hands together. "Can I ask a question?"

"Absolutely."

"Did I do something wrong?"

He glanced at her then back to the road. "Hell no. Why would you think that?"

"You seem upset."

He signaled and changed lanes. "Doc, I am the farthest thing from upset."

Now she was really confused, relieved, but confused nonetheless. "Then, I don't understand."

They stopped at the next traffic light. Derek leaned across the center console to her. "Let me help you understand. I want you. I want you so fucking bad that I was about to take you in that parking lot. And that's not happening. No way I'm fucking the sweetest thing I've ever had in my arms in a goddamn gravel parking lot in Chandler."

Oh, wow.

That was... *The sweetest thing he's ever had in his arms...*

Wow.

Rayna's nipples rose to hard peaks behind her bra. Thick waves of lust spread through her, making every inch of her body pulse with need for him. She squeezed her thighs together and swallowed. "Oh."

"Oh is right." He straightened in the seat and proceeded through the intersection.

"Can I ask another question?"

A small smile played along his mouth. "Please do."

"I assume we're going to my house. Do you want the address?"

He merged into the left turn lane. "I already know it."

She jerked her body to face him. "What? How?"

He glanced at her and then made a left onto the freeway. "I'm a cop, remember? Consider it a hazard of the job."

"Oh." Rayna frowned and, after facing forward again, stared out the windshield.

"Not a big deal, Doc."

It kind of bugged her that he'd looked her up in the system. But he was right, hazard of the job was the best way to put it. Then again, had he figured this would be the case? That he'd be taking her home? Good grief, had he planned this?

Rayna studied his profile as suspicion and doubt welled up inside her. What if he thought... Oh dear, was this just some sort of fling for him? Did he think she was the kind of woman to have a one-night stand?

As they were getting closer to her exit, she twisted her hands together in her lap. This was bad, so bad. How stupid could she be? Ugh! Rayna knew better than this. She swallowed the bile rising in her throat. "Derek, I don't do this. This isn't me."

He glanced at her. "I know."

She frowned as frustration beat through her gut and mind. "What do you mean *you know*? What does that mean?"

Derek signaled and headed off the exit that would lead to her neighborhood. When he got to the end, he stopped and leaned over to her again. "It means, I know you don't do this. You don't go home with someone on the first date. Hell, probably not even the fourth date. I also know that the things you said and how you've responded to me sexually isn't typical of you, either." He cupped the back of her neck and pulled her closer to him. "But I also know that with *me*? This *is* you. It will always be you." He stroked his thumb over her bottom lip, and she couldn't help the sigh that escaped *or* stop the tingles that one little touch inspired. But he wasn't done talking, and all Rayna could do was gaze into his eyes and listen. "What does that all mean? It means, what you're giving me, Rayna, it's *only* for me. And that means everything to me." He pressed a quick kiss to her lips before he pulled away and, since the light was now green, made a left off the freeway off-ramp.

Feeling a little dizzy, Rayna slowly settled back in the passenger seat. She touched her fingertips to her still tingling lips. "Oh."

A laugh blurted out of Derek that was so real and honest, so pure, it rippled over her skin and cradled her body in a new kind of heat. One that settled right in the center of her heart.

He reached across the center console for her hand. Rayna laced her fingers with his and once more focused on his profile. Good grief, she had not expected this from him, any of it. There was so much more to Officer Derek Hansen than she'd thought. And there was so much more she wanted to know.

But at that moment, she knew enough. And maybe Derek knew her, more than she knew herself even. Which was crazy, but felt true because he got it. Her fear, her hesitation *and* her unexpected desire.

He understood all of it...a whole lot more than she did.

Chapter 7

Derek pulled into the driveway of her quaint but definitely not small house and killed the engine on the Dodge. As he opened the driver's side door, he glanced at her. She was nervous, no doubt about it, but she was also all in.

He nodded at her and stepped out of the truck. She'd already opened the door but, coming around to her side, he gave her his hand to help her down. His truck wasn't raised so high she couldn't manage it, only a few inches really, but he'd rather be there to give her his support anyway.

Derek had a feeling there weren't a great deal of people in her personal life that she accepted help from. In fact, Derek bet he might be the only one. He closed the passenger door, took her hand and led her up her walkway to the front door. "Keys?"

"I don't have them."

"What?"

She sucked her lips between her teeth then let out a little laugh. "I usually go in through the garage."

He moved to her and pulled her close. "You park your car in there, huh?"

"Yes." She smiled, the porch lights making her eyes sparkle. "I almost never come in and out via the front door."

He bent and ran his palms along her back and down to her ass. "You should still keep your keys with you. Safer that way."

"Yes, sir."

At her answer, Derek gave her ass a little squeeze, and she giggled. Though what he really wanted to do was swat it instead. *Slow your roll, Shirley.* One step at a time. They weren't there yet. "Lead the way, before

I start doing all the naughty things I want to do to you in your front yard and your neighbors call the cops."

She giggled again before turning and heading for the garage. She punched in a code, one that he knew was far too easy for someone else to figure out, though he kept that to himself. Derek was greeted with the ass end of her dark blue Volvo S60. "Nice car, Doc."

"Thanks." Rayna gave him a smile over her shoulder.

He followed as she continued through the garage and into the large mud room/laundry room. They made their way from there into the kitchen. Derek realized something was missing. Jesus, fuck, really! She didn't have—

"Rayna, you don't have an alarm?"

She turned and faced him, her eyes wide and both brows raised. "Uh, no?"

He shook his head, looked down at his feet, put his hands on his hips and sighed through his nose. Drawing on any reserves of calm he had in his body, he paused another moment before finally speaking. "Okay, look. I'm gonna have to take my cop hat off for now, and also my alpha male hat." He dropped his hands and pulled her against him. "Scratch that, probably not the alpha hat, but I'll table the alarm discussion for now."

She smiled and rose on tiptoe, circling his neck with her arms. "Thank goodness, because I think I rather like the alpha male part. Even if he is a little nosy, not to mention bossy."

Jesus, she felt so fucking good against him he could barely stand it. "What about the cop part?"

She drew in a breath. "Jury's still out on that."

"Hmm. Guess I'm just going to have to plead a good case."

"I hope so." With a small smile on her lips, she shrugged one shoulder.

Derek had no clue what to make of her comment regarding him being a cop, but he wasn't about to dive into it tonight. Instead, he took her lips in a slow kiss, dragging his tongue over hers, tasting her, tempting her and enjoying every moment. It was a different kind of intensity than what they'd shared in his truck outside the bar. It was softer, but it was awesome just the same.

She sighed when he broke from her lips. Derek brushed her hair away from her face and gazed down at her. "How about a drink?"

A devious smile spread across her lips. "Tequila?"

"Perfect."

She stepped away from him and moved to an area to the right of the kitchen. He followed her into the small galley space that connected the kitchen and formal dining room. The same bottle of tequila that Tish had likely tapped into earlier was sitting on the counter.

Rayna picked up the bottle. "I don't have any margarita mix, so I'm guessing a shot is okay?"

"I'll survive." He leaned a hip against the counter.

She smiled and reached into the cabinet above her, retrieving two shot glasses. Derek took the bottle from her, and when she set the glasses down, he filled both. After he set the tequila down, he handed her one of the glasses. "No salt this time?"

She took the shot in her hand. "No. But that's okay. What shall we drink to?"

He raised his glass. "How about breakfast in bed?"

She tilted her head to the side, her eyes dancing as she grinned. "Sounds like a plan to me."

He tapped his glass to hers, and they both drank the liquid down. The fiery burn hit his throat and settled hot in his stomach. He managed to not cringe, because tequila was definitely not in his top-ten picks for straight-up shots, but since his Doc liked it, he'd deal with it.

Derek took her empty glass and put them both in the sink in her kitchen. When he turned, she was still standing in the butler's pantry, hip resting against the counter and a grin on her face.

"Did you do that to help me relax?" She moved into the kitchen and right up to him.

Derek placed his hands on her hips. "Yes."

"Very thoughtful of you." She traced the line of his collarbone with her fingertip. "Did you need some relaxing, too?"

"Big strong alpha males aren't supposed to need relaxing, but truth be told, yes, a little." He gazed down at her, torn between wanting to move slow with her, take his time, and wanting to fuck her right there on the kitchen floor.

She swiped the tip of her little pink tongue along her bottom lip. Derek smoothed his palms up her sides but resisted the urge to move them higher and take her full breasts in his hands. Her nipples were hard, protruding through the thin fabric of her bra and sweater. Just begging to be touched—and he was desperate to give her that as well as feel them in his mouth.

She gazed up at him and, completely under her spell, Derek gave in to his urge. Keeping his touch light, he shifted his hold and dragged his thumbs over the ridge of her nipples through her top. Rayna jerked forward and let out a gust of air, laced with a whimper. Instantly his cock was hard.

This was their beginning.

Their jumping off point.

As he gazed down at her, Derek knew for sure he needed to start as he meant to continue. He'd be as close to vanilla as he could tonight, and for as long as necessary. But eventually he'd coax out what he knew was hiding inside her.

Drawing in a calming breath, he dropped his hands and took one small step back from her. "Take your shirt off for me."

* * * *

Rayna froze as all at once the room went fuzzy, her vision going dim. As her eyes were about to close, she reached for the edge of the counter to hold herself up—but then something inside her snapped to attention and every molecule within her fell into a sort of hyper-clear focus.

She blinked, zeroing in on the one and only thing in her line of sight: the dominant, gorgeous man standing in front of her.

His face was serious, almost impassive, though his brilliant green eyes held an emerald fire that betrayed his absolute desire for her. Rayna felt that desire to her bones. Her heart pounded in her ears, racing faster than a rocket ship. Her skin prickled with an ache to be touched, to be soothed by him.

There was no question, no hesitation...nothing for her to decide.

The things he'd said when they were still in the parking lot about being a dominant man became very clear now. This man, this incredible man, had given her a direction, a command actually, and with every fiber of her being, she wanted to obey it.

Different, so very different.

She wasn't in charge. He was. And as a result, a strange sort of comfort arose in her. Drawing in a deep breath, she pulled her shirt over her head and placed it on the counter.

Derek stepped forward and ran his knuckles over the swells of her breasts above her bra. "So pretty. Your skin is like fine china with a beautiful pattern on it."

She sucked in a breath as he placed a tender kiss to each mound then, with his fingertip, traced the edge of the lace where it met her skin. *More? Please touch me more?* "Derek..."

Looking up at her from his bent position, he met her gaze. "Now the bra."

As soon as he straightened, she reached behind her back and unhooked the clasp. As she let go, the bands came loose and she rolled her shoulders, allowing the straps to slide down her arms, the bra tumbling to the floor at their feet.

His eyes flared for a split second, so fast she wasn't sure it'd even happened. With her heart pounding and her breath sawing in and out of her lungs, she watched him as he took in her bare chest.

Blessed with a natural C-cup, her breasts were firm and full. And good Lord, although she never much gave it thought before, Rayna prayed that he liked them, was pleased with them. The thought was foreign, and she almost covered her nakedness with her arms.

Far in the back of her mind, Rayna's controlling nature was screaming for her to put her clothes back on and get away from Derek. It should never matter what anyone thought of her body!

But it did matter. It mattered above all things—at least right then. Controlling nature as well as logic and reason be damned. Maybe she'd gone crazy, maybe it was the little bit of alcohol she'd had, but wanting him to like her body, ultimately, pleasing Derek mattered to her.

"Fucking gorgeous. Look how hard your nipples are for me, Doc." He licked his lips then licked his thumb and flicked it lightly over one nipple.

Rayna jerked at the feather light touch, and a whimper bubbled out of her. She went to clasp her hands together but thought better of it. Instead she linked them behind her back. Good grief, she'd never in her life been this turned on.

The anticipation of more, of what he'd do next, was driving her mad, but also serving to build her arousal higher.

He glanced at her. "It's almost as if they're begging to be pinched and sucked and bitten." He focused back on her breasts and flicked his thumb over the other nipple. "So pretty! Fuck, love how your areolas are all puckered tight, tempting me."

Trembling from head to toe, Rayna didn't know if she should respond in some way or just wait for a direct question. Or maybe fall to her knees in front of him and beg—she moaned at the thought of taking him into her mouth.

Before him, she rarely had sexually explicit thoughts, and if she did, she certainly didn't act on them. Moreover, she never, in her life, craved a man's touch like she was craving Derek's.

All of this was so new and foreign, but she wanted it...welcomed it. Rayna closed her eyes, trying to sort all of her jumbled thoughts out. This wasn't normal for her, but like he'd said in the truck, with him, for him, it felt like the most normal thing in the wor—

A sharp sting resonated from her nipples, spreading up her chest and reaching every nerve ending in her body. She gasped and snapped her eyes open to find Derek kneeling in front of her so he was eye level with her breasts.

He had her nipples pinched tightly between the fingers and thumbs of each hand. Twisting a little as well as tugging.

"There you are." He jerked his chin toward her. "Stay focused, baby. Stay right here with me and keep out of the maze of thoughts that I've no doubt are swarming your brain."

"Okay, yes."

He pinched tighter, and Rayna threw her head back as the sweet pleasurable pain rang through her entire body, settling in her core. "*Ohhhhh!*"

"Too much?"

"No, no. It's..." She shook her head and sucked in a breath as he pinched and tugged a little more. "Oh, God!"

Tingles spread over her skin, pebbling it with goosebumps, and she panted, drawing in as much oxygen as she could manage. Her clit throbbed, and her stomach clenched with a need so deep it felt as if she was going to blow apart from the inside out.

It was heaven and hell combined...a decadent euphoria so divine Rayna could barely comprehend the waves of intense feelings rolling through her. But she didn't want it to end.

"Fucking hell, you're incredible." In the next second, Derek let go and immediately cradled the underside of her breasts in his palms and pressed his face between her cleavage.

With the stinging, delicious pressure gone from her nipples, waves of relief coupled with the heavy feel of her breasts sent another round of sensations through her, and Rayna's core clenched down on itself, aching to be filled.

He needed to do something!

She *needed* him to do something.

The ache, the need, the pleasure mixed with pain overwhelmed every one of her senses. As she dragged in breath after breath, desperation for more filled her, only serving to drive her desire higher. "Derek...Oh, God, Please? *Please?*"

God help her, she needed to come!

* * * *

"Please what, Doc?" Derek tilted his head back and gazed up at her. He knew where she was, knew what she needed.

Even though he intended to give her the relief she was begging for—loved that she was begging for it, too—he wanted to take her a little deeper.

She drew in a strangled breath. "I need you inside me. Please?"

He slid his fingers between her legs, tracing the seam of denim covering her pussy. "Is your cunt wet for me?"

She nodded, her long red hair flowing forward and back with the abrupt movement. "Yes. Very. My panties are soaked."

"Perfect." He unbuttoned her jeans and slid the zipper down. "Do you need to come for me?"

Again she nodded, jerking her head up and down. "So bad. So, so bad. Please?"

"Mmm. I like that." Derek tugged her jeans over her hips and ass, revealing her black panties.

For fuck's sake, he was mesmerized. They weren't lace, but simple cotton. Sitting back on his heels, he traced the edge of the thin elastic seam resting against her lower abdomen. Her underwear, by standard definition, were not something anyone would find sexy.

But to him, they were the sexiest fucking thing on the planet. The simple bikini-cut panties were exactly what he'd expect Rayna to be wearing. It might seem silly to some, but Derek believed that something as simple as a woman's underwear could tell a man so much about who that woman was as a person.

No frills, no drama, no bullshit. Just honest, simple, and pure.

Derek pulled her jeans the rest of the way down her thighs, then helped her step out of them. Next he removed her panties. After placing them aside, he focused on the naked beauty in front of him.

She had a fine patch of strawberry-blond pubic hair over her mound that he couldn't wait to feel against his skin. Derek caught her gaze. "Spread your legs a little farther apart."

Trembling, she did as he asked. Overwhelmed with the anticipation of what delights her body held for him, Derek gave in to his desire and slid two fingers through her slit to the mouth of her cunt— Goddamn! *Soaked!* *She was fucking soaking wet!* His cock throbbed behind his zipper. "Oh yeah, that's perfection. I bet you taste sweeter than honey."

Circling her opening with the tips of his fingers, he pressed his thumb against her tight, swollen clit.

She bucked against his touch and let out a deep moan. "Please..."

She was stripped bare before him and dripping with arousal, and Derek let his gaze roam from the juncture between her thighs where her arousal coated his fingers, then up her soft stomach, and further to her beautiful breasts before focusing on her even more beautiful face. "I'm in awe of you." Still trembling, she gave him a slow blink and licked her lips. Holding her gaze, he drew his fingers away and sucked them into his mouth. Her taste hit him like a sledgehammer, and his prick jerked in his pants.

With a growl, Derek got to his feet and, in one motion, scooped her up by her arms and settled her on her granite countertop. She let out a half squeal, half giggle as he let her go and took a step back from her.

"When you smile at me like that, looking at me the way you are right now?" He shook his head, unsure if he should share his thoughts yet.

She rested her hands on the edge of the counter on either side of her hips. "Go on."

"Part your legs for me first." When she did, he continued—though his mouth was watering for a taste of all that glistening arousal clinging to her damn near perfect, pink pussy. Yeah, he'd share. She was worth the risk. Derek cleared his throat. "Makes me want to give you whatever you want."

"Whatever I want?" A small smile arched her mouth.

"Yes."

"Will you let me see your body, please?"

Yeah, it was time to give her that. Derek loved the power he held with her naked and him fully clothed, but he was ready to put the semi-dominant play aside...for the moment only. He nodded. "Yes, especially because you asked so sweetly."

She smiled, and Derek kept his gaze locked on her as he unbuttoned his shirt. Her eyes went wide as he parted the two halves and the fabric slid off his arms to the floor.

With him bare-chested in front of her, she pressed her hands to her cheeks, which had gone an adorable shade of pink. "My goodness, you're incredible. I don't think I've ever seen a man with a body as gorgeous as yours."

Derek was used to women reacting in positive ways to his muscular physique. However, with Rayna it felt real and genuine. Of course, it also didn't hurt to know that he was her first, of sorts—as far as built guys went anyway. The look in her eyes made Derek want to puff up his chest with pride, maybe pound on it a little too. Considering he wasn't a caveman, at least not normally, he'd keep that reaction under wraps. Instead he smiled. "Thank you."

"Do I get another request?"

He pursed his lips and stepped forward. "Yes, but not yet."

She smiled. "Anticipation?"

"Now you're getting it." Derek smoothed his palms up the tops of her legs, sliding his thumbs along her inner thighs as he spread her legs farther apart. God she was soft. "Your skin feels like satin." He looked down her body to her bared cunt. "Your pussy is a pretty shade of pink, too." He parted her glistening folds with his thumbs. "Wet and swollen, begging to be licked." Derek looked back to her eyes. "Do you want me to lick and suck your pussy, Doc?"

Her breath hitched and then she swallowed. "Yes, please."

Derek stroked his thumbs along her folds, parting her labia and watching as her already swollen clit protruded ever so slightly from its hood. "Fuck, look at that!" Without wasting another minute, Derek bent forward, raised her knees in the air and sucked the hard nub between his lips.

A loud gasp came out of Rayna, and her hands landed on top of his head. Her taste hit his tongue, spreading through his veins like a wildfire, and he let out a rumbling growl before pulling away so he could lick at the mouth of her cunt. Her soft curls tickled his nose as he licked at her core and dragged his tongue through her folds to suck her clit again.

Rayna moaned, panted, and then tilted her pelvis forward, opening herself for him even more. He was drowning in every single sweet drop of her. Her taste, her scent, the sounds she was making...all of it had him gloriously drunk on her.

Derek couldn't get enough—knew there was no way he'd ever get enough of her.

* * * *

"Oh, God! *Ohhh! Derekknnnggghhhahh!*" Rayna's back arched as her climax exploded.

Rippling waves of pleasure pulsed through her, tightening her stomach as her core clenched on the two fingers he'd pressed inside her. With his face still buried between her thighs, Rayna's legs shook harder than an earthquake, and she grabbed at the short strands of his hair, holding onto him as she rode each pulse of her orgasm.

Derek straightened and stepped between her parted thighs. As he pressed his forehead to hers, he continued to massage her still spasming clit with his thumb. After licking his lips, he closed his eyes. "Never in my life have I ever had anything as fine as what you just gave me."

Still trying to catch her breath, Rayna swallowed past the sudden lump in her throat. His words, and the tenderness in them, shocked her. They weren't meant to be titillating. On the contrary, they were unbelievably romantic and had a different kind of warmth filling her limbs.

She wasn't sure what to say in response to him. Once again, he'd surprised her, and with every part of her, heart and soul, she couldn't help but believe him. She had to say something—needed to give him *something* in return.

In an effort to express what his words meant to her, Rayna touched her fingertips to his cheek. He opened his eyes, and she let herself drown in their soothing shade of green. "Never in my life has anyone ever said something so romantic to me."

Derek sighed through his nose and then took her lips in hard kiss. Tingles broke out over her skin, and she wrapped her legs around his waist. She was ready for him, more than ready.

As he kissed her with more passion than anyone ever had in her life, he continued working her clit, building it again. Making her mindless, making her want to scream and beg for more. Rayna yanked from his lips. "I need you. Please. I need you now."

"Right here?"

"No." She pressed on his chest, and he took a step back. Rayna slid off the counter, took his hand and led him from the kitchen, through the entryway hall and into her bedroom. As she entered the dark room, she turned to face him. "Here."

"Much better." Derek pulled her against him, kissing her, as he walked them toward her bed.

When the backs of her legs hit the frame, he scooped her under the arms, as if she weighed nothing at all, and lifted her onto the bed. Rayna fell back onto the soft comforter and gazed up at him. Yes, she was shorter than the average woman, but she wasn't thin or petite. Somehow, Derek made her feel like she was small, delicate and lighter than a feather. And beautiful. He made her feel beautiful, too.

Derek pressed a soft kiss to her lips before he straightened, kicked off his shoes and undid his jeans. He pushed his pants down his hips, reached inside his boxer-briefs and freed his engorged penis. As he gripped the length, he sucked in a breath. "Been dreaming about this for too long, Doc."

Her heart melted at his words, even as her clit pulsed in need. There really was no halfway with him. The man was either all in where she was concerned, or really good and laying it on thick when he wanted to get laid. She hoped it was the former, but either way, there was no turning back now. She didn't want to.

With wide eyes, she watched him stroke his length, watched how the muscles bunched in his chest and how his abs tightened. Good grief, the man made for an amazing sight. Rayna held her hand out to him. "No more waiting."

Derek nodded, pulled his wallet from his back pocket and produced a condom.

Sheesh, she hadn't even thought of that. Rayna sat up. "Let me help with that."

She took the little foil package from him and tore it open. Derek pushed his jeans the rest of the way off, and then bent to kiss her again.

With her head tilted back and his tongue in her mouth, Rayna ran her fingers over the head of his penis and then trailed them down the length. His skin felt like satin under her touch, his mouth tasted like heaven. Heat spread over her skin as lust infused every part of her body.

As she rolled the condom down his shaft, his body stiffened, his erection pulsed in her grip and, still kissing her, Derek groaned into her mouth. The sound was so primal, so sexual, she felt her body respond in kind, her core clenching down on itself, aching to be filled by him.

Rayna broke the kiss on a gasp, and as she panted, she scooted back on the bed. Derek followed. When she'd landed somewhere near the center, she lay back, and he settled between her parted thighs.

Perched above her, his weight balanced on one arm, he gazed down at her. Rayna trailed her fingertips over his chest, tracing the line of his pec muscles, and then continued down to his abs. He was chiseled like a Greek god. And just as breathtaking. "You're beautiful."

"So are you." His tone was soft. His eyes even softer. But every other part of him was rock-hard...just for her.

Derek placed his big palm on her breast bone, then smoothed it down her body, over her tummy, and found her clit with his thumb. Rayna's breath hitched, and she raised her pelvis off the bed.

As she settled back down, she felt the blunt tip of his penis against her opening. Moaning, Rayna tipped her hips forward again.

"Oh yeah, let me feel you, Doc. Show me how bad you want your cock." As he continued to work the tight bundle of nerves with his thumb, he pressed the bulbous head inside her. "Fuck yeah! Sweet as honey and tight as a vise."

The combination of his words, his touch and the feel of him finally penetrating her had Rayna's core clamping down on the head, clenching it. "Derek! Oh, please, more?"

In one motion, he rolled them, and as Rayna shifted, adjusting herself to straddle him, his erection sank deeper in her channel. "Take all you want, Doc."

Sucking in her breath, she sat up, seating him fully inside her. She was filled, his thick shaft held tight in the clench of her core. Electric tingles bounced up and down her spine as she adjusted to his size. Gazing down at him, Rayna couldn't move, didn't want to move. The moment was too intense, too incredible. "Derek..."

"I know." He splayed his palms on her waist, then moved them up to her breasts. Derek pinched her nipples before running his hands back down her body and finding her clit with his thumb again. "Ride me, Doc. Take your cock. Let me give you what you need."

No longer able to stop herself, Rayna started moving. With her hands pressed to his chest for balance, she rose up, sliding along his length and then back down again. Drawing in a breath, she repeated the motion, feeling her body relax around his size but...

He was so large, his body, his penis...all of him. Rayna felt almost awkward trying to find a rhythm. Though she wasn't an expert by any means, she also wasn't inexperienced, but for some reason she had no idea what she was doing. Not wanting to spoil the moment, she bent forward and hovered her lips just above his mouth. "Show me, please?"

Derek's eyes went wide for split second before he took her lips in a harsh kiss and his hands came down on her bottom in an easy slap. With a groan, he gripped the flesh and guided her hips forward and back, sliding her along his shaft.

Slow and steady, the angle allowing her to also grind her clit against his pelvis. Over and over, moving her on him, kissing her, nipping at her lips, her tongue. Possessing every inch of her body and soul.

Rayna's core clenched around him, the bundle of nerves in her clit tightening and pulsing. Sweat broke out over her skin, and she shivered as he moved her, forcing her to ride him faster. And once again, he built it.

She was going to come really hard for him. Again.

Chapter 8

"Fuck yes, ride that cock." Derek gripped her ass harder, feeling her tight cunt clench around his dick.

Rayna's body glistened from head to toe with a light sheen of sweat. Her nipples were stone-hard, tight little pebbles he was dying to nibble on. He'd be damned if he let go of her ass though. She'd wanted him to guide her, and he was happy to do it. "Give me those fine tits. I need to suck your nipples."

A high-pitched whimper came out of her, and she bent forward, cupping her full breasts in her palms. Derek took one tight bud into his mouth, swirled his tongue around it before dragging his teeth over it.

She arched when he bit down, but she didn't stop fucking him. Yeah, he was guiding her, but she'd begun moving all on her own. He pulled away from her sweet nipple. "You like my dick, Rayna?"

"Yes!" She thrust her pelvis forward.

"Say the words for me. Say you like my dick." Screw it, he took one hand off her ass, grabbed the other breast and sucked that nipple into his mouth, doing the same as he'd done to its mate. She let out a loud moan, and he let it go. "Say your cunt loves my cock."

"Oh, God, I..."

She never swore, and he respected that, but in bed...in bed she could be different, and Derek knew she had it in her. He pinched her nipple, tugging it a bit. "Say it for me, Doc."

"Derek, I don't know—"

He ran his free hand down her body and found her clit with his thumb. She bucked against him. "Say it, baby, because when you unleash that, you'll come hard for me, and I want to feel that sweet pussy milking my cum from me."

Gazing down at him, riding his dick like she was born to do it, Rayna moaned, whimpered. Arching her body, taking all he was giving her. Goddamn, she was everything he knew she would be, and more. "Let me hear you, Doc."

She closed her eyes. "I love your... Oh, God!" She threw her head back. "I love your cock."

"Fuck yeah, baby!" Derek took hold of her ass with both hands again. Gripping the soft flesh, he lifted her and slammed her back down. "Again."

She flipped her head forward to look at him, her hair wild and flowing all around her shoulders as she bounced on his dick. She swiped her tongue over her bottom lip. "I love your cock."

"Fuck, that's sexy." Derek sat up and wrapped an arm around her ass and pulled her against him, pressing her pelvis tight to his so she could slide up and down his shaft. "Does your pussy love my cock?"

"Derek! God, *yesssnnggghh!*" She grabbed his shoulders, her blunt nails digging into his skin.

"Say it for me." He nipped her bottom lip. "Tell me and then come for me."

She nailed him with a hard gaze filled with lust and passion and pure sex. "My pussy loves your cock." She moved faster. "So much. So, so much."

Derek cupped one breast before moving his fingers to her nipple. "Want to feel that cunt squeeze me. You feel how hard my dick is for you, throbbing inside you?"

"Don't stop!"

"Filling your tight pussy?"

"Derek!"

"So sloppy wet for me? Give it to me, Rayna."

"*Yessss! Now!*" She threw her head back, and her orgasm exploded through her.

Derek felt every ripple of her cunt as it took her over, and as she kept moving on him, he only lasted another moment before his own orgasm hit like an earthquake. "*Fuuuuuck!* Oh my God, baby!"

In a frenzy, Derek wrapped his arms around her waist, holding her still against him as his climax took him over and he spurted his release over and over, filling the condom, until he was spent.

He fell backward, taking her with him, trying to catch his breath, but also not wanting to let her go yet.

Actually, not wanting to let her go. Ever...

* * * *

Rayna lay on her side, boneless and completely sated. She'd had two orgasms and talked dirty for the first time in her life. All with a man she'd never thought she'd ever be interested in or date, let alone have mind-blowing sex with. To add to all of that, he was a cop. Which was crazy...

Lying beside her and facing her, Derek trailed his fingertips up and down her back. "I like being the first of things for you."

"The first?" Did he think she was a virgin or something? Yeah, it'd been a while and he'd said she was tight, but she couldn't have been *that* tight. "Derek, did you think I—"

He trailed his fingertips down her lower back and lightly through the cleft of her bottom, grazing her anus. She gasped at the unexpected sensations. No one had ever touched her there and—

Rayna felt his lips at her ear. "Did I think what?"

"That I was... Oh my." Dazed, she dragged her teeth over her bottom lip as he continued teasing her rear end.

"Does that feel good?"

Rayna moaned again. "Yes. Really good."

"Anyone ever touch you here before?"

She swallowed. "No."

"Another first." He nipped at her earlobe. "Tell me, sweet Doc, you were saying? You were what?"

Rayna sighed, giving herself over to wherever it was he wanted to take her. Unsure if she was even thinking straight anymore, she ran a hand up his side and tried again. "Um... Did you think I was a virgin?"

He chuckled and cocked his head back to look at her. "No, why would you think I thought that?"

She swallowed as nervous confusion crept up her spine. Okay, she really must not have heard him right. And...he was still touching her butt. "I thought you said..." She cleared her throat. "Um... Okay now I feel foolish. Sorry. I thought that's what you meant when you said firsts."

"Ah, I see now." He leaned forward to her ear and ran his lips over the edge. "No need to feel foolish. What I meant was, you said you've never seen a body like mine before. Then you said you've never had anyone say such romantic things to you. Also, I know you've never talked dirty before."

Rayna couldn't help but smile a little, and then her breath hitched as he licked the sensitive spot just under her ear. "Never had your ass played with, either, and the way you're responding to me right now as I tease this tight little hole...just... Goddamn, Doc." He groaned as she trailed her hand down to his erection and gripped it with both fists, and then he thrust his hips forward. "All those firsts, they're all for me. All mine."

With only a few sentences, her feelings of foolishness disappeared. Knowing she was giving him something she'd never even considered would be cherished had sheer power pulsing through her veins. "I like that."

"Thought you might." He thrust his hips forward again, sliding his length through her fists. "Fuck, that feels good."

Rayna moaned, holding his thick erection in her hands, feeling it pulse and grow harder as he thrust himself into her fists. Derek growled and nipped at her shoulder and then palmed one of her breasts.

Heady lust swirled through her body. They were nowhere near done pleasuring each other yet, and sleep was nowhere in sight, either. Losing sleep in exchange for the way Derek was making her feel was perfectly fine with her.

Besides, sleep was overrated anyway.

Chapter 9

"I don't even want to know what time it is, I just know it's too early." Derek pressed his nose into the back of her messy and utterly sexy red hair. "Your hair smells like coconut. It's delicious. It's also making me hungry."

Rayna giggled as she silenced her alarm clock before snugging her backside against him a little tighter. "My hair is definitely not edible. And I'm hungry, too. But coffee first, please?"

"You're reading my mind." He smoothed his palm down her soft hip. "You want me to make a pot, or shall I run to the Starbucks on the corner, assuming it's open?"

She laughed again. "It's open, but I can get up and make us some instead."

She started to turn over, but Derek stopped her. "No, you stay right here. All nice and warm and soft—" He smoothed his palm around her waist to her tummy. "If sustenance wasn't a priority, I would not be leaving your side right now. Trust me on that." He pressed a kiss to her shoulder. "Stay here. I'll go grab coffee and a couple egg sandwiches from Starbucks. Won't take long. Plus, I do believe I mentioned something about breakfast in bed. Another reason why you need to stay put."

She turned her head but raised the sheet to cover her mouth before she spoke. "That's right, you did."

"Cute." With a chuckle, he pressed a kiss to her cotton-covered mouth then pulled the sheet down. "Don't stress the morning breath, babe. There isn't anything about you I don't find beautiful."

Her eyes went wide, but she tugged the sheet back over her mouth. "Only a crazy person would find morning breath beautiful."

"Then you may as well call me crazy because when it comes to you, that's how I feel." He smiled and rolled away from her. "Not feel crazy, but feel that you're beautiful. Anyway." He chuckled.

She laughed, and the sound of it rippled through Derek like a soft melody. After he found his boxer-briefs and jeans, he turned back to her as he slid them on. She'd rolled over to face him. Her light red hair splayed on the pale yellow pillowcase, her lips drawn into a sweet smile, her eyes still a little sleepy.

How he got so lucky to have spent the night with this amazing, smart woman, he had no clue. But he sure as hell wasn't ready to let her go...if ever. Jesus, she took his breath away, and all he wanted to do was climb back into her bed and pull her close to him again.

Just going to get coffee, Shirley. No reason to be all separation-anxiety-ridden. Derek gave himself an internal eye roll as he looked around the room for his shirt but didn't see it.

"Hey, do you remember—"

"I believe you left it in the kitchen."

"I believe you're right." He bent and kissed her forehead, then straightened. "Stay put. I'll be back."

"Okay, but I'm gonna brush my teeth."

He crossed his arms. "Nope. Don't do it. Ride or die, baby. We both got morning breath, and soon we'll have coffee and egg sandwich breath." Derek chuckled when her eyes darted to his bare chest. "Promise me."

"You're nuts. But okay, fine. You want morning breath, then you got it."

"Perfect." Derek turned and walked out of her bedroom.

As he made his way down the hall into the kitchen, he found his shirt on the floor in the corner, slipped it on, and buttoned it as he walked out to the garage. Once in his truck in the driveway, he fired up the engine and then realized he hadn't asked Rayna how she took her coffee.

Grabbing his cell from his front pocket, he shot her a text. It was likely her phone was in the kitchen, and maybe she wouldn't reply. If not, he'd just grab some cream on the side and a variety of sugar along with the typical blue or yellow sweetener packets for her.

As he exited her neighborhood onto the main road, his cell buzzed with a reply from her.

Doc Rayna: *Two Splenda and extra cream.*

Derek: *You got out of bed, didn't you?*

Doc Rayna: *Yes. But I didn't brush my teeth, I swear! LOL*

Derek chuckled and pulled into the Starbucks parking lot. After he parked and turned off the truck, he replied.

Derek: *Best get your gorgeous ass back in that bed before I'm back,
or I'll have to paddle it.*

She sent him back the flushed-face smiley emoji with the big eyes.
Derek laughed and got out of the truck. After ordering their sandwiches
and coffees, he fixed hers as she'd requested, fixed his own, and then
headed for her house.

Opening the garage using her code, which he'd easily memorized,
Derek carried their first meal together to her bedroom, wondering when
the hell he'd become such a sap for the romance. Derek frowned. Screw
it, it felt good, so he was running with it.

"Honey, I'm home!"

She laughed, and again the sound rippled through him, warming parts
of his body he hadn't realized were cold. When he walked through her
bedroom door, he found her sitting up in bed. He almost stopped dead in
his tracks to take in the sight of her.

Blankets pulled up, tucked just beneath her arms to cover her gorgeous
breasts, hair still a sexy mess, but the remains of makeup that'd been there
from the night before were gone. He set the tray of coffees and the bag of
food down on the nightstand. "Did you brush your teeth?"

"No, sir, I did not." She smiled.

He raised a brow as he opened the bag. "Do I need to do a kiss test?"

She giggled. "I'll take a kiss, but only after I get a swig of coffee in."

"You cleaned up your makeup, I see." He handed her a napkin and her
breakfast sandwich.

"Well, of course, I mean, morning-after smeared mascara is not in
fashion. Plus, I might be pale, but the goth look isn't really becoming on me."

"Psshaw. Who said?" He handed her her coffee. "Here, I brought an
extra Splenda for you, just in case."

With a bright smile, she took the coffee and extra sweetener packet.
"First, thank you for the extra Splenda. Second, as far as who said? Pretty
much any woman in the planet says. I may not wear makeup often, but I
do know it's actually an unwritten rule. But!" She raised a hand in the air.
"I didn't brush my teeth, so I still get points."

He chuckled. "Fair enough." Settling on the bed so he could face her,
he took a sip of his coffee. He watched as she did the same then took off
the lid and poured the third packet of sweetener into hers. "Coffee okay?"

"Yes. It's perfect." She took another sip before setting it down. Then
she grabbed her sandwich and took a bite. "Mmm."

"Agreed." He bit into his own sandwich.

"Do you work today?" She sipped her coffee. "Oh my goodness, I just realized... Who's taking care of Axle? Shouldn't you get home to let him out?"

He smiled and swallowed his mouthful. "Not working today. Axle has a dog door to the side yard, which is penned in. He'll be fine for a little longer." He sipped his coffee.

"Takes the pressure off, on both sides I suppose." She smiled. "I've heard that some PDs around the county don't like it when their handlers treat their dogs like family pets. That doesn't seem to be the case with you and Axle."

Derek nodded. "It's true. I believe the sheriff's office is like that. Basically, they want their officers to keep it all business. But I can't see doing that. He stays in the house with me, hence the dog door."

"Seems cruel to do that. I never understood why." She took another sip of coffee.

"They feel it interferes with the way the animal performs at work." Derek shrugged. "I don't agree. If it ever does with Axle, I'll make changes with him. Until then, he's fine." He took a sip of his coffee. "I assume you're going into the practice today, yeah?"

"That's good to hear." She glanced at the clock. "Yes."

He leaned over and gave her a quick peck on the lips. "How much longer do I have you?"

She licked her lips. "Office opens at seven thirty, and I usually get there before seven to prep for the day."

Derek glanced at the clock. Damn, it was already six. "How long do you need to get ready?" Of course, she'd bitten into her sandwich right as he'd asked the question, and now she was smiling, her lips pressed tight together, so she could still chew. Derek laughed. "Sorry."

He bit into his own sandwich as he waited for her to finish chewing. He really needed to let the woman eat her breakfast, especially because she was likely going to have to get ready soon. Maybe they could do their part in the community and shower together? Save water?

His dick came awake behind his zipper at the thought of her creamy skin coated with hot water and bubbles from her soap, and Derek took a sip of his coffee to keep from moaning.

"It takes me about thirty minutes I guess. Maybe a little less?" With a shrug, she took the last bite of her breakfast.

"Seriously? I don't think I know any women who can get ready that fast. You're something beyond special."

She frowned, her brow furrowed, but her lips curved into a bewildered smile. "That's silly. I am not."

"Doc, I'm telling you." He bent close to her, hovering his lips just above hers. "I think you might be a unicorn."

"A... Oh my." Rayna's eyes went soft, and she let out a little sigh.

Derek took her lips in a tender kiss. The woman didn't wear a lot of makeup, and her hair was either pulled back in a ponytail or loose with its natural waves flowing down her shoulders.

She was always beautiful as far as he was concerned. Simple. Pure. Natural... Considering the women Derek knew, and had known, Rayna was an anomaly. An amazing rare find.

Unicorn was *the perfect* description for her.

* * * *

"Thank you for my breakfast, and for getting me home safe last night." Rayna felt her face get warm, and she smiled, almost giving in to her urge to look away from his penetrating gaze. "And also, the other stuff, too."

Holding her tight in his arms, Derek rubbed his big palms up and down her back. "*Especially* the other stuff." He grinned and touched his lips to hers.

For the first time ever in history, Rayna didn't want to go to work. Unfortunately, that wasn't a choice she had at the moment. She tipped her head back as he deepened the kiss.

With a rumbling groan, he pulled away from her. "You'll text me your schedule when you get it, so I can take you to lunch today?"

"I will." She licked her lips.

"Good. Now, get going. Before I drag you back into that house and have my way with you. Again." He gave her another quick kiss before he let her go and opened her driver's side door. "Your chariot awaits."

Again... Lust filled her stomach like warm honey. As appealing as that threat sounded, she needed to get to work, so she tamped it down and focused on other things. Rayna smiled. *Her chariot.* He'd said the same thing last night when he opened his truck door for her.

Who said chivalry was dead? Definitely not Derek Hansen, that was for sure. With a shake of her head and a smile that practically made her cheeks hurt, she slid into the driver's seat of her car. "Thank you, good sir."

"Anytime, m'lady." He gave her one more quick peck on the lips. "Have a good day, Doc."

After he'd closed the car door, Rayna hit the ignition button and watched him in the rearview as he started up his truck and then backed out of her driveway. The exhaust rumbled as he pulled away from her house. With a sigh, Rayna donned her sunglasses, put her car in reverse and backed out, too.

Good grief, she was going to be sore. She could already tell by the minor ache in her abs when she twisted to look over her shoulder while backing up, and then straightened to put the car in drive. She'd used muscles in the last six hours that she obviously hadn't in... Rayna tried to think back to the last time she'd had sex.

Sheesh, had it really been four years? She stopped at the traffic light at the main intersection just outside of her neighborhood. There had to have been another time and she just couldn't remember. Right?

Ugh, she could call Tish and ask her, but the thought of doing that was just...no way. It was bad enough Rayna likely had cobwebs between her thighs. She should've sent Derek in there with a Swiffer Duster, for goodness' sake.

Rayna laughed out loud and shook her head at her silliness. Well, he'd certainly done a darn good job of cleaning house for her. Three, or was it four orgasms? Yes, the shower this morning made for four. More orgasms than she ever remembered having with anyone.

Safe to say, the cobwebs were long gone, and Derek had knocked the dust off of every inch of her body. And now, according to his declaration, she was a unicorn. She supposed that meant her vagina was now coated in glitter.

As she stopped at the next intersection, taking her to the freeway, Rayna laughed out loud once again and turned up the news on the satellite radio. She glanced to her right, and the guy in the car beside hers was watching her, a flirtatious smile on his face.

What the? Baffled, Rayna cocked her head back and frowned. Why on earth was he— A horn blew behind her. She jerked her head back in the direction of the road and noticed traffic had already moved forward through the light. She and the gawking guy in the car next to hers were both holding up traffic.

Good grief. Rayna rolled her eyes and hit the gas. Getting her head back in the game, she made her way to work. For the first time since she'd opened the practice, she was going to actually leave the building for lunch.

Apparently the "firsts" hadn't come to an end. And maybe, if she was lucky, they wouldn't. Then again... A thread of insecurity spun through her mind. Officer Derek Hansen *could* be too good to be true. Rayna frowned and rubbed her forehead. Insecure wasn't a sandbox she ever allowed herself to play in.

Letting out a sigh, she focused on hope—whether foolish or not—and helped it form its own thread alongside doubt. So far the man was showing her he was everything she never knew she wanted. But oh, she sure wanted it now.

Maybe Derek was a unicorn, too.

Chapter 10

"Did you put a tracking device on my phone or truck?" Derek laughed as he pulled out of Rayna's neighborhood.

He hadn't gotten more than a quarter mile from her house and his cell was ringing, Jeff's number showing up on his nav screen in the dash.

"Negative. But if I said yes, it'd be damn fun watching you try and find it."

"Asshole."

Jeff laughed. "Love you, too, Shirley."

Derek smirked and pulled out into morning traffic. "Why are you up so early? More important, why are you calling me?"

"Duh, I want the deets. Did you two like...ya know, *dooo ittt*?"

"You are such a chick." Derek chuckled. "All I'm gonna say is she has a really nice house."

"Tease."

"Yeah, yeah. What about you and Tish? Any sparks?" Derek merged onto the freeway.

Jeff let out a groan that practically rattled the truck's speakers. "That woman, she's fine...F. I. N. E. Fine as they come, thank you, Steven Tyler. But she is one hundred and fifty percent blind to me. Closed off like Fort Knox."

Derek frowned. "You sure about that? I mean, I thought Rayna was blind to me, too, but turns out, she wasn't. Maybe you should do like you told me to do: ask her out."

"*Shewww.* Yeah, that's the thing. I never take my own advice, my friend. I'm usually full of shit."

Derek nodded, even though Jeff couldn't see him. "I'm well aware."

"Yes, yes you are. Anyway, you gonna see the good doctor again?"

"That would be a hell yes. I'm planning on taking her to lunch today. It's still early, so I figure I'll go home, take Axle on a run and then head to the gym." He changed lanes.

"Sweet! Rio and I will meet you at your house in fifteen."

"Okay, but—" The screen went back to the radio display. Derek chuckled. He and Jeff often worked out together, but they didn't usually run together. Maybe his best friend was feeling a little lonely after not hitting it off with Tish.

By the time Derek pulled into his driveway, Jeff was waiting for him. Rio, his canine partner, sat at attention beside him, Rio's rare gray coat with black patches shining bright in the sunlight.

After shutting the truck down, Derek got out and headed for the pair. He clasped Jeff's hand and glanced down at Rio. Derek bent forward and stroked over the dog's fur. "The ladies are gonna start calling you silver fox, my man."

Jeff chuckled. "Pfft, too much of a baby for that yet."

Rio's tail wagged side to side, sweeping any dust from the driveway. "You ready to go hang out with Axle?" Derek straightened. "Let's go get him."

After heading to the front door, Derek unlocked things and moved into the house. A few feet in and Axle was right there, sitting in the entryway to the front room. "Brought you a friend, dude." Derek turned and looked back at Jeff.

Jeff stepped inside, Rio hot on his heels, nearly knocking him over to get to Axle. "Hey, Rio! Jesus, trying to walk here!" Jeff shook his head, frowning. "Excuse him. Like I said, he's still a baby."

"He's four, Jeff." Derek laughed and continued past the dogs into the kitchen and tossed his keys down on the table.

"Exactly." Jeff grinned. "Barely off the boob."

Derek rolled his eyes and gave a short whistle. Axle came running and stopped in front of Derek. Staring down at his partner, Derek crossed his arms. "You been good?"

One ear going floppy, Axle tilted his head to the right.

"Perfect. You keep the bad guys away while I was gone?"

Axle *hurumphed* and then tilted his head to the left.

"Good job." He stepped away from Axle, opened the freezer, grabbed an ice cube from the bin and moved to the small rug he kept on the floor in front of the sink. "Just because you were a such badass watchdog when I was gone, you get your treat."

Axle's ears perked straight up.

"*Hier!*" As Derek dropped the ice cube onto the small rug, Axle obeyed the German command to come and ran over, snatching up the ice cube in the blink of an eye and crunching it in his strong jaw.

"Still can't believe his treat is ice cubes." Jeff stood in the kitchen doorway, arms crossed. "Craziest shit I've ever seen."

"Right? But he loves them." Derek headed toward his friend. "Just gonna get changed."

"Don't do your hair, Shirley. It's warming up out there. We need to get a move on."

"Yeah, yeah. I won't shave my legs, either."

Jeff chuckled. "How's Megan enjoying her summer vacay?"

"She's good. I think they spent a few days in Deadwood this week," Derek called over his shoulder as he entered his bedroom.

"Damn, that must be awesome. Always wanted to go there."

Derek stripped off his clothes and tossed them on the floor by the bed. After grabbing what he needed from his dresser, he pulled on a pair of his tight spandex running shorts, and then a pair of loose shorts over the top. Last was a shirt, socks and his running shoes.

He came back to the kitchen. "I know. I gotta say, it's really cool she gets to RV all over the country this year. Hannah is big enough for it now, so that's why they took the opportunity."

"Nice." Jeff stretched his arms over his head. "You ready?"

"Yup." After hooking Axle's leash to his collar, he moved to the front door. "After you."

Side by side, Derek and Jeff started their jog down the street until they made it to the three-mile path that weaved around and through Derek's neighborhood. The paved trail wasn't as good as running along the Western Canal that stretched from Tempe to Mesa, but it got the job done when time was limited.

Nearing their second mile, Jeff spoke up. "How old is she again?"

"Who?" Derek glanced at his friend.

"Megan? Your daughter?"

"Oh, that was random." Derek cleared his throat. "She's ten. How do you not remember this?"

"Come on. I remember, I just forgot. Besides, how is that random? We were just talking about her at the house, remember?"

"I know. I just...forgot." Derek gave his best friend the side eye.

Jeff chuckled. "See? Anyway, what's that face for? Wait... Did you think I was talking about your doc?"

Derek frowned as annoyance pricked the back of his neck. Because he did in fact think Jeff was talking about Rayna. "No."

"Uh-huh. But speaking of, how old is the doc?"

Called that one. Derek shook his head and chuckled. "Christ, you're nosy."

Jeff laughed. "Nah, I'm just bored."

"Nosey *and* bored." They turned the corner and proceeded along the stretch of path that ran behind the neighborhood. "She's thirty-two."

"That's adorable."

Derek glanced over at Jeff. "Adorable? Really? I take that back, you're not nosey and bored. You're nosey, bored *and* incredibly weird."

Jeff laughed. "I love you, too, Shirley. But I really think you should stop flirting with me like this."

Derek blurted a laugh and almost stumbled. He caught himself, thank God, because kissing the pavement and jerking Axle to a sudden halt while he tumbled ass over teakettle was not his idea of fun.

"Careful, Cinderella."

"Yeah, yeah. If you'd shut up, I'd be fine." Derek chuckled and rolled his eyes. "Two more miles to go."

"Did you tell her about Megan yet?"

Derek drew in a deep breath. "Seriously? We just had our first date."

"So."

"Let me guess, you think I should just come out and be all, 'Hey Doc, so you like kids? Yeah, I've got one. She's ten and awesome and does that work for you?'"

"Pretty much." Jeff coughed. "Not sure what the big deal is."

"No wonder you're single." Derek swiped his palm over his forehead. "It's not a big deal, I just don't think that's first date information."

"Shirley, did you sleep with the girl?"

Derek glared at him but didn't answer.

"No need to answer, I can see it in your eyes. It's a big fat affirmative. So sleeping with her is first date acceptable, but telling her you have a daughter isn't? You make no sense."

"Jesus, it's not like Megan's a secret or anything. It makes plenty of sense to get to know each other first. I'll tell Rayna about my daughter soon enough."

"All right, fine. But note, I'm not saying you need to intro her to Megan, but my advice would be to at least tell the woman you have a daughter sooner rather than later."

"I thought we established that you were full of shit, so your advice doesn't hold much credibility."

"That only applies to me, myself and I. For you? I'm spot on. Every time." Jeff chuckled.

Derek drew in an exasperated breath. So he hadn't told Rayna about his daughter yet, so what? As he'd said to Jeff, it wasn't as if Megan was a secret or anything. Derek just didn't think it was the right time to bring something like that up. Not yet anyway.

Plus, if Rayna had no issue with him having a child, she'd probably want to meet Megan, and he couldn't do that until he knew things between them were a sure thing. After all, once he told Rayna about Megan, he'd also have to tell her about his ex, Stephanie. That could be a risk, too. Not all women were interested in divorced fathers his age, nor did they want to deal with the possible drama of an ex-wife.

Even though Derek and Stephanie were only good friends, and as a result, they co-parented their daughter way better than even the courts dictated people do. Concerns aside, Derek had nothing to hide.

He'd tell Rayna about his daughter...as soon as the time was right.

* * * *

Rayna: *He's taking me to lunch today.*

Tish: *Awwww! How sweet! But tell me what I really want to know: Was it good?*

Knowing exactly what her friend was digging for, Rayna rolled her eyes. Normally she'd ignore the question, pretend Tish hadn't asked. But the truth was, Rayna was nearly busting at the seams to share.

Unfortunately, her office staff was not on the list of people she could tell something like this to. In fact, the only person on the list was Tish. Which meant Rayna was going to gush all over the place, or as much as texting would allow anyway.

Drawing in a deep breath, she typed a reply.

Rayna: *Good doesn't even come close to describing what I experienced last night.*

Tish: *Wait, are you saying it sucked? Because if it sucked, that's really going to suck.*

Rayna: *What? No, it didn't suck. How on earth did you come to that conclusion?*

Tish: *Oh! Sorry. LOL I thought you were being sarcastic.*

Rayna: *LOL I swear, you are the reason why people shouldn't converse via text because you interpret everything incorrectly.*

Rayna: *To make it as specific as possible for you: It was amazing, earth shattering, unbelievable! And every part of my body aches today and in the best possible ways. Better?*

Tish: *HOLY WOW! Yes, totally better! And I am sooooo jealous.*

Rayna: *LOLOLOLOL!*

Good grief, Tish was nuts and always way too open sexually. But she was nuts in a way that made Rayna want to be as open as her friend was. There wasn't anything Tish was afraid to do, or experience—or not do, for that matter. Last night with Derek was the first time Rayna could ever recall coming anywhere close to being as open as Tish was. It felt really, *really* good.

Rayna: *So, I take it no fireworks with Jeff last night then?*

Tish: *Oh, hell no. That guy. No. Completely turned off by him. I wouldn't let him come near me with someone else's dick.*

Rayna: *Oh, wow. I'm sorry. =(Okay well, I'll text you after lunch. Maybe we can find time for a call.*

Tish: *No worries. And yes, if I block some time on my calendar just for you, will you share all the naughty and delicious details? Pretty please? With sugar on top?*

Rayna laughed again. She'd already shared a lot, and giving the intimate blow by blow to Tish wasn't in the plan. But since Rayna had opened the door by sharing what she had, it seemed the slope was a slippery one. Getting into the nitty-gritty was going to happen regardless.

Rayna: *I'll do my best.*

Tish: *YASSSSS!*

Rayna: *I swear, you really scare me sometimes.*

Tish: *I know. But you love me anyway. Talk later!*

Rayna shoved her phone in the back pocket of her scrub pants and pushed away from the desk in her small office. It was time to get to work. Hopefully the day would be smooth and she'd get to have lunch with Derek.

Rayna exited her small office and moved to the tech counter—smile firmly in place. "Good morning, Gina."

"Morning, Doctor. You look happy this morning." Gina smiled as she checked medical stock in the cabinet above her.

"Thanks. A little tired, but what's not to be happy about? It's Friday." Rayna slid the stack of patient files closer so she could go through them. "What do we have on the docket today?"

Andrea came over. "Late night?"

Rayna glanced at her. "Yes, actually. Tish talked me into going out last night. We had fun, though."

Andrea laughed. "Something tells me with Tish, there's always fun involved."

"This is true." Rayna held up one of the files and looked at Gina. "How's Sparkles doing this morning?"

"Looking pretty good, though he's moving a little slow. He ate some soft food when I came in. So far he's tolerating it."

"Great. I'll check him after I get done with this first patient." Rayna stepped away and headed for exam room three to do a yearly checkup on a six-year-old corgi named Sampson.

The first few hours of the morning flew by, patient after patient, dogs, cats and one teddy bear hamster named Brittany—who actually turned out to be a boy. As Rayna filled another cup of coffee, her cell vibrated in her back pocket.

She pulled the phone out and swiped the screen.

Derek Hansen: *Thought you were going to text me your schedule?*

Oh, no! Rayna's eyes went wide. She'd been so busy texting like a silly schoolgirl with Tish when she first got in to the clinic, and then reviewing patient files, she'd completely forgotten to message Derek. Considering she'd barely stopped thinking about him all morning, she was baffled by how she'd managed to screw up one simple little task.

Rayna: *I'm so, so sorry, Derek. I got caught up, and then starting seeing patients. I can't believe I did this.*

Derek Hansen: *It's okay, babe. I understand. I can only imagine how busy things get around there. Do you have time for lunch though?*

Rayna: *Thank you for understanding. Give me just a minute to check the schedule.*

Moving down the hall, she stopped just behind the front desk. "Hey, Billy, what time did we book in lunch today?"

"Hey, Doc Michaels." Billy smiled. "Let me see... Yes, it's looking like one to one thirty is blocked for lunch. Did you need me to shift anything?"

"Hmm." Rayna ran her teeth over her bottom lip. "What's the one thirty appointment?"

"Let me check." Billy scrolled through the office scheduling system. "Looks like a new patient checkup. A beagle puppy named Augie. Probably the usual lab tests and vaccines."

"Shoot." She bit her bottom lip, knowing there was no way to push the appointment later. She'd just have to make it work. Unless... "What do we have at twelve thirty?"

Billy raised a brow and then looked back at the computer. "Well...we have Caspian coming in for a nail trim. You usually do a quick checkup on him after he's done."

"Right, right. Okay, let me know as soon as he's here. I'll check him before the nail trim. That way I can head out for lunch a little early."

Billy grinned. "Lunch date?"

Before she could stop it, a small grin arched Rayna's lips. She rolled her eyes, mostly at her own corny giddiness. "Maybe."

"Yay!" Billy clapped. "I can't wait to hear all about this."

"Oh dear. Don't know what I am going to do with you." Rayna giggled. She couldn't help it. Sheesh, talk about another schoolgirl moment. She rolled her eyes again. "Going back to work now."

Still smiling, Billy turned back to his computer. "I'll call and see if Caspian can come in early."

Instead of commenting that it might not be a good idea to move a patient around so that Rayna could go have lunch, she decided to let Billy do what he did best, which was handle her scheduling. If anyone could pull that off, it was Billy. Either way, she was happy to have at least forty-five minutes free for lunch with Derek.

When she got back to the main treatment area, she sent the targeted time to Derek and then got back to work. Sweet anticipation thrummed in Rayna's veins. The wait to see him was bittersweet. Here she was, all dressed up in her un-sexy green scrubs, her lab coat, and her hair pulled up in its standard, un-exciting ponytail.

Would he still find her attractive? Would he kiss her hello? Would he back her against the wall in exam room four like he'd done last week when he'd shown up to ask her out? Wait, maybe it was better if she left the clinic and met him somewhere.

Grabbing her phone, she typed another message.

Rayna: *Did you want to meet somewhere? There's lots of places close by.*

Derek Hansen: *Works for me. Is there someplace you'd like to go?*

Rayna: *There's a small family owned lunch cafe called Double Decker in the plaza across the street. Meet there?*

Derek Hansen: *Perfect. Can't wait to see you.*

Rayna sighed, and a smile curled her lips. Warmth bloomed in her chest, and she knew as a result her skin was flushing pink. However, this time she didn't care. Rayna couldn't wait to see him either. She had two more patients to attend to before Caspian was in for his trim.

After that, she was free. At least for forty-five minutes anyway.

Chapter 11

"I'm running late." Rayna set her cell phone down and hit the speaker button.

"You're always running late." Tish laughed. "Do you need me to come over and help you get ready? Some tequila perhaps?"

Rayna ran a brush through her hair, trying to get the length to cooperate into some sort of organized display. "I had a late appointment. And no, definitely no tequila, thank you very much."

"What dreamy place is he taking you tonight?"

"He won't tell me. Says it's a surprise." Rayna added a little spray to her hair.

"So, it would seem like you're over your cop hang-up."

Rayna frowned and glanced down at her phone. "No. Not over it. Just not going to focus on it. Besides, we're just dating. I'm keeping it casual because, for the first time, I'm having amazing sex, and I don't want to complicate that with feelings. And hello, not like I'm marrying the guy."

"Honey, some guys cheat. But lots of guys don't."

"I know that, Tish." Agitation itched along the back of Rayna's neck, and she shoved it aside, focusing instead on adding a touch of mascara.

Apparently, Tish wasn't done. "Just because he's a cop does not automatically mean he'll be a liar or cheater like your father. Let's face it, your dad was an asshole."

"I know that, too." Rayna tossed the mascara aside. "Good grief, can we *not* talk about this right now? It's not exactly going to set my night off on a good note."

"Yes. Sorry. I just... Sweetie, I'd hate to see you miss out on something awesome because of an old idea."

"Not an old idea, plus—" Rayna paused, listening. "Crap, he just rang the doorbell. I'll call you tomorrow."

"Okay! Don't do anything I wouldn't do!"

"Oh dear, that's a scary thing coming from you, Tish." Rayna rolled her eyes. "Bye!" Flipping off the bathroom light, she rushed from her bedroom, down the hall and to the front door.

Of all the subjects to bring up, the one regarding her cop father, and his constant lies and also frequent infidelities during his marriage to her mother, was not one Rayna needed to have in the forefront of her brain right before seeing Derek—a cop she was now, against her better judgment and hard lessons learned thanks to dear old Dad, casually dating and having regular sex with.

Pushing down her heated agitation as best she could, Rayna swung the door wide and froze. All annoyance and thoughts of her father flew from her brain. Her breath caught in her lungs, and her skin got tight and warm. *Oh my.*

The sun had barely begun to set, and he was still wearing his sunglasses. Rayna wasn't even sure what clothes he wore on his amazing body, because she couldn't get past how absolutely mind-blowingly sexy he looked in, of all things, sunglasses.

He slid his shades down a little to stare at her over the tops of them. "Doc, I'm really getting concerned with your ability to be safe in your own home."

Oh dear, looking at her like he was right then? All serious, beyond sexy and, well, dominant—her nipples went stone-hard. She swallowed past the glue that coated her tongue. "Um..."

He removed his glasses and stepped to her, so close their bodies were almost touching. "Um?"

Sucking in a deep breath, Rayna tilted her head back to stare up at him, and her clit started throbbing. She needed to say something, she was sure of it. But with him so close, smelling so good, looking so good, Rayna could not manage a coherent thought...other than: "I want you."

One corner of his mouth twitched, and he stepped closer, effectively pressing his body to hers. "Is that so?"

Rayna nodded and stepped backward, but only because he was walking them that way. Every inch of her body was burning with lust now. And he hadn't even touched her yet. Good grief, was it always going to be like this?

It'd been just over a week, and she'd seen him at least four out of those seven days. Each time he'd taken her out somewhere. Mostly dinner, lunch or coffee, but usually in some off-the-beaten-path place that she'd never heard of.

Trish called them dream dates, and honestly, Rayna couldn't argue it. Plus, before, after, and sometimes even in between, they'd been having sex. So much sex, Rayna was sure her libido would need a nap. But apparently not, because it was wide awake and revving for more.

When they'd cleared the entryway, Derek swung the door closed, then wrapped an arm around her, picked her up, raising her to his lips, and kissed her.

Rayna gripped the sides of his neck, curling her fingers around to hold him tight, and moaned as his tongue dove into her mouth. Derek growled, turning them, and her back hit the wall in the entryway.

When he pressed against her, Rayna felt his erection through his pants... and oh yes, this was too good. Too mind-blowing. Too...everything. Hot, wet, fast and furious, and she welcomed every glorious moment of it.

Derek broke from her mouth and pressed his forehead to hers. Breathing heavy through his nose, he licked his lips. "Fuck, you taste good. As much as I want to fuck you right here and now, I'm not going to."

Dizzy from his kiss, his touch, his scent and taste, Rayna swallowed and tried to focus. "May I ask why?"

"Because we got a reservation in Cave Creek for dinner."

Rayna felt the lust in her body settle into a sweet warmth in her stomach. "Oh."

He set her back on her feet. "While we drive there, we're talking about your habits."

Rayna blinked. "My habits?"

"Yup. The bad ones. Grab your purse, Doc. Clock is ticking." He moved back to the front door.

She frowned as confusion filled her brain. What on earth was he talking about? "Bad ones?"

"Like I said, we'll discuss it in the truck." Derek chuckled and opened the front door. "Meet you out front. Assuming you're heading out the garage door, so how about you start by locking this one when I close it."

"Of course. Don't be silly." Still perplexed, Rayna moved to him.

"'Of course,' she says. 'Don't be silly,' she says." With a chuckle, he shook his head, while rolling his eyes to the sky, and then bent, pressing a quick kiss to her lips before slipping his sunglasses back on and closing the door.

Now it was her turn to roll her eyes. And yes, she did as he said, locked the door. But not because he told her to, because not locking it would be foolish and unsafe. Yet, for some reason, Derek thought she wasn't being safe. In her home. Hmm...

For the life of her, Rayna had no idea why he thought that. So, yes, as soon as she got her butt in the truck, as he said, they'd discuss it because she wanted to unravel this little mystery. Grabbing her purse, she moved through the house to the kitchen and out to the garage.

Derek was waiting for her, his back against the grille of his truck, arms crossed over his broad amazing chest. Legs crossed at the ankles. As she hit the enter button on the garage keypad, she took in his attire.

Gray short-sleeve button-up, dark blue jeans, and black boots. Gorgeous. Rayna bit her bottom lip and moved to him. He took her arm and walked her around to the passenger side, opened the door for her, like he seemed to really like to do and then—

"Your chariot, m'lady." He smiled and helped her up into his truck.

Rayna giggled. She couldn't help it. He was so sweet to her. Under all those hard muscles and his bossy, alpha cop demeanor, he was a total romantic at heart.

Yes, another dream date for sure.

* * * *

"So, let's talk safety." As he navigated onto the 101 freeway, Derek reached across the center console and took her hand in his.

She leaned toward him. "Wait, real quick before you start. How's my sweet Axle?"

"He's fine. Nice try with the distraction." He chuckled and looked over at her.

"I beg your pardon, sir. I'm not trying to distract you." She grinned. "I genuinely miss him, especially since you haven't brought him in for his weekly checkup."

"Very cute. I'll bring him over next time I spend the night, deal?"

"I'd love that! Yes. Deal."

He glanced at her again. "Can we talk safety now? While there's still enough driving time for my lecture?"

"Yes, let's. I have no idea what you're talking about, but I can't think of anything else I want more than a lecture from you." She giggled.

He smirked. "Now, Doc, don't go being more cute when I'm trying to be serious."

"Oh, well, in that case..." She let go of his hand and turned in her seat to face him and gave him something close to a frown. "How's this for serious? Wait, let me try again." She turned her head slightly, dipped her chin, pursed her lips and raised one brow. "How about now?"

"Lucky I'm driving, else I'd spank your ass for being so sassy. Albeit, cute as hell, but still...sassy."

At her intake of breath, Derek glanced over, and the expression on her face had completely changed. Her blue eyes were wide, her face was a little flushed, and she had her teeth planted in her bottom lip.

Huh...did his Doc want to be spanked?

"You'd spank me?"

Derek glanced back to the road, pausing as he weighed his options on how to answer that question. Screw it, may as well just see what happens. He glanced at her from the corner of his eye. "Hell, yes, if you earned it, I'd spank you."

"I've never been spanked before." She cleared her throat. "I think I might like it."

Her tone was so low, he almost missed it. Thank fuck he hadn't. This woman, Jesus, she was like opening a present every damn day. She'd like it, he knew she would. It was building, each time they had sex. Every time he took her, she gave him a little more control, and Derek wanted more. "Good. Another first just for me."

He took her hand once again and squeezed. Knowing she'd need to process her latest sexual realization, he decided that was enough on the spanking topic for the moment and redirected. "Now, stop changing the subject. Let's get back to safety."

"I didn't change the subject. You did!" She laughed.

"Changing the subject again, I see? Sassy. So sassy."

"Oh dear. I give up." She laughed again, and Derek felt it tingle from the top of his head down his spine. "Tell me about my safety issues, please."

He sighed. "There's just so many, I have no idea where to start now."

Laughing again, she pulled her hand free and swatted his arm. "No fair!"

He shrugged. "I know, but I like hearing you laugh." He grabbed her hand and brought it to his lips.

He liked hearing her laugh as much as he liked making her moan. The moaning was beyond amazing, though. But Derek held that extra bit of information back from her. She already had him beyond enthralled, caught in her spell, there was no getting free. He'd give her all that detail later, but slowly, and in a way that she'd know it was real.

She slid her hand from his and stroked his cheek with the back of her fingers. "I like that you make me laugh, even if you are a little bossy and annoying at times." She bent over the console and pressed a soft kiss to his cheek and then settled back in her seat. "Tell me what my safety needs are, Officer."

Derek's cock pulsed behind his zipper. Yeah, totally under her spell. He cleared his throat, glanced at her, and did his best not to drown in her pretty blue eyes so he could stay on topic. "Your garage code is a problem."

She brushed her hair off one shoulder. "How so?"

"It's your birthday, Rayna. That's way too easy for anyone to figure out."

"Oh. Well...I hadn't really..."

He glanced at her, and this time she was frowning. "Yeah, I get it. But babe, you gotta change it. Come to think of it, please tell me that's not the code you use for your debit card, because if so, you gotta change that, too." He heard her blow out a breath. "Okay, that's an affirmative."

She crossed her arms. "All right. What else?"

"I got there tonight, rang your bell, and you didn't check the peephole before opening the door."

"Of course not, Derek, I don't have a peephole."

"Exactly, Rayna." He reached across and put his hand on her thigh.

"Ugh...okay, fine. You're right. I'll hire someone to put in a peephole. But in my defense, I never use the front door. And it's not like I have many people coming by. I'm at the clinic all the time."

"No need to hire someone. I'll put the peephole in for you."

"Oh, no. That's not necessary. Really, I can just hire a handyman."

Not gonna happen, some strange guy at her house. No way. Derek frowned. "You're seriously going to deprive me of giving you something I want to give you to keep you safe?"

"Well no, but Derek, that's not your responsibility. I can't accept that."

"Yeah, Rayna, you can. Because I'm offering it. I want to do this for you, and I'd appreciate if you'd let me." He gave her thigh a squeeze. "Besides, it's just a peephole."

"I know, but..."

Layers, she had so many damn layers around her. Good thing he was up for breaking through them. "Look, I get that you're used to doing things on your own. Nothing wrong with that. But it's okay to let someone help once in a while."

She gazed out the passenger window. "I know it is."

"Good, then it's settled. Tomorrow, I put in a peephole."

"Fine."

"Then we put in an alarm system." He braced.

She jerked to face him. "A what?"

"An alarm system, Doc. You got one at the clinic. I've seen it. You need one at your home." He nodded as he exited the freeway and stopped at the light.

"Derek, I don't—"

"Speaking of that, please tell me the code for the alarm at the clinic isn't also your birthday." Since the truck was stopped, he turned his head to fully look at her.

She opened her mouth and then shut it. Opened it again, then shut it once more. He wanted to laugh, but he was also not happy with this knowledge. She was a smart woman, but he knew she just wasn't thinking.

He shook his head. "Yeah, that's another affirmative. Tomorrow morning, you're changing that and you're setting an appointment with the alarm company that monitors the clinic to install one at the house."

She frowned. "Fine. But let it be known right now, you're definitely too bossy."

"May as well get used to it."

"You're also annoying."

He smirked. "Should probably get used to that, too."

"Whatever." She crossed her arms.

He chuckled. "Cute but sassy. Definitely in need of a spanking."

"What*ever.* And by the way, you can get used to that." She crossed her legs.

"Get used to which? The spanking or the sassy?"

She rolled her eyes, but her lips twitched in a grin she was trying not to give him.

He pulled her hand free from its tucked position and brought her fingers to his lips. "Would love to get used to it, Doc. Can't imagine anything better than your cute and your sassy. Cherry on top is spanking that fine ass of yours before sinking deep in your tight pussy."

She squirmed. "Land sakes, Derek! Everything inside me just got warm!"

He drew in a deep breath, knowing she was getting wet for him. He liked that a whole fuck of a lot. Plus, was that an accent he just heard come out of her? "And this is a problem how?"

She faced him. "Because we're goin'ta dinner and all I can think about is sex with you."

"Anticipation, Doc." He winked, and since the light turned green, he pulled out into traffic. "By the way, was that a Southern accent I just heard?"

"You shush." She shook her head and pressed her lips together.

Derek laughed. He'd feed her, then take her home to her place, and spank her, at least once. Then he'd fuck her...definitely more than once.

Especially if she really liked the spanking.

Chapter 12

"Nnnggg*hhyesssss!*" Rayna arched, or tried to, but she was on her stomach, pressed to her mattress, and Derek was leaning on her, his entire upper body holding her down...spanking her.

Spanking! Her!

And she freaking loved it.

Loved! It!

"Jesus, fuck, Doc! Your ass is the prettiest fucking color pink I have *ever* fucking seen in my life." He smoothed his palm over the hot flesh of her buttocks.

Rayna moaned and again tried to arch to him. It was the strangest thing she'd ever experienced in her life. The sting of the pain and how it brought forth pleasure. It didn't make a bit of sense. Yet, apparently, it made complete and total sense to her body.

Since she'd started having sex with Derek Hansen, barely two weeks ago, her body wanted a lot of things that seemed to make sense to it, but they were things she'd never in her life given much thought to.

He'd started this new phase of their sex life a week ago. While on their way to dinner, as he lectured her about the safety she wasn't taking in her home, *and* with her money, he'd also told her that she was sassy, and for that, he was going to spank her.

She'd wanted to be appalled, truly she did. However, the minute he'd said it, her nipples had gone hard as pebbles. And her pussy—yes, pussy, because she was now using the same terms he used, not only because he regularly commanded her to say them when he had her naked, but also because the words no longer felt vulgar or undignified. On the contrary, even in the privacy of her own thoughts, they now felt titillating.

Rayna didn't curse, part of her Southern woman upbringing she'd guess, and that remained intact. She'd never talked dirty in bed, either. But with Derek, she did. Because he liked it. Because he wanted her to.

For the love of all things holy, when he got her riled up enough, her Southern accent would sneak out. With Derek she did a lot of things she avoided or had never done before. So yes, when Derek told her he would spank her, her nipples got hard and her pussy got wet.

Rayna loved it, and she hated it. And she didn't want any of it to stop. *SMACK! SMACK!*

A groan punched out of Rayna, and her pussy convulsed. *Oh, God!* The feel of his broad hand as it came down on her flesh was agonizing... and it was bliss.

"Fuck yeah! Let me see, baby." Derek slid his fingers along the crevice of her buttocks, between her legs, and found her center. He dragged the tips of those fingers through her wetness, then moved them to her clit, and Rayna whimpered. "Oh yeah. Drenched for me. Sloppy wet. You want my cock?"

With desire pulsing through her veins, Rayna drew in a breath and forced herself to speak. "Yes."

"Say it." He drew his fingers back and pressed them inside her. "I want the words from your sweet lips."

Her inner walls clenched down on the penetration, and another strangled moan punched out of her. So good. "Derek...please?"

"Love when you beg, Doc. Now, say it for me." He pulled his fingers away and smoothed his palm over her heated buttocks.

Another sting of pleasure from his caress bolted through her, and her clit pulsed. God help her, she loved this. She knew he loved it too, so she gave him what he wanted. What they both wanted. "Please, baby. I want your cock."

"That's what I'm talking about. Don't move." At once his weight was gone, and she heard the tearing of the foil packet. Knew he was putting on a condom. The bed dipped, and her hips were pulled up. Rayna raised up on her hands. But then his palm was pressed to her upper back, between her shoulder blades. "No, baby. Stay down."

Rayna's chest hit the mattress again, and then she felt the tip of him slide through her folds. "Derek, yes, please..."

"Is this your cock, Rayna?" He pressed the tip to her opening.

"*Yessss.*"

"Say it. Tell me." He gripped her butt cheeks in his palms, pulling them apart.

The sting from the spanking and now the added sting of him stretching her anus sent another wave of pleasure through her. Rayna was going to orgasm before he even got inside her. "My cock! It's mine. Oh God. Please, baby!"

"Fuck yeah, it is." Derek thrust in, fast and hard, filling her. "Goddamn, this cunt!"

Perfection.

Bliss.

Rayna fisted the sheet beneath her as he drew out then drove in again, his hips slapping against hers.

Still holding her ass in a tight grip, he let go with one hand and slid it to her middle back. Pressing down, he pinned her there. His weight causing her body to arch deeper, angling her bottom just a little higher for him.

Derek took her hard and fast, harder than he had before, and she welcomed it. Wanted it. Needed it. Pure, unadulterated, raw sex. Each time he slid in, the head of his penis grazed her G-spot.

Rayna closed her eyes as her breath came out of her on a slow and deep moan. She welcomed it, letting it build. Her core rippled, convulsing around his thickness. Her clit pulsed. She was going to come.

"Feel you squeezing my dick." He drew out fully, to the head, then drove back, this time slower but still hard. "Gonna come with you, Doc."

Again, he slid out fully, letting her feel the rim of his bulbous head before he drilled back in. The perfect angle, sending all her senses spinning as her pussy clenched and her need to climax rose higher. She was going to die, just fly completely apart.

Lost in the haze of pure sex and need, the sounds they were making together penetrated her ears, driving her higher. Rayna moaned, whimpered and gave herself over to him and her orgasm.

And still, he kept going.

Like a rubber band snapping, Rayna's body jerked hard as her climax hit with a force so overwhelming, she buried her face in the mattress and screamed.

Slamming in deep one last time, Derek came over her, and with his weight atop her, Rayna's body slid flat on the mattress. His gorgeous cock pulsed hard in her core, spurting his release into the condom, as her walls clenched, over and over again, around his length.

He pressed his lips to her ear. "Milking your cock, baby. Taking every drop from me."

"Can't help it." Rayna closed her eyes as the aftershocks of her orgasm started to settle.

"Trust me. Didn't say I minded it." He chuckled, and as he did, his penis jerked inside her.

Rayna moaned, and her core clenched down on him in reaction.

Derek let out the closest thing to a growl she'd ever heard. "Jesus...love that."

She loved it, too.

The spanking. The fucking. The moaning.

All of it.

* * * *

"You good?" Derek stroked his fingers up and down her bare back, wondering how in the hell he'd gotten so lucky.

"Mmhmm." She was curled soft and sweet against him, her head on his chest, her soft breath tickling his skin.

"Good." He gave her a small squeeze and smiled as she cuddled a little closer. Yeah, he'd for sure gotten lucky, and there was no way he was going to fuck that up. Derek closed his eyes as warmth filled his gut.

In the darkness of her room, lying in her bed, with the sweet sounds of her breath in his ears and the softness of her body pressed against him, Derek's next thought was to tell her about his daughter. The time was right.

He wanted Megan to meet her. Hell, he wanted Stephanie to meet Rayna, too. His ex would love Rayna for him. In fact, Stephanie, being the friend she was to him, would know Rayna was right for him the minute she met her.

Derek drew in a breath, ready to say what he'd been waiting to say, but then stopped himself as her petite body gave a slight jerk against him. She was falling asleep, and that was...wow...nothing like it in the world.

He turned his head and pressed his lips to the top of her head. He'd tell her in the morning. Or maybe tomorrow night if he got to see her after his shift. Either way, it'd been a couple of weeks, and clearly they had a good thing going.

No signs of it stopping, it was time to tell her. There was no reason not to.

Chapter 13

A few days later, Rayna stepped inside the bar and looked around for Derek. The Dry Desert Brewery was a place she'd heard about but hadn't been to. Honestly, she hadn't had a reason to until now.

He'd texted her earlier, letting her know he and Jeff were heading out for a few drinks after shift and he wanted her to meet him. Apparently, Jeff wanted to see Tish again, too, so Rayna had texted her best friend to meet up as well.

Walking a little deeper into the crowded, dim space, she found Derek sitting at the end of the bar, Jeff right beside him. After navigating around a few more people, she caught his gaze, and he got up from the barstool and came to her.

"Hello, beautiful." Derek circled her waist and brought her to his chest. "Best part of my day, seeing you."

Heat rose in her cheeks, and she smiled. "You are far too sweet to me."

"No such thing." Derek bent and pressed his lips to hers.

Rising on tiptoe, she circled her arms around his neck and got lost in the taste of his lips and tongue, and the feel of hard muscles pressed against her body. In an instant, her panties were wet, her clit was throbbing, and her nipples were tight points. Rayna moaned, and Derek pulled her a little tighter against him.

God, she really loved how good the sex with him was. So good that she'd pretty much pushed the fact that the man was a cop out of her mind entirely. Rayna just didn't think about it. Things were much easier that way.

"Holy shit, get a room, would you?" Tish laughed.

Rayna broke the kiss and looked over at her best friend. "Sorry. I ju—"

"Not sorry." Derek chuckled. "Hi, Tish. You look great, as usual."

"Thank you, Derek. As do you."

Jeff walked up. "Glad to see someone got them to come up for air. Thought I was going to have to get a bucket of water."

"That's because you don't know how to behave in public." Tish rolled her eyes and then glanced at Rayna.

"I could use some training. Are you woman enough to take the job?" Jeff grinned.

Still in his embrace, Rayna rose to Derek's ear. "Not even five minutes and they're at it."

"Foreplay." Derek glanced to her then back to Tish and Jeff.

"Pfft. Whatever. I need a drink." With another eye roll, Tish walked past them toward the bar.

"All she had to do was ask." Jeff shrugged, gave them a crooked smile, and followed after Tish.

"Oh dear." Rayna dropped her forehead to Derek's shoulder.

"It's fine, baby. I actually think she's warming up to him." He caressed her lower back, and tingles skittered up her spine.

She tipped her head back. "Seriously?"

"Affirmative." He grinned and gave her another quick kiss. "Let's find a table."

"Okay." She glanced around. "It's really packed in here for a Wednesday night. Is it always like this?"

"Yeah. It's their weekly beer tasting and trivia night, which tends to draw a good crowd." Derek took her hand, pivoted, and headed toward the back corner of the bar.

"You come here a lot then?"

He came around a table and pulled a chair out for her. "Yes. Well, I used to."

Rayna sat and looked up at him. "Why not anymore?"

"Because I've been busy." He grinned. "What do you want to drink? You want to try one of their beers?"

She smiled. "Busy with what?"

He bent to her, his lips brushing her ear. "Busy with you. Touching you. Kissing you. Fucking you. And enjoying every moment of it."

A bolt of lust shot through Rayna's body and settled in her clit. "Oh my."

"Annnnd they're at it again." Tish moved in front of the table, Jeff close behind her.

Peeking around Tish, Jeff grinned. "What *are* we going to do with them?"

Tish glanced over her shoulder. "Heel, boy. Now sit."

"Yes, ma'am. Woof." Jeff laughed.

As they both sat, Rayna couldn't stop the giggle that came out of her. "You two are—"

"Well now, look what the cat dragged in!"

A set of arms came around Derek's waist, and immediately he straightened and turned around.

What on earth? Rayna looked at Tish, but Tish was looking at whoever had walked up. *Who was it?* Clearly, by the sound of the voice, it was a woman, that much was clear, but Derek was still blocking Rayna's view. The expression on Tish's face sent a chill down Rayna's spine, and she scrambled to her feet. "Derek?"

With a strange look, Derek peeled the woman's arms from around his waist. "Good to see you too. Let me introduce you to Rayna." He looked at Rayna. "Babe, this is an old friend, Stacie."

Oh no. No, no, no. Rayna's mouth went bone dry as she took in the very busty, very tall, bleach-blond woman standing next to Derek with her palm held out to Rayna.

"Oh wow! How cool. Nice to meet you."

Rayna managed somehow to swallow and tried to find her voice. She cleared her throat and shook the woman's hand. "Likewise."

"Was starting to wonder what'd happened to this guy. He's usually here a lot and then, poof, he just up and disappeared." The blonde smiled at Derek, rubbed his upper arm, then returned her gaze to Rayna.

Rayna instantly hated her.

"Anyway, we were just about to sit down. Good to see you, Stacie. Take care." Derek nodded and stepped away from the woman and then rounded the table.

"Always good to see you, too, Derek. You keep in touch." She smiled and then looked at Rayna. "Have fun."

"Thanks." Rayna sat and tried to remember how to breathe as the blond bombshell walked away.

This was why.

Exactly why...

And she'd forgotten.

Rayna had let herself forget.

Bile rose, burning the back of her throat.

"I'm not sure I like her." Tish locked eyes with Rayna.

"Eh, she's harmless. Nothing to like or not like." Jeff chuckled.

"Babe, did you want to try a beer? Check out what they have on the menu." Derek leaned close to Rayna, beverage menu in hand, opened for her to see.

There was a ringing in Rayna's ears, and she blinked and looked at Derek. What did he just ask her? She glanced at the menu then back to him. "Um... Can you just order whatever you think I'd like? I'm going to run to the bathroom."

"You okay?" He rubbed her arm.

"Yes. Of course." She managed a small smile. God, she needed air.

Tish went to stand. "I'll go with y—"

"No." Rayna got to her feet, staring dead into her best friend's eyes. "I'll be right back."

Tish nodded, but her eyes were wide as saucers.

Derek clasped Rayna's hand before she walked away. "Hey. Not so fast."

She glanced back at him. "Hmm?"

He tugged on her a little, indicating he wanted a kiss. Rayna bent to him, gave him a quick peck on the lips, then walked away. She wanted to run, but of course that would be way too obvious.

How could she be so stupid? So trusting? This was exactly why she never, ever wanted to be with a cop.

She needed to go, to get away from him now.

And never look back again.

* * * *

"Uh, Tish? Can I ask you something?"

"Uh, sure, Derek." Tish stared at him with an expression that looked far too much like a glare.

"She's upset. Any idea why?"

Tish took a swig of her beer and slowly placed the bottle on the table. "What makes you think she's upset?"

"Because I can tell she is." He looked back toward the bathroom then back to Tish.

Tish spared a look at Jeff, then rested her forearms on the table and leaned forward. "How can you tell?"

"Seriously? How could anyone *not* tell? I'm not blind. It's all over her face. She's upset. It's so obvious it felt like a punch in the gut when I looked at her."

"Wow, hot *and* perceptive?" Tish rolled her eyes.

"Shirley is the most perceptive guy I know. For realsies." Jeff chuckled.

Tish glanced at Jeff. "I'm not impressed."

"Not fucking around right now." Derek scowled at his best friend, and then directed his highly annoyed stare back to Tish. What the fuck was going on? Frustration rose inside Derek like a tidal wave. Jeff's games weren't a surprise, but how could Tish be breaking his balls when her best friend was in the bathroom upset?

He shook his head and stood. "Forget it. Fucking Stacie comes over and now my girl is upset. I'm going to see if she'll talk to me."

As Derek came around the table to head in the direction of the bathrooms, Tish got to her feet and stopped him. Christ, he did not need this. "Can you just chill out? Give the girl a minute, okay? She obviously just came face to face with a Barbie doll who you likely used to fuck."

"Look, not that I care what you think, but Stacie is nobody to me. Never was. Never will be. I get how it might've looked, but it's not my fault Stacie flirts with the world and loves starting shit. So, either fill me in, or let me go figure out if I can fix it."

Tish nodded, and then her expression softened. "Look, it's not Stacie. Well, it sort of is, but not how you're thinking. Stay here. I'll deal with it."

"No way." This time it was his turn. He caught her by the arm as she went to brush past him. This wasn't how this was going to go, and Tish needed to understand that right now. "Tell me what it is."

Tish looked down at his hand and then to his eyes. "Listen, King Kong, I got it. You need to trust me."

"This isn't about trusting you, Tish. It's about Rayna. You want to handle your girl, I get it. I respect it. But I have no shame in telling you that she is the one for me. *The one,* Tish, and I have no intention of losing her, so give me a break and tell me what this is really about."

Tish drew in a deep breath, and as she glanced over her shoulder she let it out, and then turned back to him. "Fine." She hit him with a resigned but hard expression in her eyes. "You're a cop."

Derek frowned as confusion swamped his mind again. "Yeah. We know. So?"

"Come on, Derek. Really?"

"Yeah, Tish. Fucking really. I'm a cop. Can you be any more vague, or are you going to spit it out?"

Tish rolled her eyes.

Irritation tingled in Derek's veins. He was getting real fucking tired of her rolling them damn eyes of hers. "Waiting."

She crossed her arms. "You know as well as I do, stereotype or not, cops can sometimes get around. First time Rayna comes face to face with one of your past fucks, you gotta figure it's not going to go over so well.

Wouldn't be a big deal for me, or anyone like me, to handle. But we both know Rayna isn't like me, or Stacie for that matter. She's different."

Of course, Rayna was different, that's what attracted him to her to begin with. But, what the fuck? Talk about guilty before proven innocent. Jesus Christ. Derek frowned. "First of all, Stacie is *not* one of my past fucks. Wouldn't lay that with someone else's dick. But that doesn't really matter because, since I'm a cop, Rayna likely just assumed I fucked the girl and probably assumes I'll do it again, right?"

"Bingo, King Kong."

"That's fucked up." He looked at Jeff. "Are you hearing this?"

"Yeah, but come on, Derek." Jeff shrugged. "Not like we don't know plenty of guys on the force like that."

"Right, but that doesn't mean *I'm* like that, too. What does she think, that when you graduate the academy it's all 'Congratulations! Here's your badge and your special license to screw everyone on the planet. Be responsible. Wear a condom!'" He shook his head. "That's wrong on so many levels, I don't even know which one to start with." Derek sat in the closest seat as a wave of defeat blanketed him.

Just because he was a cop, she automatically didn't trust him? What the fuck was up with that? The wind had just been knocked right out of his sails. He had real and serious feelings for Rayna, didn't want anyone else but her, and couldn't even imagine touching another woman.

Derek ran his palm over his hair and cupped the back of his neck. For fuck's sake, he may not be a saint, but that didn't mean he was a sinner, either.

Tish placed her hand on Derek's arm. "Look, just trust me. It's gonna be fine. But I need you to not take it personal. There's more to it than you realize."

"How can I not take any of that personally?"

"Because it's not about you. Honestly, it's not even about the blond Barbie." She squeezed his arm. "I'll be back. Jeff? Keep your boy here. If you do, you'll get a reward."

"Don't tease me, girl." He winked. "No worries. We're not going anywhere."

"I never tease." Tish stepped away.

With an unexpected amount of disappointment pulsing through his heart, Derek looked at Jeff. "That's fucked up, Jeff. If that's how she is, how she thinks, then I seriously misjudged her."

"Nah, Shirley. I'm sensing it's old baggage more than anything. Plus, you heard Tish, she said there's more to it. Just slow your roll and see what happens."

"Fine." All Derek could do was lean back in his seat, cross his arms, and shake his head.

He glanced over toward the bathroom as a feeling of helplessness pulsed in time with his heart. She'd basically profiled him due to his job. Which was just too fucked up to fathom, or maybe Jeff was right and it was old baggage. For the sake of his heart, he hoped that's all it was.

"Everyone has baggage..."

"True story. Just depends on how many bags." Jeff sipped his beer.

Confusion filled Derek, and he raised his brows. "Huh?"

"I'm agreeing with you. Everyone has baggage, just saying it depends on how many bags they have."

"Shit, I said that out loud? Christ, this little blip of what-the-fuckery really has me twisted." Derek leaned forward and glanced in the direction of the bathrooms again. "Fuck's sake, I don't know what to do." Derek shook his head.

"Like I said, slow your roll."

Derek nodded and tried to look anywhere but in the direction of the restrooms. Even though his first reaction had been anger, he truly didn't like that Rayna was upset. No matter what the reason was.

The instinct to make it better, to make her smile again, hit him so hard in the gut, he wasn't sure how to get past it. Sitting still sure as hell wasn't helping the matter. Worse, the fact that *he* was the cause of the hurt in her eyes had sliced through his heart like a hot knife through butter.

Fuck, where were they?

* * * *

"All right, Rayna. Enough theatrics. Come on out."

Rayna rolled her eyes and stared down at Tish's shoes visible on the other side of the bathroom stall. "Geez, Tish, I'm going to the bathroom."

"No. You're not going to the bathroom. You're in there sulking and beating yourself up. And telling yourself that you never should've gone out with him to begin with, but then you think about how awesome he is, and then you ruin that by thinking about your dad."

Good grief, was her best friend living inside Rayna's head?

"For real, Rayna. Don't make me crawl under this stall. I'm wearing new jeans."

"Ugh, fine." Rayna stood, opened the stall door, and walked past Tish to the sinks. "I don't want to talk about it."

Tish moved beside her. "Fine. I'll talk. You listen."

"Whatever." Rayna rolled her eyes at her friend and washed her hands. Talk about déjà vu. Weren't she and Tish in the ladies' room just a couple weeks ago and Rayna was upset about a similar thing? But, heck, in retrospect, that seemed way less of a big deal than this time. Yeah, and this was exactly why she should not be with Officer Derek Hansen.

"He's never fucked her, and has never wanted to, either. She's just one of those silly, desperate women that like to cause trouble."

Rayna stared down at her fingernails. "So? It doesn't matter. Women like Stacie are always going to come on to him, flirt with him. Eventually he'll give in. Nature of the beast."

"Oh! Thank you for participating in the conversation. But what you're saying is nuts. You really think, in your heart of hearts, after the last few weeks you've spent with him, that he's really and truly that kind of man?"

Rayna bit her bottom lip. From what she knew so far, did she really think Derek would be "that guy"? Yes. No. Argh! Rayna threw her hands up as frustration raced through her veins. "I don't know, Tish. My mother never thought that my dad was that kind of man, and look what happened to her. You never really know a person. *That's* what I believe. So, no, maybe Derek wouldn't cheat right now. But someday maybe."

Tish frowned. "When did you get this fucked up?"

"That was mean." Rayna looked at the ground and tried to swallow past the lump that'd risen in her throat. "I've always been this fucked up. You just didn't realize it, apparently."

"Rayna, come on." Tish clasped her palms on Rayna's forearms. "I'm sorry, you're right. That was harsh. But, honey, this is your chance. That guy out there? He is *nothing* like your father. You gotta know that. Derek really cares about you."

Hope filled Rayna's chest, mixing in with all the doubt. She looked at her best friend. "How do you know?"

"Girl, you should have seen how freaked he was when you walked away. He knew instantly that something was wrong."

Rayna blinked back the tears that had filled her eyes. She'd been wearing mascara on and off over the past couple of weeks; she wasn't going to ruin it with stupid tears. "He did?"

"Yeah, he even got pissed at me when I joked around with him, teasing that he was both hot and perceptive. Well, to be honest, I was just being snarky. But whatever."

Rayna laughed; she couldn't help it. She already knew he was perceptive. "He really is perceptive, and smart, too. You should see him with his canine partner. He's really sweet to him, but in a tough guy kind of way. It's adorable."

"Yep, I bet. And now your face just completely changed. I bet you have no clue that even happens, do you?"

Rayna looked into the mirror. "What changed?"

"I swear, you live in a little bubble." Tish let out a mock snore. "Look at your face, I mean really look at it. You're glowing right now. Five minutes ago, you looked like someone had killed your dog—" Tish cringed and so did Rayna. "Sorry, I know you hate that reference. Anyway, my point is, you wear your emotions all over your face. Hell, all over your body. Happy, sad, angry, whatever you're feeling, is stamped all over you. I see it all the time, but I'm used to it. But Derek sees it, too. Don't you get what that means?"

Rayna looked at her best friend through the mirror. The lump was back in her throat, and her stomach had gone into a knot. Afraid of what Tish was going to reveal to her, Rayna barely managed a whisper. "No."

Tish drew in a breath and shook her head. "That man out there?" She pointed in the direction of where Derek would be located in the bar. "He's into you. I mean, he is *really* into you, Rayna. Meaning he already cares about you in a big way. So, if you care about him at all, you *have* to give him a shot. A real one."

Rayna sucked in a sharp breath as a whole tornado of feelings sped through her, sending her emotions into a tumultuous storm. Great, like she needed that—and right on cue, her chest and face grew hot. Ugh!

She grabbed a paper towel, ran it under the cold water and pressed it to her neck.

"You okay?" Tish gave her a gentle smile.

Rayna nodded as she let the cool cloth do its job. "Yes. It's just...I don't want to have feelings for him. I mean, I really love the sex." She shook her head. "The sex has been... I can't even describe it, it's so good. But more than just sex with him scares the heck out of me."

"Hate to break it to you, Rayna, but if all you wanted was sex, then seeing another woman touch him wouldn't upset you like it did. You wouldn't care."

"Ugh, why do you have to be so logical?" Rayna frowned and swallowed down another lump. "As much as I don't want to admit it, you're right. I guess I failed at keeping my heart out of it. But can you blame me? He's a dream guy out of some sort of fantasy. Fantasies like that don't happen in real life to people like me. It's crazy to think someone as awesome and smart and gorgeous as Derek would look my way. He should be with someone like Stacie."

"Everything you just said about him is exactly why a man like Derek would never be with a woman like Stacie and exactly why he only has eyes for you."

Rayna sniffled and wiped away a single tear that escaped. "Crud! My mascara is going to run."

Tish laughed. "Never thought I'd ever hear you say something like that."

"Oh shush." Rayna swatted Tish's arm. "Don't just stand there. Help me fix it."

Tish grabbed some toilet paper from the stall. "Just wait. Don't wipe, just dab. Dab..."

Rayna leaned close to the mirror and did as Tish instructed. When she'd cleaned herself up as best she could, she pressed another damp paper towel to her cheeks and neck.

"You ready to go back out there? I'm thinking Jeff had to sit on him to get him to stay."

Rayna drew in a deep breath and then let it out. Slow and easy. Derek cared about her. Because of that, Rayna had to believe that maybe, just maybe, this could be it for her. Fifty-fifty shot of it working out, if she was going to be real about it. In the grand scheme of things, those weren't bad odds. "Yes, I'm ready."

* * * *

Out of patience, Derek took his shot and made his way toward the bathrooms when Jeff got up to get them more beer. He wasn't going to knock, or maybe he was. He wasn't really sure. He just knew he couldn't sit and wait, because he was coming out of his goddamn skin.

Before Derek got to the hall, both women emerged from the ladies' room. Derek slowed his approach.

When Rayna spotted him, she stopped.

Tish kept going, but as she got near him she leaned his way. "Told you." She gave him a wink and then kept going.

Derek turned his focus back to his Doc. When he reached Rayna, he had to resist the urge to touch her, pull her into his arms. Which sucked and felt all wrong. "You okay?"

"Yes." She looked down. "I'm sorry."

It was such a classic submissive action, and he loved that about her. Except, with her eyes cast down, he ached to connect with her, bring her closer to him. There was only one sure way to do that.

"Eyes, Doc." Derek ran his fingertips up the side of her biceps. When he did, she glanced up and caught his gaze once more. He cradled her shoulder with his palm and stroked her soft skin with his thumb. "You have nothing to be sorry for. I'm the one who's sorry. Stacie is kind of an asshole, and I need you to know that she is no one to me other than someone I've known for years. More of an acquaintance really. Nothing more."

"Thank you for reassuring me. It means a lot. But I *am* sorry, Derek, because I totally overreacted."

He nodded. "You're human. I understand but...I gotta ask, the fact that I'm a cop? Tish mentioned something. Can we talk about it?"

She cast her eyes down again and shook her head. "Maybe at some point. Just not right now, if that's okay? Just, please don't take it personally."

Derek sighed through his nose. If she needed time, he'd give her time. "Okay. I understand."

"Thank you." Rayna rose on tiptoe and wrapped her arms around his neck. "What I'd much rather do is have fun with you, try some beer that I probably won't like, and then go home and get naked in my bed with you."

Hope and lust spiked in his blood. "That's the best idea I've ever heard." He took in her expression, checking for signs of her true mood. There were still residual traces lingering from her being upset, but it was well on its way out the emotional door and she was definitely in a better headspace. "I ordered you a beer."

"I'm nervous." She smiled.

"Bah, no need. I got you, baby." Derek gave her a wink, pressed a soft kiss to her lips, then took her hand and led her back toward the table.

Whatever the deal happened to be, whatever her issue with him being a cop was, he'd deal with it. When she was ready, she'd share, and he'd work through it with her. Whatever it was.

Because she was worth it.

Chapter 14

Derek pulled into Doc's driveway and shut the truck down. After he got out and was about to head for the front door, the garage opened. He stopped, crossed his arms and leaned a hip against his bumper.

The rising door gave him the first glimpses of her, starting with the cowgirl boots she wore on her feet and then—God help him—her smooth bare legs. Next, her thighs, where the short, flowy skirt she wore skimmed her heavenly flesh. All his breath left his lungs as he watched her being revealed, inch by inch, before him. Then came the snug waistline of the dress, and equally snug top, which enhanced her fucking delectable breasts. But then, finally, her fresh and naturally pretty face.

The beautiful face he'd never been able to forget since the first day he laid eyes on her six months ago.

They'd been dating for three weeks.

Three weeks of losing his breath at the sight of her. Twenty-one days of kissing her sweet lips, touching her velvet skin. Of burying his nose in the coconut scent of her hair. Twenty-one days of gazing into the clear-blue-sky beauty of her eyes. Three weeks of—almost every single day that made those weeks up—the divine pleasure of burying himself between her luscious thighs.

The best goddamn three weeks of Derek's life!

"You were heading for the front door, weren't you?" She smiled as she stepped out, hit the enter button on the keypad, and the garage door closed behind her.

"Have I told you how beautiful you are today?"

She stepped up to him, dropped her overnight bag at her feet, and then held her little purse behind her back with both hands. Tilting her head back, she met his eyes. "No, but you did yesterday. And you spoil me."

"No such thing." He placed his palm on her narrow waist and pulled her close to his body. "Besides, even if I do, you deserve it. Nothing's too good for my Doc."

"What'm I going to do with you?" As she smiled, a blush rose on her cheeks.

"I can think of a lot of things for later. But for now, I'll take a kiss." Lust filled Derek's veins, coursing through every inch of his body. He dipped his head and took her lips with his.

Her taste flooded his senses, and Derek squeezed her side, letting the headiness of the chemistry that swirled consistently around them tingle along his skin. Rayna moaned, tangling her tongue with his, giving him all of herself.

Jesus, he loved that about her. The woman never did anything half-assed, at least not from what he'd seen so far. Letting out his own moan, he pulled from her mouth. "As much as I am loving how good you feel right now, I need to get you into my truck and then get us on the road."

She sighed. "*Oooookayyyy.* If you insist."

"Sassy." With a chuckle, he grabbed her bag, took her hand and walked her around the front of his Dodge. After opening the passenger door, Derek held his palm out. "M'lady, your chariot awaits."

She giggled as she always did when he said that to her, then took his offered hand and stepped onto the rubber tread of the running board, climbing up into the truck. "Thank you, good sir."

He smiled and closed the door. Opened the back door, set her bag on the seat and closed things up. They were heading up to Prescott to see a buddy of his, Jason DeVore, play an acoustic set and also spending the night there. Coming back around to the driver's side, Derek slid behind the wheel and cranked the engine. "Ready?"

"Absolutely!" She smiled her sweet smile and shot him a wink.

Derek drew in a slow breath as he backed out of the driveway. They'd gone on a lot of dates in the last three weeks, several actually. Some lunches, some breakfasts and lots of dinners, plus anything fun he could find for them to do in the Valley during the summer. More than a few of the dinners had been spent at her house, due to her late hours at her clinic, as well as his duty schedule. Those nights had been his favorite. Dinner on the couch, as they watched a movie, Axle lying on the floor at their feet, had become a comfortable, regular thing for them.

After backing out of the driveway, he threw the transmission in drive and got them on their way. Derek reached across the center console and took her hand in his. Holding hands had become something they always did too. He wouldn't trade any of it.

Things were amazing, more than amazing between them. The sex? God, the sex had just gotten better and hotter, each time. Every time they were naked, a little more of Derek's dominant side emerged, and a little more of Rayna's submissive side rose to it.

The amazing part was, it all seemed to be happening naturally. They hadn't needed to discuss it too much, either, but Derek thought it might be a good idea to broach the subject. Taking advantage of the two hours they'd be in the truck on the way to Prescott, where neither of them had any distractions or were tired from working, was wise. He also hoped to talk about other things.

One of those other things being telling her about Megan. Another week had passed since he'd decided to tell her. One distraction or another had gotten in the way, and he knew it was beyond time.

Even so, talking with Rayna, about any number of topics, had turned out to be the best part of each day for him. She was easy to talk to, she listened. She gave her opinion when he needed it. He had no reason to think sharing with her that he had a child would go any differently, but he had to admit he was a little nervous still.

"Can I ask you something?"

"Of course." He smiled at her.

"When are you going to take me to your place?"

A cold chill ran down Derek's spine. Talk about timing. This was it, he should just tell her about Megan, but he still wasn't sure he could. "Well, honestly? It's not very nice. Typical bachelor pad, not a lot of furniture. Not very big. Just a basic three-bedroom ranch."

"I don't care if it's small or not very nice. It's where you live. I'd love to see where you live."

Fuck, she was sweet. Sweeter than he deserved. "All right. I'll take you. Just...let me get it a little cleaned up, okay?"

"Okay." She smiled. "So how was your morning? Did you take Axle to the park, go for a run with him?"

He glanced at her and then made the left onto the San Tan freeway. "I did, yes. You'll be proud, I also let him run around and just be a dog for a little while, too."

"Aw, I love that you do that for him, honey. It's so good for him, you know? He's a busy boy, and like the rest of us, he deserves downtime, too. Stress relief is important."

"Agreed. When I got him home, he passed out on his memory foam bed. He was still out cold when I left to come get you." Derek chuckled. "Anyway, Jeff is going to check on him tomorrow morning for me."

"Perfect. He's a good friend." She smoothed her thumb over the back of his hand. "Have you given any more thought to the animal Reiki sessions for him?"

"Nah, I mean, Jeff really prefers to have a 'private' and 'special' massage in his own home."

Rayna laughed. "I meant for Axle, silly! And, ew, I don't want to know about Jeff's...massage preferences." She laughed again.

Derek laughed, too. He couldn't help but tease her a little. His Doc was always so serious, she needed her own kind of stress relief. Laughing was incredible medicine. God knew it was what kept Derek sane considering the emotional and stressful grind of police duty.

"I knew what you meant. I just love teasing you." He raised their linked hands and pressed a kiss to her knuckles. He glanced at her. "You really think it would be good for Axle?"

A soft smile spread over her lips, and an even softer expression filled her baby-blue eyes. "Absolutely, honey."

"Okay, I'll make an appointment next week."

"Good!" She smiled.

Derek kissed her knuckles once more before resting their hands down on the console again. A sense of warm contentment settled in his gut, making his heart beat in a way he was more than open to.

Honestly, with Rayna, there wasn't anything he wasn't open and welcome to. He wanted more with her—Derek wanted the whole deal. It was early on in their relationship, yes. They were getting to know one another at a consistent, steady pace forward and with every minute he spent with her, he fell a little more.

Not a surprise since he'd spent six months wanting her, dreaming of her, knowing she was *his* one.

Good thing he was happy to let things take their natural course. He just prayed that course would eventually lead them down the path that meant forever with her.

White picket fence and all.

* * * *

"Have you always had dogs?" Rayna twisted the cap off her water bottle and took a sip. "I mean, did you grow up with them?"

"Yes. We had cats, too. Not a ton of them or anything, just a couple over the years. Same with dogs. My parents are definitely pet people."

She smiled and gazed out at the desertscape along the freeway. "They sound like my kind of people."

"Told you already, they'd love you. My sisters would love you, too."

"I'm sure I'll meet them soon enough." Rayna took another sip of her water.

Things were moving along with Derek in a really positive way. Since that first date three weeks ago, they'd seen each other non-stop. At least between and around their busy schedules.

Aside from the cop thing, Derek was turning out to be an amazing guy. Considering her past, and in spite of the fact that she hadn't planned to, Rayna was falling for him.

A cop.

She was falling for a cop.

Dad was going to be so pleased... Not. Her momma on the other hand was going to give her "the talk." The one she'd been having with Rayna since her father had moved out of the family home.

Her momma's heavily Southern-accented lecture played through Rayna's mind. She could hear her as if the woman was sitting right beside her. *You stay away from them cops, Rayna Christine. Not any of 'em are any good. Not a damn one of 'em.*

"What about you? Pets?"

Jerked from her stroll down not-so-fond memory lane, Rayna snapped her eyes in Derek's direction. "Drove my momma crazy. I think I brought home a new stray every week."

Derek laughed. "Dogs? Cats?"

"All of the above. Plus I had my share of rabbits. One time I found an injured squirrel, knew better than to touch it, but came home crying my eyes out. Begging and begging for them to let me nurse it back to health. Daddy about busted a vein over that one."

Derek laughed again. "That's so sweet though. Did they let you?"

"Oh my word, no. Squirrels are cute and all, and I know of people trying to raise them from babies, but they really shouldn't. They really can't be tamed. Have you ever seen a squirrel bite on a person? Vicious little suckers."

"Uh, not that I can recall. But I'll take your word for it." He reached over and took hold of her hand. "You know your Southern accent is slipping out again."

"Oh dear." Rayna shook her head and felt her face flush hot. She cleared her throat. "Doesn't happen often."

"Yeah but I kinda dig when it does happen, Doc." He squeezed her hand. "Especially when we're in bed and you're naked."

She rolled her eyes as instant lust bloomed in her tummy. "Your fault for gettin' me so riled up."

He chuckled. "What about your brother, Jonathon is it? You don't talk about him much. Is he married? Kids?"

Relieved he hadn't continued with the sex talk, Rayna crossed her legs, hoping to quell the throb that he'd so easily kick-started, as well as get her accent under wraps again. She took a sip of her water. "Yes, my brother. Jonathon—JJ for short. He's married. But no, no kids. Not yet anyway."

"That's a shame. Bet your parents would love grandkids. Most parents do."

"Tell me about it." She smiled and shook her head. "My momma won't stop poking and prodding and nagging JJ. She's had her shot at me, but of course, I'm not married so she nags me about that instead."

"Yup. I get the same. But at least my older sister, Rachel, has her two boys. Keeps Mom and Pops occupied, or distracted is a better word." Derek chuckled and let go of her hand to take the wheel in both of his. "You ever want that stuff? Marriage, kids?"

Eyes wide, Rayna glanced at him. All at once, the throb between her thighs was gone. Goodness gracious, where was he going with this? Drawing in a slow breath, she tamped down the lump of panic that'd risen, clogging her throat.

Breathe... They were having a nice conversation. That was all. He wasn't proposing marriage or anything, just talking with her. But she had no idea how to handle this, and she sure wasn't used to having to answer it, at least not to anyone other than her momma.

Screw it, she was just going to lay it out for him. No reason not to. She cleared her throat. "You want the polite answer or the honest one?"

"The honest one, of course." He spared her a quick glance before focusing back on the road to round a mountain corner.

Thanks to Momma and Daddy, marriage is a big joke. Didn't work for them, no reason it would work for me. "Truth is, I've been so busy with my career, it's always been on the far back burner in my mind. And now, I'm not sure that sort of thing would fit into my life." Rayna cringed at her cowardly answer. So maybe she hadn't been *totally* honest, but she'd come close enough. She wasn't about to split hairs over it.

"Which thing? The marriage or the kids?"

"Both, really."

"Interesting." He changed lanes.

Wait, what? Shifting in the seat, Rayna faced him. "Why is that interesting?"

"You're so...maternal? Not sure that's the right word but, either way, with Axle you're very loving. Almost motherly." He shrugged. "Guess I kinda figured you for someone who'd want kids."

Maternal with Axle? "I don't know if I'd say I'm maternal. Caring might be a better word. But...regardless, kids and animals are two different things."

Derek glanced at her. "Of course. I mean I realize that. But...I don't know, in some ways, they're kinda the same, don't you think?"

She took a swig of water. "Yes, I guess if you mean the potty training, feeding and general discipline. But it's not like I have to send a dog to school."

"Not true!" He laughed. "Dogs go to school all the time. Some of them even have jobs. Case in point: Axle."

"Okay, fine." Laughing, she rolled her eyes. "But it's sure as heck not a four-year degree or master's program I'm paying for."

"That is true." He grabbed her hand and pulled it to his lips. "Guess we're both right."

Rayna smiled, watching his profile as he drove. What a strange and twisty conversation they were having. Childhood pets, sex, marriage, kids, back to pets. Her head was nearly spinning. The only thing that might make her head actually rotate on her shoulders was if he asked her about the cop thing.

Rayna had been waiting for that question to surface. It'd been almost a week since the incident at that bar, and honestly she wasn't sure why it hadn't. But for whatever reason, he hadn't brought the subject up.

"Okay, next topic." He smiled at her then focused back on the road. "You think you might be ready to tell me why you have issues with cops?"

Rayna's mouth dropped open, and her heart jumped up into her throat. "I never said I had issues with cops, Derek."

Blowing out a harsh breath, she leaned forward and turned the fan for the AC up a notch...because even though it was summer out, which meant triple-digit temperatures, and they were halfway to Prescott, where it was cooler, *now* she was sweating.

Good grief, she'd just jinxed herself.

* * * *

"Okay, you're right, you didn't. Tish said you did." Knowing he should probably stop talking, Derek risked a glance at her. She didn't look happy, but his desire to understand her was sincere, so he had to try.

She raised both brows about as far as physically possible. "That's right. What did Tish say exactly?"

Anxiety crept along the back of Derek's neck, and he cleared his throat. "Just that you didn't like cops because some of them get around, women-wise."

She frowned and crossed her arms. "What else did she say?"

Man, sharing about his daughter was a clear no-go now...at least until he figured out how best to lay that out for her, and he *really* should not have raised the subject about cops. Judging by the look on her face, her body language and her tone, he'd clearly ventured into territory she did *not* want to discuss with him.

The last thing Derek wanted to do was have an argument, their first one to boot. Shit. He hadn't figured she'd be so closed off about it. "Babe, it's fine. It was no big deal. Forget it, okay? I shouldn't have brought it up."

"Too late. Please tell me what else she said."

He sighed through his nose. "Okay, fine. All she said was that I shouldn't take it personally and that there was more to it than I realized."

"Well, I told you not to take it personally at the time, too."

"I know you did."

"Did Tish say anything else?"

"No. That was it." Taking a chance, he reached across the console and opened his palm. She looked down at his open hand, and after a few too many seconds, she threaded her fingers with his, but didn't look back up at him.

He gave it another couple of seconds before he spoke up. "Hey..."

She kept her eyes down. "Yeah?"

"We don't have to talk about it, babe. Really. It's okay."

Finally she gave him her eyes. "As much as I know that's not fair to you, I appreciate it. And like I said, you shouldn't take it personally. I just need time to sort—"

"Doc, it's okay. Someday, if I'm lucky and I earn your trust, I hope you'll share it with me."

She gave him a small smile. "Stop being so wonderful, okay?"

"Not sure I can give you that one, Doc." He laughed, but beneath it was the knowledge that she still didn't trust him. He hated that because the truth was, it hurt.

With a small giggle and a roll of her eyes, Rayna bent forward and pressed her lips to the back of his hand. Derek's heart melted at her show of tender affection.

He really wished he wasn't driving at the moment so he could give that back to her. So as soon as they got to their destination he planned on showing her how very much he appreciated her. As far as Megan went, he'd figure that out too. Crisis averted, for now at least.

"So, I have a question."

He smirked. "Hopefully I have an answer."

She giggled. "Did you bring your handcuffs?"

Having just taken a swig of his water, he almost choked. Derek managed to swallow and then looked at her. "I'm sorry, what?"

"Uh..." Her eyes went wide, and she dragged her teeth over her bottom lip. "Well...did you bring your handcuffs?"

Wow! Was she? No way. Well...maybe? Derek looked back at the road. Only one way to find out. "I have a set in the glove box, also zip ties. Why do you ask?"

She pulled her hand free of his and twisted it with her other. "Oh dear, I really hope you don't think this is weird. But if you do, it's okay. I think. I mean...well, it'll just have to be okay."

"I can pretty much guarantee there's not much of anything I find weird." Derek had no clue what she was going to say, but he was praying to God it was that she wanted him to use them on her. Christ, if that was the case, he might bend a knee right then and there and ask her to marry him. *Okay, slow your roll, Shirley!* No need to get all jump-off-the-deep-end crazy.

Man, the thought of her in wrist restraints? Goddamn...

When she stayed quiet, he prompted. "What's on your mind, Doc?"

"Well..." She looked away from him, focusing on the windshield. "I was wondering if you might want to use them on me."

Ding! Ding! Ding! Jackpot! Derek's dick went rod-hard. "Absofuckinglutely!"

She jerked her attention to him. "Really?"

"Oh, hell yeah, really! You want that, I'll give it to you. Fuck, Doc, that kind of play? I'd love to have that with you. I mean, we've already kinda been heading that way, don't you think?"

A shy smile arched her lips. "Yes. I mean, I think so." She shrugged one shoulder. "I have no experience with it, but I like what we've been doing so far."

Derek had seriously just died and gone to heaven. His version of heaven anyway. "You think you want to explore more, in addition to restraints? Maybe other things?"

"Can we talk about what those other things might be?"

"Affirmative." He nodded. "It's really about doing what you're comfortable with. Babe, we can try anything you want. If you don't like it, we stop and don't do it again. Simple."

"Okay." She dragged her teeth over her plump bottom lip and then nodded. "Yes, okay."

He took her hand in his again. "Okay."

Derek would tap the brakes for sure, but someday, no doubt, he was going to marry this woman. When a man knows what he wants, he goes after it, and Derek was no different from any other man.

Except for the fact that he happened to be head to toe alpha male—who was totally into a little dominant or bondage play, or both.

Bottom line, Derek wanted Rayna, for always.

The woman was perfect for him.

Chapter 15

"After you, Doc." After opening the door into the hotel room, Derek stepped to the side to let her pass.

"Thank you." She smiled and stepped by him into the room.

Derek closed the door and stepped a few feet into the space. He tossed the key card onto the small dresser and focused on Rayna. The rest of the ride up to Prescott had been filled with three things: sexual tension, anticipation, and light conversation.

Rayna *had* to be nervous. Hell, he wasn't exactly the picture of calm. The plan was a nice dinner and then see the band, but before they did any of that, first they needed to talk...because later that night, he planned on binding her wrists, like she'd asked for.

"This room is amazing." She smiled and set her small bag down on the chair in the corner.

"Agreed." He smiled and motioned to the bed. "Can you sit for a minute? We need to talk."

"Of course." Without hesitation, she moved to the foot of the bed and sat. "Is everything okay?"

"Everything is very much okay." Derek stepped in front of her, squatted down so he could be eye level and took her hands in his. "We just need to talk through some things before we go any further."

"Okay." She dragged her teeth over her full bottom lip.

Jesus, he loved when she did that, so much so, it was all he could do to not get a hard-on each time he witnessed it. Somehow, he reeled himself in so he could focus on what needed to be discussed.

Establishing this foundation, this understanding between them, absolutely needed to happen. Derek stroked his thumb over the back of her hand. "As you know, I'm a dominant man, Rayna."

A soft smile arched her lips. "Yes. And I like that about you."

"Glad you do. You also know, I enjoy talking dirty."

A slight blush rose on her cheeks. "Yes, I like that, too."

"I know you do." He couldn't help but smile back. "Then there's the spanking."

Her eyes got big, and then she closed them, letting out a sigh. "Yes, I really like that."

"Yeah, I really do, too. In fact, I love it. Love making your skin all pink and feeling how wet that makes you." He cleared his throat and did his best to ignore how hard his cock had gone. "But there's more to it than that."

"Okay. Tell me." She leaned forward a little.

He drew in a breath and continued. "I like things different, Doc. Maybe a little rough too—though not too rough. Know that I'll never hurt you. Not the bad kind of hurt, anyway, if that makes sense." He smirked when she nodded and let out a little giggle. "Yeah. Like I mentioned in the truck, I'm open to all things sexually, and anything you want to try with me, I'm happy to give you. You can ask me anything, and I'll answer you honestly and openly."

"I appreciate that."

Relief filled his chest. This was happening, and he was so ready to take her there. He sighed and gave her hands a squeeze. "This might be a lot for you to take in or process, and I don't expect you to jump in with both feet, but at the very least, I need to make sure you're okay with where we go sexually tonight. We can go as fast or as slow as you want or need. Either way, I need you to tell me which way you want to go. I need you to communicate with me, before, during, and even after, so I know how you're doing. Is that clear for you? Are you good with that?"

"Yes." She blew out a breath and smiled. "I'm nervous, and excited and...curious. Is that weird?"

"Baby, no. Never weird." He leaned forward and gave her a soft kiss. "Nothing we do, or try, or anything you end up liking is weird. I don't want you to ever think that."

"Okay."

"Okay." He nodded. "Do you need to freshen up before dinner?"

"No, well, do you think I need to?"

"Doc, I think you're fucking beautiful no matter what, so no, I don't think you need to. But if you want to, then that's okay, too." He smiled and stood, pulling her to her feet.

Rayna circled his neck with her arms. "Thank you."

He placed his hands on her hips. "For?"

"For everything." She rose on tiptoe and pressed her lips to his.

Derek pulled her body tight to his and melted under her touch. He never thought a woman would or could ever have this kind of effect on him, but here she was. Living and breathing, and in his arms.

Rayna might be the one submitting to him sexually, or would be later that night, but Derek had done the same with her. He'd submitted: body, heart, and soul, and as a result, given her all the power.

For him, there was no turning back now.

* * * *

"Here's to overnight trips!" Rayna raised her glass.

Derek smiled and raised his. "Yes, and how about, here's to more of them."

"Oh, even better!" They clinked glasses, and she sipped her margarita. Barely able to sit still in her seat, she was a ball of nervous energy and excitement. He'd planned this trip for them. He'd driven. He'd booked the hotel and made the dinner reservation. All she'd had to do was pack a bag.

Scary because she really liked the way it made her feel. It was nice, refreshing. Moreover, it was a relief. And yes, that was all really scary. Outside of her patient appointments, which her staff handled, Rayna wasn't used to anyone doing the planning or scheduling for her.

They'd finished dinner and moved on to the bar where the band he wanted to see was playing. When they were done here, they'd head back to the hotel.

Then...he was going to use his handcuffs on her.

Handcuffs!

Handcuffs that *she'd* asked for.

Dear Lord.

Rayna set her glass down and reached for a napkin. What was it going to feel like? The pasta she ate was sitting like a brick in her stomach. Not because it didn't taste good, on the contrary, every bite had been delicious. Unfortunately, right now, nerves were winning the digestive battle.

"Pretty quiet over there." He put his warm palm on her knee. "You okay?"

I'm terrified and turned on at the same time. "Oh, yes. Fine. Just checking out the crowd." She smiled and placed her hand on his. "It's a colorful gathering."

"Definitely. Lots of tattoos and beards." He chuckled and glanced around the outdoor patio of the bar. "Fun for all ages. Oh hey—" Derek stood and clasped palms and hugged a bearded guy carrying a guitar case. "Good to see you, man."

"Yeah! You, too. Thanks for coming up." The guy smiled.

Derek's palm came to her shoulder. "Jay, this is my girl, Rayna. Rayna, this is Jason."

His girl...

Oh dear. That felt good.

Really good.

They hadn't discussed labels, commitments, or exclusivity. She hadn't given it much thought. Really, to be honest, she just hadn't allowed herself to think about it.

"Ahhh." Jason smiled at Derek then focused on her. "I see, I see." His smile was warm and reached clear to his eyes. "A pleasure to meet you."

She took his offered hand and couldn't help but smile, too. At the musician, but more because Derek had called her his girl. "Likewise."

Jason turned back to Derek. "You guys staying the night or heading back down to the Valley tonight?"

"We're staying. Got a room at the St. Michael." Derek massaged her shoulder as he talked. That was another thing he'd done for her. She'd always heard about the historic hotel they were staying in. Had always wanted to stay there, someday. It was on her list of all the other things she was going to do "someday." But now, here she was, doing it. All because Derek was giving it to her. *His girl...*

"Oh, sweet! Maybe you'll catch a glimpse of a few ghosts." Jason laughed.

"You never know." Derek laughed, too. "Not much a badge and set of cuffs do in those situations, right?"

Rayna's stomach jumped, and a rush of heat flooded her lower body... not because they were talking about the fact that the St. Michael was allegedly haunted. No, it was because he'd mentioned handcuffs. Good grief. Rayna uncrossed and re-crossed her legs at the instant throb that started between her thighs.

In the matter of two minutes he'd not only melted her heart, he'd also managed to wet her panties. Rayna was sure he had no idea he'd done either.

"Gonna go set up. Good to see you." Jason smiled and then looked down at Rayna. "Nice to meet you."

She nodded and managed to speak even though she was aching with arousal. "Same to you."

"Later, man. Shot of Jameson coming your way in a bit." Derek shook the guy's hand again and then sat once more.

Speaking of shots. She leaned over to Derek. "A shot sounds fantastic."

"Yeah?" A corner of his lips arched in a grin. "Tequila?"

"Oh yeah. Tequila for sure." She bent closer and pressed a kiss to his cheek.

Gazing into her eyes, he moved his hand from her shoulder to the nape of her neck, taking it in a soft grip in his warm palm.

"One tequila for my girl."

My girl...

* * * *

Derek watched Rayna from his seat as she stood, clapping along to his buddy Jason DeVore's song, "Wasted Youth." She liked the music, but then again, it wasn't hard to like Jason's songs. The guy had an intoxicating fun vibe.

Derek hadn't paid much attention to the show because he'd watched her all night...hell, he didn't want to stop watching her. In his eyes, she was so beautiful and sexy, he wasn't sure he could stop staring at her even if he tried.

They'd had a couple drinks: beers for him, margaritas for her. Plus, they'd done a shot right before the start of the show. Rayna had been nervous, not that she'd told him so. He'd known it, though. Felt it rolling off her in hot waves. She'd needed the shot.

Now her nervous edges had smoothed out. Now she was feeling relaxed, enjoying the music and having a good time. Now she was smiling and flirting with Derek, and each time she did that, he was thanking God he'd taken Jeff's suggestion three weeks ago and finally asked the woman out on a date.

Their relationship was going to turn a corner tonight. She'd taken another step in the direction they were already heading sexually...she'd asked to be bound. Derek was more than happy to oblige her. In fact, he was fucking elated.

There was still the matter of his daughter to discuss, and he'd get to that. Truth be told, considering their convo on the way up to Prescott, he was even more nervous now about how she'd react. Either way, before any more time passed, he needed to tell her.

Derek ran a fingertip along the back of her bare thigh, just below the flowy skirt of her dress. She glanced back at him. He gave her a crooked smile. "Having fun, Doc?"

"Oh, yes." She bent to him and placed her hands on his shoulders. "Awesome show. Thank you."

"You're welcome." He captured her lips in a quick kiss.

As she stroked her tongue over his bottom lip, Derek groaned and cupped the back of her head in his palm.

Yeah, fucking elated didn't even begin to cover it.

Chapter 16

Rayna sat, perched on the edge of the wooden desk chair in their hotel room, with lust pumping through her veins like a river of hot lava.

She was naked, except for her panties. Her heart raced, thudding in her ears. Her nipples were hard as stone, and her clit pulsed and throbbed, aching to be touched.

Derek hadn't used the cuffs, but instead secured her hands behind her back with a set of plastic industrial-grade zip ties from his glove box. Much to her surprise, she'd been a little disappointed. She had really wanted to feel the cool metal of the handcuffs against her skin, but Derek was worried they'd be too hard or rough on her soft skin.

This tender concern of his had only served to amp up Rayna's arousal even more than it already was—which, considering the minute he'd pulled her arms behind her back and secured them, she'd soaked clean through her panties, she didn't think it was possible to be more turned on, but she was. She really, really was.

And so far, this was the most erotic thing Rayna had ever experienced in her entire life.

"You look so fucking beautiful. I'd love to blindfold you." He thrummed both of her nipples. "I wish I'd brought something for that."

Rayna sucked in a breath and swallowed. "I've never been blindfolded before."

He squatted down in front of her. "We've got plenty of time to try that soon enough. The anticipation is just as hot." He gazed down her body then back to her face. "Fuck, you're beautiful, Rayna."

More of the tender and sweet. Rayna felt her throat get tight and heat rise up her chest. The things he said to her, she just...she knew he meant them. He really thought she was beautiful. She could feel it from head to toe. "Thank you."

As far back as she could remember, Rayna had kept control, maintained discipline in all things. It was exactly how and why she'd gotten as far as she had in her career and been successful with her practice.

He circled around, stopping behind her. "Spread your legs."

The idea of being bound and then directed, or ordered to do something, should appall her. It didn't. None of the things they'd done so far together did. The spanking had been a huge deal for her. The fact that she'd enjoyed it so much, another shock for her.

Here she was, bound and at his mercy, ready to take whatever he was going to give her and open to all he would make her feel.

Sure she was nervous, but she wasn't scared. There was a difference. A huge one. Rayna knew she could tell him to stop, and he would. He'd respect her wishes. Derek would take care of her. Rayna was safe. He wouldn't hurt her...not physically anyway.

But it was quite clear to her, in that moment, from a consenting sexual point of view, she had no control over anything. Not him, and sure as heck not herself.

There was freedom in this newly found lack of control. Without another thought, Rayna let go...of every and any illusion of power. And as she did, a sense of ease filled her mind and limbs, spreading through her body.

Still at her back, Derek threaded his fingers through the length of her hair. "Love your hair."

Rayna closed her eyes and just let herself feel. She felt the press of his fingertips at her scalp, massaging her. Then she felt them brush through her hair again, then the sting when he gripped the strands.

He pulled the length to the side, then she felt his warm breath and then his lips at her neck. "You taste so good."

Rayna's head lolled from the side to the back of her shoulders as he caressed her neck and shoulder with his lips and tongue. He smoothed one hand from her shoulder down to one breast and cradled the underside of it, while stroking his thumb over the nipple.

She moaned and her body quivered.

"Are you wet for me?" Rayna moaned again, and he moved his hand down her stomach to between her parted legs, cupping her mound. "Oh fuck yes, baby. You are. Soaked right through your panties."

A whimper came out of her when he pulled his palm away from her core and went back to her breast, this time tracing an outline around her areola with his fingertip. "You need to be fucked don't you?"

Another body jerk and stomach jump. And another flood of arousal coated her panties. "Yes."

He chuckled and pulled away. "Not yet."

Rayna felt the chill from his body leaving hers as he moved to stand in front of her. The room was dim, the only light coming from the bathroom—though it was plenty for him to see her, because she could see him clearly, too. He was, as usual, beautiful. But he was still fully clothed. "Can I see your body?"

He raked his gaze up and down her body, and she felt it like a physical touch. "This what you want?" He started unbuttoning his shirt. Taking his time with the first button, then the second—he stopped. "You didn't say please."

Funny, she always said please when she asked him for something, in and out of bed. Or when she begged him. Of course, that was always when they were naked. She readily said please and begged him as if it was instinct to do so.

Rayna tipped her head forward and licked her lips. "Please?"

"Good girl."

Good girl...

Another kind of thrill bolted through Rayna, making her skin tingle from head to toe, and she drew in a deep breath through her nose and blew it out through her mouth, to keep her head from spinning.

With her eyes intent on his body, she watched as he finished unbuttoning his shirt, slipped it off his broad shoulders and laid it on the dresser. Her breath hitched, and her clit pulsed. For heaven's sake, she would never get tired of seeing his incredible body bare.

"You want more?"

She swallowed past the dryness in her throat. "Yes, please?"

He nodded, and his lips pursed into a smirk. "Okay, I'll give you more. But to be clear, you stay right where you are until I say otherwise. Got it, Doc?"

Her stomach jumped. "Yes."

"Perfect." Derek unbuttoned his jeans, pushed them and his boxer-briefs down his thighs, and palmed his erection. With a short groan, he stroked from root to tip. "This yours, Rayna?"

"Yes." Her throat no longer dry, she swallowed the water filling her mouth. She'd never had him in between her lips before, though she'd wanted to. Good grief, he was beyond gorgeous, and sexy, and so totally male, she was overwhelmed in every wonderful way possible.

With her hands bound behind her back, completely at his mercy, Rayna couldn't think straight anymore, but at the same time, she was beyond clear about what she wanted. All animal instinct, she was ruled by the desire to taste him, feel the shape of him in her mouth.

Unable to hold herself back any longer, and without his permission, Rayna met his gaze and stood. He was so strong and powerful, and her desire to please him, even if it meant defying him, drove her forward.

She loved what he was giving her, loved being bound. Loved the alpha male side of him and that he'd taken control of everything happening between them. But she needed this, and for the moment, Derek said nothing, only watched as she walked to him and got down on her knees. "I need you in my mouth."

With his erection still held in his fist, he stared down at her, one corner of his lips curved up in a grin. "You got up, even though I said you should wait. Maybe you need a spanking."

She gazed up at him. "I'll take the spanking, just first...let me suck my cock."

Yes, Rayna said that.

That was her.

Because, yes, she'd meant every word as if they were her last.

* * * *

Sexy.

Sassy.

Beyond fucking hot.

The sight of Rayna, arms bound behind her back, down on her knees in front of him, had his dick throbbing to the point of almost pain. She'd never sucked his dick before. He hadn't let her. A fire sparked in her eyes, the expression of need he saw there undeniable, Derek sure as hell wasn't going to stop her this time.

Mustering every ounce of control he could find within himself, and with his prick still fisted in his palm, Derek gazed down at her. "Say please, Doc."

With her eyes trained on his shaft, she dragged her teeth over her bottom lip. "Please, may I have you in my mouth?"

Goddamn... Derek took a step closer. "Give me your eyes and open your mouth for me."

Without hesitation she looked up, caught his gaze, and opened to receive him.

"Perfect." Shifting his pelvis forward, Derek traced her lips with the engorged head, painting them with his arousal. "Keep that sweet tongue in your mouth until I say. If you're a good girl, and listen, I'll let you have a taste soon."

Rayna moaned and closed her eyes.

Derek tapped the head on her bottom lip, then traced her lips again. Her breath was warm on the shaft, and her pink tongue looked so wet and inviting it was all he could do to not lose his damn mind. "Is this your cock?"

She nodded, gazing up at him again. Derek dragged the head lower, rubbing it along her chin, then back up to her lips. He pulled back a bit. "Close your mouth." A look of confusion came over her face, but she did what he asked. God, she was killing him. "Good girl."

Shifting closer once more, he pressed the tip against her closed lips. "Slowly, so I can watch you let me in, Doc." As he pressed forward, as he'd directed, her lips parted to receive him. Taking first the tip then the head as he pressed deeper. He stopped with her lips wrapped tight around the rim. "Suck me like this."

As the wet heat of her mouth enveloped him, Rayna's eyes fluttered closed and she started suckling him. *Holy fuck!* Derek groaned, gripped the back of her hair and held her there for as long as he could stand.

"Need to feel more of you." Unable to hold back any longer, he pressed forward, sliding farther in her amazing mouth. She moaned again, taking him deep. He felt the back of her throat and pulled back, only to slide back in. "That's it. Just like that. Keep those perfect lips wrapped tight. Fuck, yeah, Rayna!"

He wouldn't last like this. Her moaning and whimpering with her full lips wrapped tightly around his prick. In and out, another groan from him, another moan from her...this one he felt in his balls. *Fuuuuuck!*

Derek jerked from her mouth. "Enough!"

"No, please—" She swallowed and licked her lips, gazing up at him. "Please, let me have more?"

Derek shook his head and got her to her feet. "Need inside your cunt. Now."

Rayna sagged against him. Framing her waist in his palms, he picked her up and took her plump lips in a kiss. Her hard nipples pressed into his chest, and he sucked her tongue into his mouth. Fuck, she was so sweet and warm against his body.

Breaking the kiss, he took her to the edge of the bed and turned her. He drew her wet panties down her legs, helped her step out of them, and then helped her get onto the mattress. Climbing on behind her, he pressed his chest to her back, splayed his hand on her stomach to hold her tight, and knee-walked them to the middle of the bed.

Derek placed a kiss to the side of her neck. "Stay here."

She nodded, and he leaned over to the nightstand and grabbed one of the condoms he'd set there earlier. After straightening, he opened the package and rolled the condom on. For once, Derek was grateful to be wearing a condom, because judging by the fact that his prick was harder than a rod of steel and ready to blow, no barrier between them meant he'd definitely lose it in a matter of seconds.

That would never be acceptable in his book, ever.

With Rayna still upright on her knees, Derek rested his ass on the back of his feet and ran two fingers down her spine, then over each bound wrist. "These still okay?"

She glanced back at him. "Yes."

After she turned back around to face the headboard, he ran his fingers down the curve of her ass. Tracing along the underside of each buttock, he could feel and see her body trembling. "You're perfect, Doc. So fucking perfect."

Continuing his journey, he had to know. Needed to feel for himself. "Is your cunt still wet for me?"

Her breath hitched. "Yes."

"Part your legs just a little wider for me." She did as he asked, and Derek slid his two fingers along one inner thigh and then the other. Her trembling intensified, and the desire to give her the relief her body needed gripped him like a vise. Though he knew that if he could hold her there just a little longer, build that need higher, it'd be worth it. "I make you wait any longer and you'll drip right down your thighs, Rayna."

She whimpered. "Need you...please?"

"You need my cock, baby?" Derek stroked along her drenched folds and found the mouth of her pussy. "Where do you need it, right here?" He pressed his fingers inside, and she jerked her hips backward. "Ah yes, right there, huh, baby? You want to fuck my fingers?"

Another whimper, and she shook her head side to side, her hair flowing around her shoulders.

"No? But you're fucking them right now. What would you rather have?" He pulled his fingers from her channel, brought them to his mouth and sucked them.

"Your cock. I need your cock, please, Derek. *Please...*" She angled her hips back. "Please take me. Please?"

Reaching up, he grabbed her hips and pulled her back and down to sit on his cock. He slipped fully inside her soaked and tight cunt, and they both let out a groan so loud the guests in the room beside theirs likely heard them. Not that he cared. "Fuck yes."

With her legs angled on either side of his, Derek bent her forward, held onto her wrists and pumped his hips up and down, fucking into her tight channel. The sounds of their flesh slapping together, their harsh breaths, and his groans, her whimpers filled the air.

Rayna's tight channel clenched on his length, and his orgasm tingled at the base of his spine, crawling up his balls. This wouldn't last long... for either of them.

"Derek..." She came down on him and rolled her hips, taking him as deep as she could get him.

Goddamn, this was so good, so fucking hot. He really wanted it to last longer, but with her moving like that, gripping his dick like she was in her core, no way that was going to happen. Reaching around her, Derek found her clit. "Ride it, Doc. Come all over my cock."

Slamming back down, her head snapped back, landing on his shoulder, and she bounced on him. "Derek! Oh, God!"

Her orgasm hit, and she froze, back arched, her tight little cunt spasming around his shaft. Derek wrapped his other arm around her middle, holding tight as he continued to rub her clit and fuck into her. "Milk it from me, baby."

"*Mmm...nngggh.*" She jerked against him, still in the throes of her orgasm.

Derek's climax hit like a bolt of lightning, racing through him, setting fire to his veins. Cupping her mound in his palm and pulling her tighter against him, he bit down on her shoulder as spurt after spurt of his release shot from his dick, filling the condom.

Still arched against him, Rayna turned her head to face him, ran the tip of her nose along his cheek, then pressed a soft kiss there.

Tender.

Sweet.

So fucking beautiful.

I'm falling in love with you... Derek ran his hands up her stomach, closing both arms around her, and buried his face in her shoulder.

Chapter 17

"I'm ready to tell you now." Rayna stared down at her hand and fingers entwined with Derek's as they drove home from Prescott.

The night she'd spent with him had been unlike anything she'd ever experienced in her life. It wasn't just the dinner or the show. Or the mind-blowing sex, either. It had been all of it combined.

It had also been falling asleep in his arms, feeling safer and warmer than she ever remembered feeling in her life. In spite of how hard she'd tried not to let feelings grow, they'd grown just the same.

And with those emotions she was now feeling for Officer Derek Hansen also came trust. Rayna trusted him.

Fully.

Completely.

Willingly.

So, it was time to tell him about her hang-up and also that, apparently, her hang-up was gone. Because of him.

Derek glanced over at her. "The cop non-issue?"

She smiled and rolled her eyes. "Yes, the cop *non*-issue."

"Should I get off at the next exit? Do we need alcohol? Coffee?"

She laughed and swatted his shoulder. "No. Stop."

"The truck? Doc, this is the 17, there aren't many places to pull over."

She raised a brow. "You want to hear this or not?"

Derek raised their hands to his lips and kissed her fingers. "Damn right I want to hear it." He smiled at her. "Thank you for wanting to tell me."

"Don't thank me yet." She drew in a deep breath, tamping down a bundle of nerves that suddenly started clawing at her stomach. "It's stupid, and again, I just want to preface this with, this isn't personal. It's not about you at all, although, I can see how it might've felt that way, or could even still feel that way."

"Okay."

"So, I guess, please try not to take it personally, and just... I hope you understand my point of view."

He glanced at her. "Got it, babe. It's all good."

Rayna drew in another deep breath. She trusted him. After last night, how could she not? Good grief, she'd let the man bind her hands and have his way with her. As embarrassing as it was, she could tell him about her father and her fear.

She swallowed and shifted in her seat to face him a little. "My father was a police officer. In Atlanta. He's retired now."

"No shit? That's awesome." He smiled and glanced at her, but then must've seen something in her expression, because his smile vanished. "Or not awesome... Okay, how about I shut up and let you talk?"

She gave him a smile, a small one, but still, it wasn't much. "It's fine, honey." She shrugged and went on. "My parents are divorced. Have been since I was ten."

He nodded. "Yeah, mine are, too, but they waited until me and my sisters were out of high school. I guess they figured after twenty-plus years together, they'd fulfilled their commitment to us kids, who knows." He squeezed her hand. "You were young, though. That had to be hard."

Rayna gazed out the windshield. "It was hard, I guess? But in a lot of ways, at least for me, it was better. My brother has his own version of it, of course." She looked down at their linked hands. "It always amazes me how two people can grow up in the same house, yet remember things completely different, you know?"

"It's probably the same for my sisters and me. Though, I don't know if we've ever sat down and discussed our childhoods in detail."

"You should. It might shock you."

"It might, maybe. I mean, not much shocks me. I'm fairly used to how people perceive and experience things differently than the person standing right next to them. Happens in pretty much every situation I deal with at work."

She moved her eyes back to him. "I hadn't thought of that." She licked her lips. "Well, anyway, this isn't my sob story or anything, so I hope you don't take it that way. I just want to explain my hang-up."

"I'm with you, Doc. Like I said, it's all good." He smiled at her.

"Okay." For Pete's sake, why was this so hard to get out? Probably because of the shame she felt climbing up her throat as well as crawling along her skin. Regardless, her issue with cops was real, and for good reason. She shouldn't be ashamed, although she felt guilty for not telling him sooner. Rayna swallowed and pushed herself forward. "So, not sure how your home was, but mine was not a happy one. My parents fought... *all the time*. Honestly, I can't remember a time that they didn't fight."

"That sucks."

"Yeah, it did suck. They didn't fight over money. Or material things. Or chores. Nothing so normal. My parents fought because my father *would not* stop cheating on my mother. For all I know, maybe he couldn't."

"That's horrible, babe. I mean, you knew? About his indiscretions?"

She looked back to the windshield. "From as far back as I can remember."

"Rayna, that's fucking horrible. Your parents should've kept that shielded from you. You shouldn't have known. As your parents, they... damn. I don't want to overstep, but seriously, they should've done a better job of protecting you from that."

Rayna shrugged. "Ya know, I never really looked at it like that, but, yes, you're right. At this point, it doesn't matter. I mean it wouldn't have changed anything."

"True, but still." He squeezed her hand, and she looked over at him. "I'm so sorry you had to go through that. It must've broken your heart, babe."

"It did." She shrugged one shoulder and swallowed down the tears that wanted to rise. Here she was, trying to tell him why she'd judged him, and he wanted to comfort her. Good grief, he really was amazing. She gave herself a moment to get things under control so she could continue.

Closing her eyes a moment, she drew in another deep breath and then began again. "I don't know how many women there were, but there were a lot. More than I can count, and believe me, for a long time, I counted. Anyway, once they got divorced, things were finally normal, whatever normal means. But when that happened, when things finally ended, I hated my father. I refused to go see him for a long time, even though the court said I had to. Not much he could do, plus he was busy...ya know, with all his women." She shook her head and looked over at him. "Point is...my point in telling all of this to you is that at age ten, I swore to myself I'd never, ever, no matter what, get involved with a cop. Plus, Momma did her fair share of drilling it into my brain, too."

There—she'd finally said it. Relief flooded her system, making her heart race. Good grief, it felt like a ten-thousand-pound weight just slid off her back.

He glanced at her and back at the road. "Rayna, you know that not all cops are like that, right?"

"Of course I know that. I mean, my head knows it. Doesn't mean my heart does, though."

He nodded. "But you dated me anyway. Why?"

She dragged her teeth over her bottom lip. "Well, honestly? I don't know."

He gave her the side eye. "Come on, really?"

"Other than the obvious, that you're the sexiest man who's ever looked at me or expressed interest in me. But...maybe it was the way you kept coming into the office."

He grinned. "Wearing you down."

She giggled. "Yes, but then that kiss..." Rayna's skin got warm just thinking about that day in the vet clinic, and she fanned herself, smiling at him. "That kiss sealed it, and I thought, why not? And don't take this wrong, but I really figured one date and then you'd see what a bore I was and that'd be the end of it."

"A bore? Rayna, you are so far from boring it's not even funny. How the hell do you think you're boring?"

"Okay, not the point. Either way, I never expected that things would continue, and they did. Here we are. And now..."

"Now what?" He glanced at her then back to the road.

"Now I'm having feelings for you. I know it's soon, so I hope that doesn't freak you out. But the truth is I feel for you, deeply, and that makes this whole thing even scarier now."

He looked over at her and squeezed her hand. "Really wish I wasn't driving when I tell you this. But I'm not waiting, so please hear me."

Good grief, what was he going to say to her? Nervous unease crept up her spine, and her hands began sweating. Ugh, how pleasant for him, since he'd kept hold of one of them the whole time as they talked.

There were only two ways this could go. He was either going to let her down—not so gently—saying he had no feelings for her and this was all just a fun fling for him, or he was going to confess that he had feelings, too. And Rayna had no idea which it would be.

"Okay. Sure."

"Doc, it's not too soon, at least not for me. I need to tell you, I've been having feelings for you for *much* longer than the three weeks we've been dating. I swear to God, from the first day I saw you a little over six months ago, I've been having feelings for you." He pulled their hands to his lips and kissed her fingers. "I hope that doesn't freak you out."

Rayna's mouth almost dropped open, but she managed to control herself. She'd suspected, and even hoped, that he might be developing feelings for her, too, but hadn't fathomed the depth of it. No wonder he'd kept coming into her office rather than taking Axle to the contracted PD vet. And no wonder he was always shy, or sweet, or joking with her—at least trying to, because she really tried to keep their interaction limited when he came in. No wonder... "Wow."

"Shit, are you freaked out?"

"No. Not at all. I'm...well, flattered? Definitely swept off my feet, but you've been doing that for a while now." She smiled.

He blew out a relieved-sounding breath. "Okay, good. I got scared for a second there." He laughed.

Relief moved through Rayna too, because she now knew he felt for her as she felt for him, but consequently, fear followed close on the heels of her solace because now...now she was *really* vulnerable.

Now her heart was really at risk.

"Look, I get it. Lots of cops cheat, hell lots of people cheat. But cops do have a bad rep. It's just the truth." He shrugged. "I know guys like that. Actually, I know female cops like that, too. But not all cops cheat, just like not all people cheat." He glanced at her and gave her hand another squeeze. "I don't cheat, Rayna. It's not my MO. I got no reason to, especially now. But here's the deal, I know that no matter how many times I tell you that, your head might hear it, but your heart won't. I don't want anyone else but you, Rayna. Haven't wanted anyone else since the day I brought Axle to you. So, I guess I'll just have to show you, and if you're willing to try and trust me, I *will* show you. I *will* prove it to you."

Rayna gazed at him across the cab of his truck. His face was a mask of seriousness. And she knew, down to her toes, that he meant every word he'd just said to her. Truth be told, there was still that small part of her that knew, even if he meant it now, that didn't mean he'd be able to follow through.

Moreover, a bigger part of her knew in her soul that he could and he would follow through. Rayna shoved that small part aside and leaned over the center console. Getting close to him, she brushed her lips over his ear. "Derek?"

He let out a sigh. "Yeah, Doc?"

"Thank you." She pressed a soft kiss to his cheek.

Derek Hansen was a cop. And Rayna was *totally* falling for him.

So be it.

Chapter 18

"Will you relax?" Derek held his phone in his hand as he grabbed a clean button-up from his closet.

"I can't. I'm nervous, Shirley." Derek heard some fumbling in the background. "How the hell did Rayna convince Tish to double again?"

"Because the woman is made of magic? Dunno, Jeff." Derek grinned and, even though Jeff couldn't see him, shrugged and raised a hand to make his point. "You ever think maybe Tish likes you?"

"Psshaww! *As if*!"

Derek stifled a laugh as he shook his head, set the phone down and pulled on his shirt. "I bet she does."

"Listen to me, Shirley. You've been dating Rayna for how long now?"

A huge grin hit Derek's lips. "Five weeks. Five gloriously wonderful wee—"

"Zzzactly. If Tish was interested in me, she'd have already gotten my number from Rayna. Or you. She didn't, so that's easy math."

Derek heard more rustling. "I don't even want to know what you're doing so I'm not going to ask about the background noises. Even though I just did. Dammit." Jeff's laugh echoed through the speaker of his phone, and Derek smoothed his palm over his face. "Anyway, you ever think maybe Tish is waiting for you to call?"

Jeff started laughing harder, like an obnoxious fool, and then finally cleared his throat. "Don't be stupid."

Derek glared at the phone. "Hey! Don't be a penis, or I'll leave you home tonight."

"I'm kidding, Shirley. Don't be so sensitive."

"Yeah, yeah. Also, keep telling me what *not* to be and you'll be home watching porn all night." Derek moved into the bathroom. "So, answer my question, Mr. Nervous Nelly."

"Fine. Tish isn't waiting for me to call because she is a beautiful, intelligent, modern, and independent woman. She goes after what she wants. She does *not* wait for it to come to her."

Derek frowned at the phone. "And you know this how?"

"Just do. Trust me."

"All I'm gonna say is this, Tish might be all those things you listed and more, but she's still a woman. And women want men to be the ones that call. Also, I'm calling you Nelly going forward."

"Ugh, you're so old-fashioned, Shirley. It's really cute. And congrats! You finally picked a good name for me." Jeff chuckled.

Derek laughed. "I'd rather be old-fashioned and cute, and get the girl, than be alone on the couch watching skinamax, *Nelly*."

"Harsh! Way harsh!" Jeff laughed. "Proud of you, Shirley."

Derek shook his head. "I'm so glad I could earn your pride. Now let me finish getting ready so I'm not late picking up the girls."

"All right. I'll see you at the Whiskey B soon. I'll get there early and grab a table."

Derek smiled and picked up his phone. "And a few shots, no doubt."

"Nahh. I'll be good. Later, tater."

"Later, Nelly." Derek hit the End Call button.

Satisfied with his appearance, he sprayed on just a little bit of cologne and shut all the lights down in his bathroom and bedroom. Heading back out to the kitchen, he found Axle napping on his big-ass designer dog bed.

He stopped in front of his partner. "Well? How do I look?"

Axle raised his head up, and then his ears perked, but one flopped to the side. "Not a good color?"

Axle tilted his head to the other side and gave a little *garumph*.

"Okay, so the color works. Glad you're good with it." Derek laughed and moved to the refrigerator. He stopped before opening the door, smiling at the pic of his daughter with her little half sister in front of a huge Fred Flintstone billboard in Bedrock City, AZ.

Next week, she'd be home from her summer adventure with her mom, stepfather, and little sister. Megan had had a blast, best summer vacation yet, according to their nightly chats anyway.

Derek missed her a ton, but the break had been nice, too. He'd had a lot of free time to devote to Rayna—

Speaking of, he still needed to tell her about Megan. He'd meant to tell her on their drive home from Prescott two weeks ago, but he couldn't bring himself to do it. She'd finally opened up about the cop thing. For real, considering the kind of man her father was, Derek didn't blame her for not wanting to date a cop.

Plus, the last thing he wanted to do that day was lay his stuff on her and give her cause to worry about his friendship with Stephanie. There was nothing between him and his ex. That chapter of his life had been closed so long ago, he could barely remember ever feeling anything but friendship for Steph. It made sense, they'd really only ever been friends. Best friends, in fact.

Plus, it was entirely possible his Doc would put on the brakes when he told her about his daughter, simply because she had said she really didn't want kids. That trip had marked a turning point for him. He'd known after the night they'd had in the hotel that he was falling in love with Rayna.

The prospect of losing her was just too scary for him to face.

Derek sighed through his nose and pulled the pic down from the fridge, then put it in a cabinet drawer. Rayna had wanted to come to his home, spend time there, and there was no getting out of that. Not if he wanted to continue with her.

So, in order to make that work, he'd taken down all the pics of Megan and any of Stephanie that were in his house. He'd also put a lock on his daughter's bedroom door and told Rayna some bullshit about that being where he stored his guns. God, he was a dick.

It was the wrong thing to do, especially because Derek had nothing to hide, least of all his daughter. But the truth was, the longer he went without sharing with Rayna, the more it started to feel like he actually *was* hiding something.

Knowing her like he did now, and knowing the story about her father, there was no way Rayna wouldn't see him failing to tell her as a betrayal of her trust. She would, he was sure, though Derek prayed she'd understand why and forgive him.

But if she didn't? Fear crept up the back of his throat. He was a cop and took on the bad guys daily, not without fear, but with a ton of determination. However, the fear of losing Rayna was more intense than anything Derek had ever felt in the line of duty. He shook his head and ran his palm over his close-cropped hair. Derek had no idea what to do.

He was screwed either way.

* * * *

Rayna opened the garage door, knowing Derek would be pulling up any second. They hadn't been back to the Whiskey Barrel since that first night they'd met up. It seemed really appropriate that finally going back meant they'd go for the double date thing again.

Plus, Jeff and Tish needed to get better acquainted. Rayna's idea, and Derek agreed. Moving back into the house, she headed for her bedroom and master bath. Coming to the doorway of the bath, she looked at her friend. "You almost ready?"

Tish was bent close to the mirror, adding more eyeliner. "Just about." She turned to Rayna. "How're my wings? Are they even?"

"Your what?" Rayna frowned and stepped closer to her friend.

"My eyeliner wings. Are they even?" Tish closed her eyes and raised her brows. "How do you not know what wings are?"

Rayna leaned closer. "Uh, not a big makeup person. How do you not know *that?*"

"True. I do know that." Tish groaned. "But, just pretend you are for a minute. Are they even?"

Rayna chuckled. "I think so, yes."

Tish drew in a loud exaggerated breath. "Okay 'you think so.' Telling ya, no help at all, lady."

Rayna leaned a hip against the counter and pursed her lips. "You seem nervous. Why?"

Tish stepped back from the mirror and fluffed her thick dark hair with her fingers. "What? No, not nervous." She turned, looking over her shoulder in the mirror, Rayna assumed to check...well, she had no idea. Then spun back to face the mirror. "Just want to make sure I look okay."

"Hmm." Rayna crossed her arms. "Thank you for agreeing to double with us again. Like I said, it should be fun."

"Well, Jeff is one of those goofy asshole but deadly good-looking guys I tend to stay away from. Plus, I can tell he's the bossy type. But for you, I'll suck it up and deal."

"Deadly good-looking?"

"Yes, but also goofy asshole. So, they cancel each other out." Tish shrugged and added more lipstick. "Plus bossy caveman. Definitely not my type."

"Okay then." Rayna nodded. "You need a shot before we go?"

"Fuck yes, I do." Tish placed her hands on the counter top and leaned on them, as if she was exhausted. "A shot would be outstanding right now."

"*Ooookay* then." Rayna stifled a laugh. "How about you meet me in the butler's pantry? Like right now? Because he's going to be here, like two minutes from now."

"Got it. Be right there." Tish spun again, this time clearly checking her butt in her jeans. "Do these look okay on me?"

"No time for this." Rayna walked out of the bathroom then called over her shoulder, "Going to get shots now."

"Not helping!"

Rayna ignored her friend, who was definitely, no doubt about it, nervous. But why? Maybe... *Wait a second!* Rayna grabbed the bottle of tequila. Maybe Tish liked Jeff more than she was willing to admit. And wouldn't that just be adorable?

With a huge grin, Rayna filled two shot glasses. Raising one glass eye level, she peered into the golden liquid. "Nothing like a little tequila truth serum to bring all things suppressed to the surface."

"Bring all what things to the surface?"

At the sudden sound of Tish right behind her, Rayna jumped and spun around.

"Ooh! Thanks!" Tish took the glass from Rayna's palm. "Come to Momma."

"Good grief, you scared me." Quickly, Rayna shook off the shudder that'd raced through her, then picked up the other tequila. "Let's drink to dates with gorgeous men."

"Oh, for fuck's sake." Tish rolled her eyes. "Fine. But if he's a goofy asshole tonight, or pretending he's all submissive when he's really all bossy caveman, I can't guarantee I won't wander away."

Rayna watched as Tish tipped the shot to her lips and swallowed it down. "You like him, don't you?"

Tish put the empty glass down. "Who? Derek? I don't really know him personally, except through you, of course. But, yeah, so far. I guess I like him."

"No. I meant Jeff." Rayna tipped her shot and swallowed the alcohol.

"No, I do not. Already said he's not my type." Again she rolled her eyes. "I mean, I'm not trying to be a bitch, he's nice enough. But I don't *like* him like him. Why would you even say that?"

Well, so much for the idea of plying Tish with booze to get her to admit the truth. Then again, two seconds after downing the shot wasn't really enough time for it to work. "Well...I don't know. I mean, you're nervous. And as long as I've known you, I've never seen you nervous. And maybe that's why—"

"Knock, knock, anyone home?" Derek called from the laundry room. An instant smile hit Rayna's lips. "Come on in, honey. We're ready."

Tish crossed her arms. "Maybe that's why what?"

"Never mind. It's not important." Rayna shrugged and moved into the kitchen to get her small purse.

Tish followed. "You don't ever say things that aren't important, Ray. Please tell me."

Rayna sighed and placed her palm on her friend's upper arm. "How about this? Let's get to the bar, have a couple drinks, do some dancing, and then I'll tell you. And I promise, it's nothing bad."

"I am the luckiest man in the East Valley right now." Derek came into the kitchen, big smile on his, to quote Tish, deadly good-looking face. "You two look absolutely beautiful!"

"You're looking pretty damn good, too." Tish smiled, grabbed her small clutch off the table and glanced at Rayna. "He's always this sweet, huh?"

"Yes, and I don't think I'll ever get used to it." Rayna smiled, not taking her gaze off Derek. When he stepped in front of her, she rose on tiptoe, circled his neck in her arms and kissed him.

Derek wrapped his arms around her waist and pulled her tight against him. He let out a little groan when she stroked her tongue over his. When she broke from his lips, he brushed his nose over hers. "Missed you, Doc."

Rayna smiled. "Missed you, too, honey."

"You two are so fucking cute, it's almost frightening. Before this goes any further and you two need privacy, maybe we should go."

Still holding onto Rayna, Derek looked over at Tish. "Frightening, huh? That makes me almost feel bad, Miss Tish. Almost." With a devious grin, he smoothed his palms down Rayna's back, stopping just above the arch of her buttocks. "So, I shouldn't grab her here? Or pick her up, like I usually do?" He laughed.

With a groan, Tish covered her face—which was now a healthy shade of pink—with her hands. "Oh, God. I'm going to go wait in the truck."

Derek laughed harder and let go of Rayna but took her hand in his. "Just teasing you, Miss Tish. Plus, the truck is locked."

Rayna giggled. She couldn't help it. She rarely got to see her best friend teased. Plus, she couldn't remember ever seeing Tish blush. The night was off to a fantastic start, and Rayna knew it was only going to get better.

Holding tight to Derek's hand, she stopped at the laundry room door to the garage and set the alarm code—at his insistence, she'd had the alarm system installed three weeks into their relationship.

All three of them scooted through as the alarm beeped in countdown mode, signaling it was going to arm itself. When she and Tish cleared the door, Derek took her house keys from her and locked the garage entry to the house. Something else he'd made her start doing.

"He's very secure, huh?" Tish nudged Rayna and laughed.

"Cop, remember?" He walked past them, grinning.

Doing her best impression of him, Rayna added, "Hazard of the job."

"That's right, baby. You tell her." He chuckled.

Tish rolled her eyes and moved past him to the back passenger door. "Yep, cute *and* frightening."

"Awesome!" Still laughing, Derek opened the door for Tish. Once she was in, he opened the front passenger door for Rayna. He paused and held his hand out to her. "M'lady, your chariot."

Taking his hand, she stepped up onto the running board and then turned and pressed a soft kiss to his lips. "Thank you, good sir."

Warmth filled her heart and flowed through her limbs. She loved when he said that to her. Had from the very start. With a smile, Rayna took her seat, and he closed her in. Yeah, she was falling for him.

More and more every day.

* * * *

"You want fried pickles?" Derek nudged her shoulder with his.

"Oh my gosh. They have those? Yes!" Eyes wide, Rayna bent closer to him, peeking at the menu in his hands. "I *love* fried pickles."

He laughed. "Look at you, you're so cute right now."

She scrunched up her nose and giggled.

Derek pressed a quick kiss to her nose and then her lips. "Yup, cute."

"Don't want to interrupt you two being all adorable and stuff, but can you pass the menu this way?" Tish held her palm open on the table.

Jeff looked at Tish. "It's frightening, huh?"

Tish jerked to look at Jeff. "Yes! That's what I said earlier! Jesus Christ, they're killing me."

Jeff sipped his drink then shook his head. "Me too."

"Look, Doc, we have fans." Derek laughed and handed Tish the menu.

"Grumpy ones." Rayna licked some salt from the edge of her margarita then took a sip.

At the sight of her little tongue, lust spiked, hot and fast in Derek's veins, and he groaned. The woman had no idea the power she had over him.

He placed his hand on her thigh and leaned close to her ear. "Reinforcing your spell, I see."

"Spell?"

He slid his fingertips along her inner thigh. "Yeah, the spell you cast on me months ago. Still there, babe. You keep licking that glass edge and I'm going to end up taking you out to the truck and fucking you in the backseat."

She moaned and placed her hand on top of his. Then cleared her throat. "Oh, *that* spell."

"Yes, *that* one." He pulled back and gazed at her. "Tying you to the bed tonight."

Her eyes went soft, and she picked up her drink and licked the edge.

Oh, yeah. Definitely tying her up and... "Spanking you, too."

One perfect brow twitched up, and she took a sip of her drink.

"Will you two give it a rest?" Tish dropped the menu on the table.

"Yeah, or get a room." Jeff smirked and crossed his arms.

Derek leaned forward. "How about you two arm wrestle again?"

Tish's eyes went wide; then she tilted her head to the side. "Gonna need more drink in me for that. Besides, I kicked his ass last time, why bother going again? I'm already in charge."

Jeff coughed. "To be honest, I'll let you be in charge anytime you want; therefore, I let you win."

"Bullshit. You did not." Tish put her hands on her hips.

"Not bullshit. Totally did. I mean, come on, you're a girl." Jeff started shaking with laughter.

Derek burst out laughing, and Rayna did, too. He wasn't sure if Jeff had a death wish, or if there was some sort of strange chemistry happening between his best friend and Tish. Derek was hoping it was the latter.

Tish leaned toward Jeff. "You did not even go there."

With pursed lips, Jeff nodded.

"Oh, come on, Tish." Rayna raised a hand in the air, motioning to Jeff. "He's kidding. Can't you see he's kidding?"

Tish crossed her arms and pursed her lips. "Where is Bethany? I want food and I want another shot and *then*—" She pressed a fingertip into Jeff's chest. "I'm kicking your ass again."

"Promise?" Jeff gave her one of his grins.

That's when Derek knew his best friend was going to ride this game out with Tish as long as it took. God bless him!

Derek hoped like hell Jeff was successful.

* * * *

.

"Ooh! Bethany?" Rayna waved their waitress down.

Tish was obviously hangry, and Jeff was deliberately trying to annoy her, which Rayna had to admit was kind of funny. But, also, not cool. Maybe once she got Tish fed, she'd be a little nicer to the guy.

Bethany came over. "Hey there. You guys need something?"

"Yes! We need an order of fried pickles." Rayna looked at Derek.

"Warm pretzels for the win, please." Derek nodded.

Rayna looked at her best friend, who was bickering back and forth with Jeff, though Rayna couldn't hear what they were saying. "Tish, what did you want to order?" When Tish didn't respond, Rayna tried again, with a little more oomph behind it. "Hey, Tish!"

"*What?*"

Rayna gave her a "look," one that clearly said: did you just answer me like that? Drawing in a deep breath, she jerked her chin in Bethany's direction. "Food, right?"

"Oh. Yeah." Tish tucked a lock of hair behind her ear. "The green chile artichoke dip, please."

Jeff rested an elbow on the table. "Oooh, yum! Are you going to share with me?"

"No." Tish rolled her eyes but then gave Jeff the side eye. "Maybe."

Jeff raised both arms in the air. "Whoohooo! I'll take the maybe for a win!"

"God help me, he needs home training." Tish picked up her drink.

"You guys want anything else?" Bethany grinned.

"Nope. We're sharing." With a huge grin, Jeff put his arm around Tish's shoulder, and she immediately shrugged it off. "Well...'maybe' we're sharing. Better bring my snookums-nookums over here a shot. *Thennnn* I'm sure she'll share with me."

"Okay then." Bethany laughed. "Tequila, Tish?"

"*Riiiiggght.*" With a grin, one it looked like she couldn't help, Tish shook her head, and then winked at Rayna. "Yes. Bring two."

"You got it." Bethany grabbed the menu and walked away.

Oh dear. Rayna was going to be in trouble now. She'd already had two shots, plus the drink in front of her. Hopefully the pickles would be enough food to help counteract the alcohol.

She didn't want to be too drunk when he tied her to the bed...and spanked her. Rayna wanted to experience every single feeling that activity would bring her. A zing of arousal shot through her, and she drew in a breath to keep from moaning.

She glanced at Derek from the corner of her eye, picked up her drink and licked the edge.

Immediately his hand was back on her thigh, and this time, he squeezed. "Sassy."

Yes, she most certainly was.

Chapter 19

"Derek..." Rayna drew in a slow breath, trying to calm her racing heart.

The minute they'd gotten in the door, things progressed quickly. They didn't go back to his place often, but tonight they had, and now she was in his bed...

With only a little bit of slack, her arms were stretched out to her sides, raised high, with her wrists bound to Derek's headboard. Her ankles were bound to the footboard, her legs spread wide, a little bit of slack there as well. In addition, she was wearing a blindfold.

Rayna was completely at his mercy. It was terrifying...and it was glorious.

"You look so beautiful." The breath of his softly spoken words feathered against her lips.

Thick, heated arousal pooled in her stomach and spread through her limbs. Her entire body trembled with it. Rayna dragged her teeth over her bottom lip and drew in another slow breath.

She felt his fingertip, at least she thought it was his finger, on the edge of her lip. "Love your lips, Doc." He tugged at the full flesh. "Love to see you bite this bottom one. Love to watch them, so full, wrapped tight around my cock, too."

Rayna touched the tip of her tongue to his finger. And then he fed it into her mouth, slowly, and she sucked it with a moan.

"Yeah, just like that." After a moment, Derek pulled his finger free, and then she had his lips.

As Derek kissed her, he trailed his wet fingertip down her neck, to one breast, and then circled her tight nipple. Rayna arched her back off the mattress, sucking his tongue into her mouth, trying to get more contact with his hand, or body...with him.

Derek pulled from her lips. "Lay still."

She moaned her frustration. "Derek..."

He pinched her nipple hard and tugged it away from her breast. The sting of painful pleasure ran through her body, arrowing right for her clit. A loud cry came out of Rayna, and she slammed her body down so hard on the bed that if she weren't lying on a soft mattress she was certain she would've hurt herself.

"Easy, baby." The bed dipped, and then she felt the light pressure of his body across her upper hips.

Rayna assumed he was now straddling her. In the next breath, his fingers were on her other nipple and he was tugging that one, the same as its mate. Rayna tried to arch again, but with his weight holding her down, she was unable to.

Searing hot pleasure ripped through her, and Rayna's stomach went tight as her pussy clenched down on itself in little spasms. She hissed and clenched her hands into fists. "Oh God! *Yessss!*"

"Love nipple play with you." Derek let go of her nipples and palmed her breasts. "Love how your skin feels, and how perfect and firm your tits are." He squeezed both breasts then pressed them together.

Next Rayna felt the hot wetness of his mouth as he sucked one nipple then moved to the other. "Love how you taste." He tugged the sensitive taut peaks again.

She could manage no words, only moans and whimpers as every single sensation his touches caused rolled through her...like waves hitting the shoreline. Rayna wanted to drown in all of them.

Derek nibbled one nipple then sucked it hard. Rolling and pinching the other between his fingers. Her clit throbbed, aching to be touched. Her pussy clenched and spasmed, seeking to be filled.

Once again, he pressed both of her breasts together. "You know what I love the most about your tits, Doc?"

"*Mmmnooo*—" She sucked in a breath as he dragged what she figured were his thumbs over each tip. "Tell me?"

She felt him shift higher on her body, and then she felt some wetness. "That I can fuck my cock right between them."

"Derek..." The feel of his erection sliding between her cleavage had Rayna wishing he hadn't blindfolded her. She knew the swollen head of his penis had to be close to her mouth as he thrust forward. Desperate for a taste of him, she raised her head and snaked out her tongue.

He drew back. "I see that sassy tongue of yours. Watched you lick salt from your glass all night." He slid forward. "Every time I saw you, my dick throbbed in my jeans. Ached to feel your tongue on me."

Moaning, Rayna laid her head back down on the pillow and bit her bottom lip.

Derek slid forward, and she felt him bump the underside of her chin. Then she felt his hand slide beneath the back of her head, grip her hair and pull her head up from the pillow. "Open for me, baby. Give me that hot tongue."

With a high-pitched cry, Rayna opened her mouth and felt him slide between her lips. She closed her eyes behind the blindfold and moaned as she sucked the head.

"Fuck yes, just like that." Derek groaned and pushed deeper into her mouth, then retreated. "Nothing prettier than those full lips around my prick."

Rayna moaned as the taste of his pre-cum hit her tongue. He was heaven in her mouth, the scent of him another sweetness she craved. With every inch of her skin tight, Rayna's entire body trembled in overwhelming arousal.

She gave herself over to all of it. With his beautiful erection thrusting into her mouth, her hair fisted in his hand and her body bound to the bed, she was utterly powerless and he was in total control.

God help her, she didn't want it to end.

But then it did. With a deep growl, Derek pulled free from her mouth. "No more." In the next instant, he scooted down her body, and she felt him between her legs.

"No!" Rayna twisted her hips, getting nowhere of course. She wasn't done. She wanted him back in her mouth. She wanted him to come, wanted desperately to feel him spurt in her mouth and down her throat as he did. "Please!"

"Stop!" *CRACK!* His fingers connected with her labia in a stinging slap.

"Oh my God!" Rayna's hips launched off the mattress as the unexpected pain turned into instant pleasure and her clit pulsed as if she'd been electrocuted. It was wonderful, and horrible, and out-of-this-world erotic. Rayna pulled both lips between her teeth, moaning.

Then she felt his palm cover her mound. "That stung, didn't it?"

Rayna nodded and sucked in a breath. "Yes."

"You liked it, though."

She nodded again. "Yes."

"Fuck me." He pulled his hand away and parted her labia. "This sweet cunt...it's all mine."

Rayna sucked in her breath and pressed her lips together. "Mmhmm."

"Say it."

She felt his tongue roll over her clit, and her hips rose off the mattress again. "Derek...baby... *Mmnnngghhh!*"

His palm landed on her pussy with another loud *snap*! "Hold still, Rayna."

"I'm yours! *Ohhhmygodddd!*" Her orgasm hit like a sonic boom as white-hot pleasure, from the sting of his palm, blasted through her. Bright spots formed in the darkness behind her closed lids, and Rayna arched her back, digging her blunt nails into her palms.

"Holy fuck! Yes you are!" Derek covered her clit with his mouth, sucking the pulsing nub between his lips.

A thick haze settled in her mind, and a guttural moan came from deep in Rayna's chest as Derek's hot mouth drove her climax higher, leaving no part of her body or mind untouched.

It was so much more than her pussy that was his.

Rayna knew he owned all of her.

* * * *

Derek was utterly, completely, and amazingly entranced by Rayna Michaels. With his head between her sweet thighs, he suckled her clit and held onto her hips as her orgasm swept through her and her body shook with every sensation.

Releasing her clit, he closed his eyes and covered her cunt with his mouth, lapping at the soaking wet entrance to heaven.

Once more she arched, her back bowing off the mattress, and Derek smoothed his palms up her body to her fine tits and massaged them. She let out another loud moan when he gave her nipples a little tug.

After one more lick, he pulled from her and ran his nose along her clit. "Need to fuck you."

"*Mmmyes.*" With her hands fisted, she tugged at her restraints and let out a sharp gasp when he nipped at her clit. "*Fuuuuuck!*"

Derek's eyes went wide, and he got to his knees, resting on his heels, between her parted thighs. He'd never heard her swear before, not like that anyway. "Doc, I just need to check." He smoothed his palms up her thighs and thumbed her clit. "Was that a good fuck or a bad fuck?"

"Oh, God!" She arched. "Mmm...a good one."

"My girl likes pain play." With his other hand, he slid two fingers inside her wet core. Fuck, she was more matched to him than any woman he could've conjured in a dream.

She whimpered and rolled her head side to side. After drawing in a breath, she shifted her hips, trying to take his fingers deeper. "Is that a bad thing?"

Derek watched her face then looked down at her pussy. The sensitive skin was flushed pink, likely from the slaps he'd given it. Her labia swollen, her little clit so hard it protruded from its hood. "Not. At. All."

Although he'd assumed, based on her reaction the other two times, that she liked it, now he knew for sure. No way he wasn't going to take advantage of that fact.

Raising a hand, he slapped her pussy once again.

Rayna's hips shot off the bed, as far as they could anyway, since her legs were bound at the ankle. Moaning, she thrashed her head from side to side harder. "Derek, please fuck me! Please!"

"Need to grab a condom, baby." He spread her labia with his thumbs and rubbed her clit again.

"No." She licked her lips. "I want to be skin to skin with you."

"Doc, I'd love that, but we haven't even talked about it."

"I'm on the pill."

"Yeah, but..." Derek knew he was clean because he'd gotten tested right after he'd met her. Since then, he'd only been with her. He smoothed his palms up her thighs and then rose to lean over her. He stroked the back of his fingers along her cheek. "Baby, listen to me, I want that with you. I do. But now's not the time to make this decision."

"Why not?" She tilted her head, pressing her cheek to his fingers.

"Because you're vulnerable right now, and overstimulated."

"Derek, I need to feel you. All of you."

God almighty, she was killing him. He pressed his forehead to hers. "Doc..."

"Please?"

Dammit... Derek leaned to the side, resting his weight on one hand. With the other, he slid the blindfold off her eyes. "Look at me." She blinked a few times, and Derek smoothed her hair away from her face. She focused on him and the sweet expression in her eyes laid him flat. "I'm going to untie your legs."

"But—"

Derek placed his finger against her lips. "Doc, just stop and let me do what I gotta do to give you a minute to settle and think."

She nodded, and he moved off of her. Going to the end of the bed, he unhooked the ankle cuff from the bed-strap, then did the same with the other, freeing both of her legs. Staying at the end of the bed, he watched her as she pulled her legs up and together.

Derek's cock was so hard he could probably hammer nails with it, but that didn't matter. He could wait. What mattered was giving her a moment to breathe. Giving her time to gather her thoughts.

Getting off the bed, he cracked the bottle of water he had on the nightstand and brought it to her lips. "Here, babe."

She raised her head and sipped. Then sipped a little more. "Thank you." She laid her head back down. "You're not gonna untie my arms are ya?"

Derek had to smile. The question came out coated with her slight Southern accent, the one that only came out on rare occasions. "Jesus, you're killing me, you know that?"

She frowned but then smiled. "Why?"

He shook his head. "Drink more water."

She drew in a breath and rolled her eyes. "Fine."

Again with the accent. Derek chuckled as he gave her a little more water. "No, I'm not going to untie your arms."

She smiled. "Good."

"Keep up that sassy attitude, and I may just make you sleep this way." He capped the water bottle and set it down on the nightstand.

"Um..."

Her eyes were wide as silver dollars, and he blurted out a laugh. "Relax, Doc. I'm kidding." He bent and kissed her lips, then climbed over her and stretched out beside her.

"Well? How'm I supposed to know if you're bein' serious or not?"

"Fair point." He smiled and traced a line down her breastbone. "How're you feeling?"

She raised a brow. "Horny."

Derek cracked up laughing again, and this time Rayna laughed, too. His chest burned, and his stomach felt funny. Intense feelings were boomeranging all over his brain, feelings he hadn't felt in years. Overwhelmed and a little scared, Derek rolled over her and settled between her welcoming thighs.

As he held his weight off of her by leaning on one arm, Rayna looked up at him and he cupped her face in his palm. Derek brushed his lips over hers, rubbed his nose over the tip of hers, and then kissed her as tenderly as he could manage.

She moaned into his lips and tilted up her pelvis.

The head of Derek's cock met the wet heat of her cunt.

She moaned again, and he pulled from her lips. With his forehead pressed to hers and their eyes locked, he slid the rest of the way inside her tight pussy. Derek closed his eyes and sucked in a breath as her warmth encased him.

"Rayna..." Emotion beat through him, and he opened his eyes and traced her cheekbone with his thumb. "I'm in love with you."

Derek had never said those words to a woman before. Not even to his ex, and he'd never known why, not truly.

But now he knew the reason was because those words were only meant for Rayna.

Chapter 20

"What are you watching?" Wiping her hands on a dish towel, Rayna stepped up to the back of her couch.

Derek glanced up at her and so did Axle from his spot on the floor by the couch. "I think it's called *Baby Boom*? Old, but great movie. I haven't seen it in a long time, though."

"Oh yes, she falls in love with a vet, right?"

"Kinda like me." He popped his brows and grinned up at her.

"Yes, kinda like you." Rayna smiled as she bent and gave him a soft kiss. "You know, just so you know, you're very much a romantic for being an alpha caveman police officer."

He laughed. "Caveman?"

"I do believe I've heard you use that word before, yes."

"No way."

Laughing, she moved back to the kitchen, hung up the towel. When she turned, Axle was sitting in the doorway, ears flopped to the sides, tail wagging. "What? You want a treat, don't you?" She laughed and moved to the freezer. Grabbing an ice cube, she stepped in front of her sink where the small rug was. "*Hier.*"

With a little half yip-groan, he trotted to her. Rayna stepped aside, and Axle moved onto it and sat. She chuckled and stroked his head. "You're a very good boy. Always listening so well." She held open her palm, and Axle gently took the ice cube. Smiling, she straightened. "And you're also a big softy, just like your daddy."

Turning off the kitchen light, she moved back to the family room and plopped on the couch beside Derek.

He scooted her closer. "Okay fine. I may have used that word before. But only because of Jeff."

"What word? Oh! Caveman." She cleared her throat and rested her head on his shoulder. "You're so funny. And so is Axle."

"Yeah? Why's that?"

"He and the ice cubes. Too funny. And you take issue with the caveman comment, but not the romantic one. That's actually far beyond too funny."

"Ice cubes make a fantastic low-fat treat." He pressed a kiss to the top of her head. "Honestly, I can't really argue the romantic thing. I'm a total softy underneath my alpha caveman exterior and bulletproof vest, and I'm not ashamed of that."

Rayna yawned. "Axle is as much a softy as you. Plus, you also like chick flicks. He probably does, too."

At that moment, Axle came trotting back out to the living room and plopped down in his now favorite spot beside the sofa.

"That's a secret. If you tell anyone, we'll deny it to the day we die."

"Your secrets are safe with me, caveman." With a giggle, Rayna curled her legs under her and pulled the soft fleece throw she had draped over the side of the sofa over her lap. "Diane Keaton is so timeless and sophisticated. How old is this movie?"

Derek scooched lower on the couch and stretched his long legs out in front of him on the coffee table, crossing them at the ankle. "Late eighties, I think. Let me see." Grabbing the remote, he pulled up the info on the film. "Yup. Eighty-seven."

She raised her head and looked at him. "So basically, when the movie was made, we were toddlers."

"Yes."

"And this is what you want to watch tonight?"

"Yes."

"Okay."

"Go with it, Doc."

Rayna giggled and laid her head back on his shoulder. "Going with it, honey."

Truly, she didn't care what they watched. Rayna didn't mind chick flicks, or action movies. Blood and gore wasn't her favorite. But a good suspense or thriller was always cool. Either way, cuddling on the couch with her man was the part that made her happy.

Her man.

Somehow in the last six weeks, he'd become Rayna's man. Then last week, he'd told her he was in love with her. She smiled, warmth filling her bones as she recalled that night. It was a memory she'd happily cherish forever.

Of course, when he'd confessed his feelings it was in the middle of incredibly intense sex, where he'd bound her to the bed. However, after he'd said those words to her, the entire dynamic of the moment shifted from unbelievably heady sex to unbelievable lovemaking. And every night since then, Derek had made love to her.

Except for last night. Last night he'd been tired, but he also seemed like there was something on his mind. She'd asked if he needed to talk about anything, but he'd declined, and they'd gone to bed early.

Derek smoothed his palm up and down her arm, and Rayna snuggled a little closer. Tonight he seemed back to his normal self, so Rayna hadn't given it much more thought.

Derek pressed his lips to the top of her head again. "You love me?"

She smiled, the warmth inside her growing. "Yes."

"You sure?"

She giggled. "Yes."

"Good." He squeezed her side.

"Oh, goodness gracious, spaghetti for a baby?" She rolled her eyes. "I may not be parent material but even I know that won't work."

"Not parent material?"

She glanced up at him. "We've talked about this."

"Rayna, that's just silly." He frowned and looked back at the television. "Oh my God. The diaper with electrical tape!"

Rayna laughed. "So sad. But I have to say, I've never changed a diaper, so I get it."

"What do you mean you've never changed a diaper? Didn't you babysit in high school?"

"Never. Too busy working a part-time job at a vet office."

"Wow, you might be the only woman I've ever met that never babysat kids."

She shrugged one shoulder. "Just never had the time is all. And my brother doesn't have any kids. And as you know, neither does Tish."

"But that doesn't mean you're not parent material."

Rayna shrugged again. "I don't know. My focus has always been my career."

Derek muted the TV then shifted and looked over at her. "Babe, I know we talked about this a few weeks ago, it was brief, but still. Are you serious when you say marriage and kids aren't in the cards for you?"

Rayna straightened and focused on him. She didn't know why he was asking her this. Because of that, she didn't know how to answer. Did he want marriage and kids? And if so, did he want them with her?

Yes, it was true that Rayna's career had always been her focus, but that didn't mean that at one point in her life, specifically when she was a little girl, that she hadn't wanted marriage and kids.

Being so young and naive, she'd always figured marriage and kids would just happen. Then after her parents' marriage blew up, she put that idea out of her mind.

Older now, she knew that marriage could be a good thing. Just because her parents' marriage wasn't successful didn't mean she couldn't have something good for herself. Intellectually she knew that. Emotionally was a different story. That's where the fear was alive and real.

Besides, even if she knew without a doubt that she wanted that kind of life, a person couldn't just snap their fingers and poof, manifest a husband and two-point-five kids. The life she'd worked so hard for hadn't exactly allowed her the luxury of time.

But with Derek—Derek made her want those things. More specifically, want them with him. She loved him, was in love with him, but it had only been six weeks. It was too soon to even go down this road.

And what if she did? What if she told him she wanted those things and—a tremor of fear spilled through her.

What if he didn't want them with her?

* * * *

"Rayna, answer me." Derek stared at her, caught somewhere in a deep well of fear and disappointment, and more fear.

"I'm not sure I know how to answer that question."

"A simple yes or no would work."

She frowned and looked down at her hands. "It's not that simple, Derek."

Shit. *Shiiiiiit!* "Babe, it is that simple."

"It's never been in the cards for me." She looked up at him, her brows drawn together. "I went straight to college after high school. Then I went to vet school. Then I worked at a practice. Then I opened a practice."

"Right, I get that. You've been busy. But...you said you don't think you're maternal. Do you really believe that?"

She sighed. "I'm *not* maternal. I've never even changed a diaper. The closest I've come to a human baby in the last five years has been when parents come into the office with theirs. And taking care of animals doesn't translate to motherhood. Why are you pressuring me about this?"

Derek opened his mouth, then closed it again. For fuck's sake, why was this so hard? How could he tell her about his daughter if she didn't even like kids? He blew out a breath and ran his palm over his head. "I'm not trying to pressure you. I'm just trying to...I don't know, I guess determine if this thing between us works out what the future might hold. If you don't like kids, or want them, I guess I'd want to know that now."

Rayna's frown deepened, and she shifted her legs from beneath her. "Derek, it's been six weeks and you want to talk about marriage and kids? That sure feels like pressure to me."

Defeated, he shook his head. "I'm sorry, okay? I didn't mean to pressure you. That's not what my intention was."

"Okay." She looked back down at her hands. "Please understand, I'm just not ready to have this conversation yet. But it doesn't mean I don't love you. I do." She covered his hand with hers. "I've never loved anyone before, or been loved by anyone, and I want to explore *that* before I start thinking about what the future holds."

Glancing down at their hands, he linked his fingers with hers then looked back to her eyes. "You've really never been in love before?"

She smiled. "Derek Hansen, I swear to all things holy, you are the most interesting and complex man I have ever met."

He shook his head, unable to stop his own smile. "Rayna Michaels, you are also complex. And evasive." He laughed. "Can't you answer the question?"

She sighed. "No, I've really never been in love before. Happy?"

"Yes. Well, no. I mean I think that's sad you've never been in love before, but it makes me very happy that I get that 'first' too."

"Good grief." Rayna rolled her eyes and shook her head. "Do you want to finish watching the movie?"

"Yes." He grinned and settled back into a comfortable position on the couch. Rayna slid close, curled next to him and rested her head back on his shoulder. He un-muted the TV, then kissed the top of her head. "Doc?"

"Yes?"

"I love you, too."

"Good." She turned her head and pressed a kiss to the side of his neck. He squeezed her side. "Good."

The movie played out before his eyes, but Derek saw none of it. All he could think about was the fact that he hadn't told Rayna about Megan yet. Or about his ex. Why couldn't she just give him a straight answer? If he had to guess, maybe she did like kids, and maybe she did want some of her own someday? But there was no way to know if he was right or not.

Withholding this information about his ex and daughter was a disaster waiting to happen. Megan was coming home tomorrow. The plan was to have her at his place overnight and then she would go back to her mom on Sunday morning, since he had to work.

Keeping this from Rayna any longer was no longer an option. He needed to try and tell her tomorrow. Or at the very least, tell her before next Friday when Megan came back to him to spend a few nights.

Fear crept up the back of his throat, and his stomach churned with anxiety. Rayna was going to hate him for not telling her. Even if she was fine with the fact that he had a kid, she was still going to hate him for not trusting her.

Caveman, his ass. Derek was a fucking coward.

Chapter 21

"Oh my God, Dad! You would not believe how long it takes to drive across Texas!"

Unable to get a word in edgewise, Derek listened as his ten-year-old daughter went on and on about her summer trip with her mom, her half sister, and her stepdad. Smiling, he pulled into his neighborhood.

"And Florida? Actually that *whole* part of the country is *soooo* hot. Way hotter than Arizona. And the bugs? Like...ugh, so gross. Mosquitos and plamettos?"

Derek laughed. "Palmettos."

"Yeah those." She shivered. "Gross. They look like those flying sewer roaches." She scrunched up her nose. "But *they are* everywhere."

"They look like roaches because they are roaches, angel."

"Ewww! Really?"

"Yup, really." He laughed.

"Steven didn't tell me that."

Derek shrugged a shoulder. "Well, maybe he didn't know."

"True." She pulled her cell phone from her backpack. "I have a ton of pictures from NOLA and lots of places for you."

He glanced at her then back to the road. "I thought your mom said no cell phones for the summer?"

"She did. She and Steven took pics, and then she added them to a shared photo folder."

"Gotcha."

"Daddy, if I had my cell phone I would've been texting you."

"Likely story." He raised a brow. "More like, if you had your cell, you would've spent the whole summer with your nose in Instagram or snapping yapping with your friends."

She laughed. "Snapchatting, Dad."

"Yeah, yeah. Either way, you would've missed the palmetto bugs and all the other cool stuff you saw." He pulled into the driveway.

"Well, just saying, either way, I could've done without the palmetto bugs." She laughed. "I can't wait to see Axle!" Throwing open her door, she hopped down from the truck and opened the back door to get her other bag.

"I got it. Here." Derek gave her the house keys. "Get inside and greet the big boy. I'll get your bag."

"Thanks, Daddy."

As Megan ran off into the house to greet Axle, Derek got the rest of her things and closed the truck up. The plan was to order a pizza, rent a movie from On Demand, and hang with his daughter.

He'd told Rayna he wasn't going to be available tonight. She'd sounded a little disappointed but didn't question why. Which was good, because Derek really didn't want to have to make up some sort of lame excuse— aka a lie. Either way, he still felt like shit about it. No getting around that.

When Derek got into the house, he found Megan on her knees, with her arms around Axle's neck and Axle panting, tongue hanging out, his jaw so wide he almost looked like he was smiling.

"Yes, I missed you, big boy! So much!" Axle rolled over, and Megan went with him. The two of them damn near cuddling on the ground. "You missed me, too, huh?" Axle licked her ear then her cheek. Megan giggled and stroked his head.

Derek chuckled and stepped over both of them and moved down the hall to Megan's bedroom. After depositing her things just inside the door, he came back out and went into the kitchen.

Megan came running in with Axle on her heels. "You want some ice, good boy?"

Axle gave a half snort, half whine and went right to the rug in front of the sink. Derek chuckled. The animal was so different with Megan than he was with Derek. When Derek gave Axle ice, or offered, Axle waited until Derek gave him the command to take it from the small rug.

With Megan, he was just a plain, everyday pet. He went to that rug and sat at attention, waiting patiently for his person to bring him his treat. Either action meant he'd been trained well, but the latter behavior was more in line with everyday dogs.

Rayna would say that it was a good thing. Derek would agree. The other K9 officers at the department would definitely agree, too.

He blew out a hard breath, and his stomach felt hollow. Damn, he missed Rayna already. More so, he missed that she wasn't there with him and Megan right now. He grabbed his cell, thinking he should text her—

"Are you ordering the pizza? Can we get all cheese?"

Derek looked up. "Of course. Do you want breadsticks, too?"

"Definitely." Megan came over and put her arms around his waist. "Missed you, Daddy."

Derek wrapped his arms around her shoulders. "Missed you, too, angel."

Okay, so maybe tonight wouldn't have been a good night for Rayna to meet his daughter. Tonight was just for him and Megan to spend time together and catch up. His daughter meeting his girlfriend could wait a few days.

Still, if he'd not chickened out last night, Rayna would know right now where he was, and why he wasn't with her, and why that was important. Instead, she had no freaking clue, and that was because he was an asshole.

Megan tilted her head back to stare up at him. "I'm going to go grab the souvenirs I got for you."

"You do that. I'll order pizza."

She nodded and ran off.

Letting out a sigh, he stared down at the phone and his last text messages with Rayna. *"I love you, too. Call you later."*

"Harrrmmpph." Axle pawed at Derek's pant leg and then sneezed.

"Yeah, partner. I miss her, too. I know. I'm an asshole."

Axle shook his head, his ears flopping with the motion, and then yawned, which was accompanied by a whine, before sitting on his haunches.

Letting out another sigh, he closed the messages window and ordered a pizza.

He'd text Rayna later, after Megan was asleep. Hopefully, Rayna would be asleep, too, and then he wouldn't have to dig his grave deeper.

God knew, it was deep enough already.

* * * *

Rayna popped a frozen burrito into the microwave. Then she went to the fridge and pulled out something to drink and set a fork and knife on the table. The micro beeped, and she grabbed the no longer frozen and definitely oozing hot meal from inside and placed it on the table. "The official meal of the single woman." She sighed. "Dinner is served."

Well now, wasn't this sad and depressing. Plus, she wasn't technically single anymore. Worse, based on the ball of sullen feelings caught in Rayna's chest, this specific meal reminded her of a life she thought was long gone.

It sure felt like it'd been at least a year since she'd spent a Saturday night alone, or was single, but that was nowhere near the truth. It'd really only been six weeks. Six weeks and she'd already gotten used to him, them... the time they spent together, and everything in between.

"This sucks." Rayna cut into her burrito and took a bite. Derek was working, at least that's what she figured he was doing. That's what he was always doing whenever he wasn't with her. He didn't go out for "guys night" like other guys did. The man didn't spend nights away from her just to "get some space."

They were always together.

So, he had to be working, right? Though he hadn't said, and she hadn't asked. A sliver of fear pierced Rayna's heart. What if he was with another wom—

"No. Nope. Do not go there, lady! Just don't." Rayna steeled her emotions and took another bite of her food. He's working. No reason to get herself all in a lather for no reason.

Derek Hansen was in love with her. He'd told her, and he'd shown her. Countless times and in countless ways. He'd proven over the past six weeks that she was where he wanted to be. The *only* place he wanted to be.

Rayna swallowed and took a drink of her soda.

But what if?

Ugh...this was going to be a long night.

Chapter 22

Derek climbed into Rayna's bed and curled up against her warm body. She was sound asleep, her breathing deep and even.

It was nearly one a.m. He'd gotten stuck late at work dealing with filing lengthy reports after the entertaining arrests made that night. One small traffic violation between two people turned into one drunk driver and the other, a dude with a shit-ton of methamphetamines in his possession, who decided to run. Morons—all innocent until proven guilty, of course.

Axle let out a groan as he settled on the dog bed at the side of Rayna's bed. Derek lifted his head off the pillow to catch a glimpse of his partner and then lay back down. Since Derek stayed at her place more than they were at his, he'd started bringing Axle over here after work, probably about three weeks ago, because Rayna didn't think it was fair to leave the animal at home alone.

She'd also bought Axle the pet bed. Plus dishes for food and water, and even toys. Yeah, the woman was a vet, but still. Derek pressed his nose into her hair and drew the scent of her into his lungs. The love and care she showed Axle always had Derek's heart melting into a complete pile of goo.

He smoothed his hand down her arm, to her waist, then around to her stomach. Snugging her back closer to his front, he closed his eyes. She let out a little sigh and then a moan, but didn't wake, only settled against him more.

Warm, soft and everything he ever wanted.

He should wake her up and tell her. Tell her about Megan. Tell her that he never meant to keep something so important from her, that he'd tried several times to find the right time, but it never seemed to come.

He needed to tell her that he didn't want to lose her. That he never wanted to hurt her. That she and his daughter were the two most important women in his life. Derek wanted to tell her how she was the only woman he'd ever been in love with, and would ever be in love with.

He needed to tell Rayna that he was sorry that he'd let her down, and that he'd never do it again.

With another moan, Rayna shifted and turned over to face him. Her small hand landed on his shoulder, then smoothed down to his chest, before reversing back up to his neck. He felt her lips graze his collarbone. "Mmm. Hi, sweetheart."

Her words were a sleepy whisper spreading through him like a warm breeze. Derek pressed his hand to her lower back and held her closer. Keeping his voice low, he pressed his lips to the top of her head. "Hi."

"You okay?" Her hand still cupping the side of his neck, she stroked his jawline with her thumb.

"Yeah, Doc. I'm good. Just ran late tonight."

She nodded. "Mmkay. Missed you." She pressed a warm kiss to his collarbone.

He cupped the back of her head. "Missed you, too, baby."

"Is Axle here, too?"

"Yeah." He stroked her hair. Now was his chance. He needed to take it. *Tell her, you idiot! Just...say you have to talk. That it's important. She deserves to know right now.* "Go back to sleep, Doc. You have to be up in a few hours."

She smoothed her hand from his neck, down his chest to his side. "Love you."

Derek pressed his lips to the top of her head and let out another sigh. "I love you, too, Doc."

Fuck, he was a coward.

Chapter 23

"You look awesome!" Stephanie held her arms wide for a hug.

"Thank you. So do you." With a smile, Derek hugged his ex and then stepped back and motioned to the bench beside them. "Want to sit?"

"Sitting is good. You'd think I wouldn't want to after being in an RV on my ass damn near all summer, but yeah, totally do." She laughed and sat.

Derek did the same. "Well, I can't say I'm any different. I'm in a patrol car all day, so you know I'm on my ass."

"Yeah, but you're way better at going to the gym than I am." She brushed some lint off her pants.

"You're chasing Hannah around. That should count, right?" He stared out at the empty playground in the center of the neighborhood where he and his ex both lived.

"This is true." She laughed.

"They both get off on their first day okay? Thanks for the pic of Megan. She looked all sweet in her little skirt and T-shirt."

"Well, you know she's a fifth grader now. Top of the heap in grade school. The skirt was a must."

He laughed. "Sorry I wasn't there. We're going to have a little diva next year."

"Lordy, I hope not. But maybe."

"Hannah started first grade, right?"

Stephanie blew out a breath. "Oh yeah, and of course I cried when she and Megan got on the school bus together."

He gave her shoulder a nudge with his own. "Sap. But don't worry. I won't tell."

"So kind of you." She nudged back.

"Too many people." He chuckled.

She laughed and slapped his arm. "Okay, so tell me how your summer went? Did you enjoy the time off?"

Derek looked back at the woman who was the mother of his child. His once college sweetheart, who he loved, still did love, but was never *in love* with. She was his best friend all four years. But they were never meant to be a couple. "I met someone."

Stephanie's eyes went wide, and she covered her mouth with both hands. After letting out a muffled squeal, she pulled her hands away and pulled him into another hug. "Oh my God, Derek! That's awesome! That's incredible!" Stephanie tipped her head back and gave him a chaste, but very enthusiastic, kiss on the corner of his mouth.

For certain, she'd meant for it to land on his cheek, but because Stephanie was so jazzed for him, she'd almost gotten his lips. Weird, but not a big deal.

"Ooh, shit!" Stephanie laughed. "Sorry. I got excited. And eww, that felt weird, huh?"

Derek laughed and patted her back. "I know. No biggie, Steph."

With her arms still around his neck, her smile faded and her expression changed. "Wait...it's serious with this woman, right?"

"Would I be telling you if it wasn't?"

She blew out a breath, gave him another squeeze, then let him go. "Oh, thank God. Of course not. I just wanted to check, because I got so excited and I didn't want to be all excited if she was just a fling. Not that there's anything wrong with a fling."

"It's all good, Steph. I know it's because you want me to be happy."

"Well, I do! It's been years for you, Derek. You deserve someone who loves you to the bottom of your soul. I found it. You should find it, too."

"Love you, too, Steph."

Her face softened. "This is why we make such good co-parents."

"Best in the whole district, I'm guessing."

"Hell, likely the whole state." She giggled and grabbed his forearm. "Did you tell Meggie yet?"

"No." He shook his head. "Figured I'd tell you first."

"Derek Hansen, you are still one of the greatest men I know. And you know that list is short." She smiled. "So, what's she like? What's her name?"

"Thanks. She's...she's everything, Steph. Her name is Rayna Michaels. She's our age. Smart, funny, sweet. She can come off as conservative, but really it's just that she's...I don't know, she's just easygoing. Not a lot of fuss."

Steph smiled, her eyes alight with happiness. "She sounds wonderful. What does she do?"

"She's a veterinarian. Axle's vet, actually."

"Oh! I remember you talking about her. Good for you! How long has it been?"

"Pretty much the whole summer. About six weeks I guess."

Stephanie patted his forearm. "Aw, I'm so happy for you, Derek. Is she excited to meet Megan?"

Derek cringed. "Well, that's the thing. I haven't told her about Megan yet."

"What, why?" Stephanie frowned.

"It's a long story. But, the short version is at first I wanted to be sure about her, you know?"

"Of course."

He nodded. "Then, she had some issues about me being a cop, you know the rep some have. But then, it just...shit. It never seemed like the right time, and now it's like I'm hiding something."

"Well, you kind of are. A big something. When are you going to tell her?"

"Tonight. I'll see her after my shift. But I'm scared shitless she's going to be furious."

Stephanie linked her hand with his. "It's going to be okay. If she cares for you, she might be mad, but she'll get over it."

Grateful for her support, Derek squeezed his ex's hand. "I hope so, Steph. I don't want to lose her."

"That's crazy thinking. Don't even let your head go there. Just tell her the truth. She'll see it in your eyes."

He nodded and stared back out at the park. "I hope you're right."

"I'm always right, Derek." Stephanie grinned.

"Except when you're wrong." He laughed. "I'll give you a call later and we can talk about schedules, cool?"

"Sounds good to me. I'll be enjoying my day with no babies in the house. I think Steven is coming home for lunch." She wagged her brows.

Derek got to his feet and held his hand out to her. Stephanie stood, and he gave her a hug. "Careful, too much afternoon delight and you'll have another bun in that oven of yours."

She slapped his arm again. "Bite your tongue!"

Derek laughed. "Yes, ma'am."

Stephanie brushed her blond hair off her shoulders. "Talk to you later."

"Definitely." Derek smiled.

Stephanie stepped away and made her way to her car. He headed across the field. Since the park was right around the corner from his home, he'd walked rather than driven. In a matter of minutes he was at his front door.

After a shower, he'd get ready for his shift and stop by the clinic to steal a kiss from Rayna before heading into work. It was almost ten in the morning already, and Rayna would be neck-deep in appointments, but he wanted to shoot her a quick text, letting her know she was on his mind.

Derek chuckled. Hell, when wasn't she on his mind?

Making his way to his bedroom, he moved to his nightstand, where he'd left the phone to charge. Unlocking it, he saw a text notification from Rayna. Perfect.

He opened the message icon and froze.

Doc Rayna: *This is over, I never ever want to hear from you again! I was a fool for believing anything you said to me, Derek Hansen, including that you loved me. You're no different from my father, or any other cop who doesn't know the meaning of the word faithful! Apparently, blondes are more your style. Have a good life with the blonde, whoever she might be.*

What? What blonde? What the hell was Rayna talking about?

Unless... No. That wasn't possible. Regardless, all the air left Derek's lungs, and his knees gave out. As if the world went into slow motion, he slipped down, landing on his ass on his mattress. An ache began behind his eyes as Derek read the message again. *Apparently, blondes are more your style.*

Fuuuuuck!

* * * *

Rayna's hands shook as if she had electricity running through them, and she could barely see the road, blinded by the endless tears flowing from her eyes as she drove to Tish's house.

Her best friend was at work, but there was no way Rayna was going home. Not for several hours anyway.

Oh God, why?

Why had this happened?

How could she have been so stupid!

When Rayna pulled into Tish's driveway, she left the engine running, grabbed Tish's extra house key from her glove box, and let herself in the front door. Once inside, Rayna moved through the house to the laundry room, opened the garage door and then pulled her car in.

Gathering her things, she went back inside and dropped everything onto the counter in the kitchen. After pulling a tissue from the box, Rayna got herself under as much control as she could, then called the clinic and asked Billy to cancel the rest of her appointments for the day...telling him she'd come down with a sudden case of the stomach flu.

God knew she felt like vomiting. Moving into Tish's living room, Rayna took a seat on the couch, and then she sent a text to Derek.

The one ending their sham of a relationship.

Maybe a text was a coward's way out, but there was no way she was calling him directly; she didn't want to hear his voice. And she sure as heck didn't want to see him. He'd likely come to her house, which was why she went to Tish's instead.

Even if he came there looking for her, he couldn't get in. He didn't have a house key, or the garage code. Or anything.

Rayna set her phone down and covered her face with her hands. Tears welled up once more, hard and fast, and then spilled, coating her cheeks and the palms of her hands. How could he have done this to her?

Falling to her side on the sofa, she curled around her knees, and wept.

Her phone rang, and she wiped her eyes, and then grabbed it. Seeing it was Derek, she silenced it. There was nothing to say. Nothing to talk about.

It rang again, and she silenced it once more. Rayna squeezed her eyes closed and held her phone to her chest. No. Definitely nothing he could say to make this better. As she figured, her cell chimed with a text. Knowing it was likely from him, Rayna looked at the screen.

Derek Hansen: *Babe, I don't even know what you are talking about. Please call me?*

Ugh! Such a liar! *Babe...* He was gutting her. Of course he didn't know what she was talking about. As if *she* was crazy, and her eyes had imagined seeing what she saw. If only that were possible.

Eyes don't lie. People do.

Fine, he didn't know what she was talking about? She was more than delighted to fill him in.

Rayna: *I saw you at the park with the blonde, Derek. Don't bother denying it. I saw you kiss. I saw your arms around her. I saw everything. Don't call me. Don't text back either. This is the last response you're ever going to get from me. This is over!*

Derek Hansen: *Holy shit, Rayna, please? Babe, I can explain. It's not what it looked like. Please let me explain?*

Bile filled the back of her throat, the bitter taste making her gag. She covered her mouth with her hand and drew in a breath through her nose. Good grief, he sounded just like her father every time he tried to get out of being caught by Rayna's mother. She *was* definitely going to get sick if she read another word from him.

Unable to handle anything more from him, she shut off her phone and set it on the coffee table. Pulling a pillow against her chest, Rayna closed her eyes and tried to forget she'd ever met a man named Derek Hansen.

A man she'd stupidly fallen in love with.

A man she thought loved her.

God, she was a fool.

Chapter 24

"Rayna, please call me back? Please?" With his stomach in a knot and an ache in his chest, Derek disconnected the call and paced in his bedroom. He was absolutely beside himself with fear, confusion and frustration.

What the hell just happened? The obvious answer was that Rayna had seen him with Stephanie at the park, but how? Derek blew out a breath. Bottom line, how Rayna knew didn't really matter. As far as she was concerned, he was guilty.

He just wasn't guilty of what she thought he was.

He tried calling again, but this time the call went straight to voicemail. Fuck! She'd either shut the damn thing off or blocked him. Neither were a choice he wanted to face. He glanced at the clock. Ten thirty... Derek ran his palm over his head and then, closing his eyes, he pinched the bridge of his nose.

He needed to report in for duty by noon, but how the fuck was he supposed to work like this? Goddammit! If he could only get her on the phone for five minutes, then he could explain.

He pulled up the number to her vet clinic and hit the Call Contact button.

"Hello, Family Animal Clinic. This is Billy, how can I help you today?"

"Billy, it's Derek Hansen, is Rayna busy?"

"Hey, Derek! Always so good to hear from you."

Derek drew in a breath, trying for all he was worth to find a shred of patience left in him. "Thanks. Is she busy?"

"No sir. She was here earlier, but then she got sick. Guess she didn't have a chance to call you yet. Poor thing."

"No, no she hadn't called me to tell me. Thanks, Billy. I'll call her cell."

"Okay. Tell her we're all thinking of her."

"Will do." Derek disconnected.

Screw this, if she could call in sick, then so could he. Considering his state of mind, there was no way work was a good idea anyway. He was way too distracted, and that's how people, namely him, could get hurt. Heading back out to the kitchen, he put in a call to the station, and for the first time ever in his law enforcement career, he took a sick day—without actually being sick.

Calling Axle to his side, he locked up the house and headed out to his truck. If she wouldn't talk to him on the phone, he was going to get her to talk face to face.

One way or another.

* * * *

"Rayna, honey, wake up."

Rayna heard Tish's voice in the distance but felt like she was a million miles away from her friend.

"Hey, are you okay?"

Rayna felt her shoulder shaking side to side.

"Rayna?"

Rayna frowned, her limbs heavy like she was stuck in mud. Drawing in a deep breath, she cringed at the ache in her chest and squeezed her eyes closed tighter as she let out a whimper.

"Rayna! What's wrong?"

Jolted by Tish's loud voice, Rayna finally opened her eyes. The room was dim, thank goodness, because her head was pounding like there was a jackhammer going to town on her brain like it was a street corner in need of repair.

She looked up at Tish, and promptly started to cry.

Tish dropped down on her knees beside the couch and pulled Rayna into a hug. "Oh my God, honey, what happened?"

"*I caught Derek with another womannnnn!*" It was all Rayna could get out through heavy sobs. But it wasn't like she needed to say anything else.

"Oh my God...honey." Tish rocked from side to side, rubbing Rayna's back. "I'm so going to kick his ass!"

"*Nooo donnn't.*" Rayna sniffled, and another wave of tears hit her. "It's *mm...mmy own faulllt.*"

Tish pulled away. "The fuck it is! It's his damn fault, Rayna. Not yours." She wiped Rayna's wet cheek, and then Tish's eyes went soft, her brows drawing together. "Honey, I'm so sorry." Tish pulled her into another hug. "So, so sorry."

Rayna sniffled and held onto her friend, trying for all she was worth to get herself under control. "*Meee too.*"

After giving Rayna another squeeze, Tish got to her feet. "Let me grab you some tissues, and then I'll make you some tea."

"Mmmkay." Rayna nodded, sniffling as she wiped her cheeks. "Sorry for coming here. But I didn't want to go home. I'm sure he already went there trying to talk to me."

"Honey, you know you can come here anytime you want. Mi casa es su casa." Tish handed her the tissues. "Tea coming right up."

Rayna took the box, grabbed a fresh sheet and blew her nose. She lay back down, trying to navigate the minefield of emotions riddling her brain. Anger beat through her veins—anger at him and at herself. And a thick block of hurt filled her heart. More hurt than she'd ever felt in her life.

After a little while, Tish was back, with two mugs of tea. She handed one to Rayna then sat on the sofa beside her. That was it. Rayna's best friend didn't say anything else, just stayed next to her. Rayna sipped her tea, and when the occasional tear slipped down her cheek, she swiped it away.

Sometimes, when a heart is broken, there isn't anything to say. Maybe not at first. Maybe not even after a little while. Maybe not ever.

And sometimes that was enough.

Chapter 25

Derek woke with a jolt to the sound of the garage door opening. Sitting up, he realized, thanks to the bright sun shining in the windows, that it was the next day.

Glancing at his watch, he cringed and rubbed his eyes. Six forty a.m. He'd fallen asleep on Rayna's couch, waiting for her. Obviously, she'd never come home.

Axle trotted toward the laundry room door and took a seat in front of it, waiting for her to enter. Derek's truck was in the driveway, so likely she was either trying to prepare herself for having to see him, or she was calling the cops.

He hoped for the former. Not that he wanted her in a place where she needed to brace herself to see him, but he'd prefer that to having to explain to the local PD, which was not the one he worked for, that he hadn't entered her house illegally.

Derek got to his feet but stayed by the sofa. She wasn't the only one who had to brace for how this was going to go. When the door opened, Axle greeted her, all floppy ears and wagging tail.

Immediately, Rayna cast Derek a look filled with so much ice, he felt the cold all the way across the room. But then, taking her gaze from his, she bent and stroked her palm over Axle's head. "Good boy. Go lay down."

Derek shoved his hands in his front pockets. "Rayna, please can we talk?"

Ignoring him, she moved around Axle and into the kitchen and set her things down. Then, still saying nothing, she proceeded down the hall to her bedroom. Derek wanted to follow, but then thought better of it.

Instead, he headed for the kitchen and started a pot of coffee. Twenty minutes later, Rayna emerged from her bedroom. Freshly showered, no makeup, hair pulled up in a ponytail and a pair of medical scrubs on.

Derek swallowed the lump in his throat.

His Doc.

As beautiful as she'd ever been.

He took one step to the side as she approached the counter where the coffee pot sat. He'd set out a mug for her, and had it prepped—the cream and three Splenda (even though she'd always said two) waiting inside it.

She filled the vessel with coffee, stirred it, rinsed the spoon, set it aside and raised the mug to her lips. She did all of this without saying a word or sparing him even a glance. The vibe radiating off of her in bitter cold waves was a clear: "DO NOT ENTER."

Derek felt it. Every bit of it. All over his body. But he wasn't about to let that stop him. This was it. He had one shot at explaining. One shot to do it face to face.

After this, if she didn't forgive him, he was quite sure she'd change the code to the garage and his access to her would be cut off. Done deal. Thanks for playing.

"I know you don't want to see me, and I know you don't want to talk to me."

She stood in silence, staring out the window behind the kitchen sink, and sipped her coffee.

"That's okay, I understand. You don't have to talk. You don't have to look at me. All you have to do is listen. That's all I'm asking for. And when I've said what I need to say, if you want me to go, I'll go."

She blinked and took another sip of her coffee.

Derek took a deep breath, knowing he needed to start talking, but not wanting to, because once he did and finished explaining, his fate, their fate, would be decided. The reality that she might not forgive him, or understand, had terror spilling into his veins and his heart galloping faster than any horse on the planet.

He swallowed, looked down at the floor, then back to her. Another breath in, and then out. "I have a daughter."

Rayna flinched, but only barely. He paused, but when she said nothing, he continued. "She's ten years old. Her name is Megan Rose, and she's the light of my life." He cleared his throat. "The blonde you saw me with is her mother, Stephanie, my ex-wife."

Rayna closed her eyes and, after a few moments, opened them again, only to stare out the window. Raising her cup to her lips, her hands were shaking.

Swallowing, he went on. "Stephanie and I were college sweethearts. Just kids. Irresponsible ones, and she got pregnant. Call me stupid or chivalric, but I did the right thing and married her. This all happened right as we graduated college, and then I went straight into the Marine Corps.

"But we knew, even before Megan was born, that we made better friends than husband and wife. What I'm trying to say is that we weren't in love. I loved her, she loved me, yes, but we were never *in love*.

"Megan was born, and we stayed together a little longer, but then divorced. She came back here to the Valley with Megan, and when I finished my stint in the service, I came back and applied for the police department.

"We're friends. We co-parent our daughter. Steph is remarried and has been for the last eight years. Her husband Steven is an awesome guy. He's a great stepfather to my daughter. They have a daughter together, Hannah. She's six and adorable. Next to Jeff, Stephanie is my best friend, hell, I look at her now like she's a sister."

He started to reach for her but stopped himself. "You have to believe me when I tell you, Doc...what you saw on the bench was nothing more than a platonic kiss meant for my cheek that was poorly aimed. That's it. I was telling her about you, and she got so excited for me she reacted by throwing her arms around me and attempting to kiss my cheek." He shook his head and pinched the bridge of his nose. God, was she really not going to say *anything* to him?

Swallowing down the emotion that the reality of the thought caused, he steeled himself and went on. "I was afraid to tell you about Megan, and about Stephanie. Which sounds lame, I know, but it's one hundred percent true. When we were first together, I waited to tell you. Naturally. There's nothing wrong with that. But after a few weeks, things were progressing with us and I wanted to tell you. I planned to tell you on our way to Prescott, but I was nervous, you know?" He raised a hand in the air, then let it fall. "What if you didn't like kids, or I don't know, what if you didn't want to deal with a guy who had a kid and an ex-wife. Plus, to be honest, the way you reacted that night we ran into that ridiculous woman, Stacie, at the Dry Desert Brewery, I was worried that you wouldn't take kindly to me having an ex-wife."

Staying silent, Rayna took another sip of her coffee. Jesus, she was like a block wall, and aside from the two flinches when he started talking, she was giving him zero emotion. None at all.

Derek cleared his throat again. "You probably remember, we talked about kids on the drive and you said you never wanted them. Or that you hadn't thought about them in your life, that it had always been about your career for you. And, suddenly, I couldn't tell you. How the hell could I tell you? But I knew I had to. I mean at some point, if we were going to have this relationship, which I wanted to have, which I still want to have, I had to tell you I had a daughter."

She blinked and looked down at her cup.

Sighing through his nose, Derek ran his hand along the back of his neck. "So, I was going to tell you on the way home that weekend, but then you shared with me about your father and why you had issues with cops. All the shit he put you and your mother through, and Jesus, Doc, I couldn't tell you then. You opened up, and I didn't want to take that away from you. Plus, an ex-wife? For fuck's sake, there was just no way you would be okay with that. I just knew it."

Unable to stand still any longer, he stepped away from the counter and started pacing behind her. "But then more time passed. And the more time that went by, the harder it became. Before I knew it, it was a secret I was keeping." He stopped and stared at her back. "I never wanted to keep any secrets from you, Rayna. But there it was. A huge fucking secret. And fuck if I knew how to get myself out of the mess I'd unintentionally gotten into. I didn't know how to tell you, and I was terrified you'd either leave me because I'd kept this secret, which never should've been a secret, or you'd leave me because I kept the secret *and* I had a kid and an ex-wife that you didn't want to deal with."

He stopped. "But, Doc, I'm telling you, what you saw on the bench... it was innocent. There's been no one else for me since I laid eyes on you over six months ago. My only crime is not telling you about Megan and my ex. That's it." He moved back to her side and looked at her profile. "That's everything. Now you know everything."

Minutes passed, felt like hours, but it wasn't. After a while longer, she took the last sip of her coffee, rinsed the cup in the sink and put it in the dishwasher. She wiped her hands on the dish towel, folded it, set it down by the sink and then turned and looked at him.

Feeling like he was going to bust out of his skin, Derek held himself still as she stared at him. She swallowed, her throat bobbing as she did. "Thank you for telling me. I need to go to work now, and I need you to leave and never come back."

Derek's heart exploded in his chest, and his hands trembled. That was it? Just...*I need you to leave. Never come back...* "Rayna..." Her name came out of him so threadbare, he barely heard it himself. He cleared his throat. "Rayna, please..."

She moved around him, grabbed her purse from the counter and stood by the laundry room door.

Waiting.

She was waiting for him to go.

Defeat spilled into his gut and spread through his limbs. So much defeat he felt like he was moving through molasses. Derek drew in a breath and walked to the door where she stood. Axle was already there, and she had bent and pressed her lips to the dog's head.

A lump filled Derek's airway, and his chest tightened with an ache he'd never in his life experienced. He looked at her, studied her, trying to memorize everything about her, everything he'd wanted to call his own. Rayna Michaels was the love of his life, and he had to let her go.

When he could take no more, but knew he'd never get enough, Derek walked out.

Chapter 26

"We're going out this weekend."

Rayna sighed and switched the phone to her other ear. "No, not this weekend, Tish."

"Rayna, come on! You need to get out of the house and out of this funk."

"I have been out of the house. I just got home from the clinic."

Tish groaned. "That doesn't count."

"It counts for me. Besides, I have to work this weekend."

"You work every weekend. I thought you were hiring another vet?"

Rayna sorted through the pile of mail on the kitchen counter. "I did. She starts next week."

"That's great! I'm really proud of you."

Rayna nodded. She didn't feel any pride; actually she felt anxiety. She'd only survived the last four weeks since breaking up with the liar because she'd been working so much. Now she was going to have time on her hands, and the idea of that had fear blazing up and down her spine on a regular basis. No, pride was definitely not what she was feeling, but Tish didn't need to know that. "Thanks."

"Okay, so we won't go out this weekend. We can do that next weekend. But, we should at least go get toes done and have lunch on Sunday."

"Fine. Toes and lunch on Sunday." Rayna sighed. She'd cancel on Tish by the time Sunday rolled around, but her best friend didn't need to know that either.

"Yay! Perfect. I'll call you later, okay?"

"You don't need to call me later. I'm fine. I'm going to make some dinner, watch some Netflix and then go to bed."

Tish laughed. "Yeah, definitely calling you later."

"Tish—"

"Bye!"

Rayna pulled the phone away from her ear and double-checked to be sure Tish actually did hang up. Rayna sighed again. Whatever. She'd just *accidentally* leave her phone in her bedroom while she watched television later. Tish would call, but Rayna really didn't want to talk more.

This had become the new norm. Tish worrying. Rayna avoiding her. Her best friend thought Rayna should give Derek a second chance. Rayna didn't agree. Second chances were never a good idea.

Fool me once, shame on you, fool me twice...

Yeah, that was a big no thanks. Rayna's mother had given Rayna's dad a million "second chances," and he exploited every single one of them. And not by being a good and faithful husband, but more as another chance to do or screw anyone he wanted, knowing his poor little wife would just forgive him anyway.

No way was Rayna going to be anyone's poor little wife. She gasped, letting out a little whimper, and pressed her hand to her mouth.

Wife...

The minute the thought passed through her mind, a piercing ache hit her chest. She'd never be Derek's wife. Besides, he'd already had one of those once. But the awful truth was, she had wanted to be his wife. She really had.

Rayna moved to her bedroom and lay on her bed. Good grief, she missed him. So much that at times it was overwhelming. Was it ever going to stop hurting? Was she ever going to stop thinking about him? And she missed Axle too.

Wasn't four weeks enough for a broken heart to heal?

Apparently not, because Rayna's heart was as raw and splintered today as it'd been the day she saw him with his ex. But then, less than twenty-four hours later, her heart shattered into a zillion pieces when he confessed to not trusting her enough to tell her about his daughter, and worse, thinking she wouldn't understand.

Who did he think she was? Some sort of cold-hearted, closed off, emotionally void person?

She wasn't.

She never had been.

Rayna had fallen hopelessly in love with him, given him her heart, and he'd been betraying her in the worst way. Worse than if he'd actually cheated on her. She never thought anything could be worse than cheating, but what Derek had done to her felt so much worse.

He'd shut her out, assuming something he had no clue about. He kept a huge part of his life from her, and he'd done it willingly. She couldn't forgive him for that, or ever trust him again.

She'd wanted kids. She'd wanted marriage.

And she'd been foolish enough to want them with Derek. Sadly, now she knew that would never happen. Other people got to have those things. Other people got to have the dream.

Rayna got to be alone, and she'd just have to be okay with that.

* * * *

With a heavy dose of self-pity pumping through his veins, Derek sat in his dark living room after his shift. There was a beer in his hands that he wasn't drinking. He hadn't turned the television on...because why bother? It wasn't like he'd watch it, if it were.

His faithful partner was lying on the floor by Derek's feet. Axle was so in tune to Derek's emotional state, he wouldn't leave Derek's side.

Derek was in hell, and there appeared to be no end in sight to the emotional burn he was living with. It'd been four weeks since he walked away from the love of his life. Four fucking weeks of misery, loneliness and regret. As a result, life had become a never-ending hell of: get up, shower, eat, work, sleep...rinse, repeat. The only variation and bright spot being the times Megan was with him.

There was no one to blame but himself. He'd fucked up, end of story. In hindsight, he should've just told Rayna about his daughter on their first date. Or hell, even before the first date. Maybe if he'd told her straight out, then they'd still be together. Either that or she would've never agreed to go on the date to begin with. The former was preferable, but truth was, he had no way of knowing what would've happened.

He only knew what did happen, and what had happened sucked. Derek took a sip of his beer, which had now definitely gone warm. Setting it on the end table, he linked his hands behind his head and closed his eyes.

Hindsight wasn't twenty-twenty, like people wanted to pretend it was. Hindsight was a fucking illusion.

There'd been so many things Derek had wanted to tell her. When he'd walked away, he'd wanted to beg, plead and stay there with her until she understood. But for obvious reasons, he hadn't.

If he had a chance to do it over again, he'd be sure to tell her how much he loved her, how much he was in love with her, and that, yes, he wanted more kids and he also wanted to get married again.

More importantly, he wanted all that with her.

Chapter 27

Derek pulled up to an intersection and stopped at the red light. Just a few hours into his shift and so far, all was quiet. He was only a couple of miles away from where Rayna's clinic was located, and once he got through this major cross-street he planned to head in the other direction.

Last week he'd stopped cruising past. After four weeks of innocent drive-bys, always praying he'd catch a glimpse of her, Derek figured it was best to stop doing that. Self-torture wasn't his deal. Not normally anyway.

He'd never been a masochist, and he wasn't about to start being one now. Cold turkey was the way to go. Of course, depriving himself was just another form of self-torture. So basically he wasn—

The sound of tires chirping caught his attention, and Derek looked toward the sound to see the car two lanes over blow right through the red light. "What in the holy fuck!"

Flipping on his red and blues and siren, Derek cut the wheel, pulled around a car that was stopped in front of him, and checked the cross intersection both ways before pulling through and going after the car.

Dammit! He needed to pay better attention. Six weeks he'd been without her, which meant for the past six weeks he'd been distracted. Distracted was not something there was room for in his line of work.

Not even a half a mile later, he caught up to the car. Unsure if the asshole was going to comply, Derek was shocked when the car slowed and then signaled before making a right into a side street lined with industrial buildings.

He followed, and as the vehicle came to a stop on the side of the road in front of him, Derek pulled up behind it. After reporting in his location via radio and providing the plate number on the car, Derek got out of his patrol car.

Axle was barking his head off, but Derek continued without him. No reason for his partner in the backseat to be involved in a routine traffic stop. The guy appeared to be alone, but Derek wouldn't know for sure until he could see clearly into the vehicle.

With his right hand poised at the butt of his service weapon, he neared the side of the car, scanning the interior through the windows, as well as the driver.

Derek's eyes went wide as the large man scrambled across the front seat, threw open the passenger door and ran.

"*Son of a bitch!*" Derek took off around the front of the guy's car and chased him. "*Stop! Police!*" The suspect ducked around the side of a building, and Derek kept going. The bastard was big, easily over six feet tall and probably around two fifty, so he wasn't fast and, wasting no time, Derek caught up to him. "*Police! I said stop!*"

A second later, the guy tripped over a pile of wooden pallets, and Derek lunged, taking him from a stumble to a hard fall onto the pavement.

They both landed with a grunt, the momentum of the fall causing them to roll over. After righting himself, Derek gripped the man's arm. The guy yanked away, breaking Derek's hold, and attempted to get back on his feet. Lunging for the man, Derek tackled him around the waist, throwing all his weight into the suspect's body.

Somehow the man managed to flip and get Derek in a headlock. "Get off, now!" With a loud grunt, Derek tried to break the guy's hold, but the bastard yanked to his left, taking Derek with him. "*Motherfucker, let go! Stop resisting!*"

Enough of this shit! As Derek tried to get a knee under himself to gain some leverage, he let go of the guy with one hand long enough to hit the remote on his belt to open the back door for Axle.

But that's when things took an entirely different turn.

Still caught in a headlock by the suspect, Derek heard the snarling bark of Axle approaching. The man yanked back, releasing Derek as he did. Suddenly free, Derek rolled to his right, and then rotated to—

POP!

Still on his knees, Derek jerked to the side, and then fell on his ass. *What the fuck was that?* The hot sting in the left side of Derek's neck barely registered, and it took him another second to realize what had just happened.

The suspect got to his feet and started to run again.

Wasting no time, Derek stood, drew his weapon, and at the same time called for backup with his shoulder radio as he took aim on the suspect. *"Stop! Drop the gun! Now!"*

Axle flew past Derek, barking furiously, and then latched onto the suspect's arm, growling and tugging at the man's flesh. The man started screaming and was on his way back down.

POP!

A loud yelp resonated in Derek's ears to the depths of his soul, and he watched in horror as Axle let the guy go, but then lunged for the dude when he started to flee again.

Fuck! *Fuck! Fuuuuck!* With Axle in the fray, the last thing Derek wanted to do was accidentally shoot his partner.

A warm, then cold, wet sensation mingled with the burn in the side of Derek's neck, but he ignored it and took aim once more on the shooter. "Drop your weapon!"

Axle tore into the fucker's arm, growling like a thing of nightmares. The man stumbled back, falling on his ass, and lost hold of his weapon as Axle held on tight. Sirens sounded in the background as other officers got closer to the scene.

Derek holstered his gun and charged forward, taking the man down onto his side. Another hard hit, the wind knocked out of both of them. With Axle's teeth still locked onto the guy's arm, Derek somehow got the man rolled over and then yanked one arm behind his back. "Stop resisting!" Derek shoved a knee in the man's lower back, freed his cuffs and caught the wrist he had hold of. "You shot me, you son of a bitch!" Derek managed to snag the other arm and then secured both hands. "And you shot my partner!"

Axle growled, shaking his head back and forth, teeth still clamped on the moron's arm. The guy let out a loud cry, likely in a lot of pain. But no way Derek was pulling the animal off yet.

The sound of other officers approaching got Derek's attention, and when they made it to him, Derek jumped to his feet and let them relieve him.

Coming around, he took a hold of Axle's choke collar and harness with both hands and pulled hard, and at the same time gave Axle the bite command. Trained to never let go of a suspect, when Axle couldn't breathe any longer due to Derek's hold, only then did he release his bite.

With his heart pounding from adrenaline, Derek moved about ten feet away from the officers now handling the suspect, went to his knees and began examining his partner. There was blood on Axle's fur, but Derek couldn't find where the bullet had entered.

Another officer stepped next to him. "Ambulance is en route for you."
Confused, Derek glanced up at him.

The officer motioned to Derek's neck. "Looks like a flesh wound, but no way to tell without you getting checked out."

Derek touched his fingertips to the side of his neck and winced. "I can wait. I need to get Axle to his vet first."

With concern racing through him, Derek probed gently at the area where the blood was the heaviest. Axle was still all sorts of riled up. Panting, yipping, tongue hanging out, tail flopping side to side. The dog was burning as much adrenaline as Derek was.

"I'll take him, Shirley."

Derek looked up from Axle to see his best friend. Relief blanketed him, making him let out a long sigh...and then a hot poker stuck him in the neck. At least that's what it felt like was happening to him now. "Okay, yeah. Thanks, Jeff. Take him to Rayna." Derek nodded and touched the side of his neck again. "Fucking hell, this stings."

What a goddamn shit show.

* * * *

Rayna stared at her cell phone screen, reading past messages from Derek that she'd yet to erase. She should erase them, but she couldn't bring herself to do it. Not yet. Closing the message window, she opened up her photos.

Resting her forearms on her desk, Rayna held her phone and scrolled through the folder of pictures titled "Us." One of her and Derek in Prescott. Another at the bowling alley, his arms around her. One of just him in her kitchen doing the dishes. Another with him, Axle by his side.

She hadn't stopped missing him. Or the dog. The constant ache in her chest was proof of that. There were days she woke and thought—hoped—maybe that would be the day she'd feel better or didn't think of him. Today was no exception.

Two weeks ago, she still couldn't wrap her mind around the fact that he'd lied, but worse, that he'd thought she wouldn't accept his child. Though, since then, Rayna had started to see it a little differently.

No lie, Tish had a hand in her changed view, but still. Each night in bed, Rayna would sift through her memories of their conversations. Recalling times when she commented about kids, or marriage, or anything that might make her sound like she wouldn't understand him. That she wouldn't accept him as is.

It was bad enough he'd thought she wouldn't forgive him for not telling her, but to think that she wouldn't want to be with him because he had a child had hurt Rayna so deeply she couldn't see around it.

And of course, that had been Tish's exact point: how could Rayna continue to be angry at the man, or not forgive him, when Rayna had reacted in the exact same way he'd feared?

Tish was right, and as Rayna explored the memories of her and Derek, their conversations, Rayna saw exactly how he could've perceived things she said, even off-handed comments, as her *not* being open to what a life with him would mean.

Of course, due to her past cop issues—Rayna groaned and put her phone down—he would definitely be afraid that she wouldn't abide by the kind of close friendship he had with his ex.

Rayna would see it as a threat, but only because she would be afraid to trust him. But she didn't have to see his ex as a threat, and she didn't have to be afraid to trust him. She could choose to be rational and logical. Rayna could choose to be brave, and she could choose to trust. Good grief, she could become friends with his ex, too. Why not?

Except now, it was probably too late. Surely he'd moved on. She hadn't, but she couldn't exactly blame him if he had.

Derek had confessed all to her and bared his soul, and she'd given him nothing but a cold shoulder and a stone-hard stare. She'd been horrible to him, and the memory of the look on his face hadn—

A loud noise followed by yelling echoed from outside her office. Rayna scrambled to her feet and threw open her door. "What's happening?"

Standing in the entryway to the back area was Jeff. Derek's best friend. Which meant... *Oh God, no!*

Rayna's two vet techs, Gina and Patrick, were hovering over a large animal on the metal treatment table in the center of the back area. Andrea, the head tech, was grabbing supplies from the cabinet, pulling down rolls of gauze and IV tubing.

With fear blazing through her veins, Rayna rushed forward. "All right, what do we have?"

She looked down at the dog and immediately realized this wasn't Rio, Jeff's partner, on the table. A cold dread filled her limbs, and Rayna closed her eyes. *God, no...please?*

"Adult male shepherd, gunshot wound," Gina said.

How was this happening? God, this could not be happening! Rayna opened her eyes to see Gina take some gauze from Andrea and press it to the wound on the dog's left shoulder. She glanced at Jeff, hoping for something, anything. He didn't say a word, only gave her a nod and then turned and walked back to the lobby. Apparently he had nothing to share, about Axle...or Derek. And that had her blood running cold.

Drawing in a deep breath, Rayna shoved the pit in her stomach aside and got her head in the game. "Okay, Axle. Easy now." She smoothed the fur on his face and then over his ear. "It's okay, good boy."

Rayna looked at her staff, and Andrea caught her gaze and started prepping Axle's front limb for an IV. Rayna smoothed her hand over the dog's shoulder. "Is there an exit wound?"

"Not that I can find yet." Patrick moved to assist Andrea.

"Keep looking." Rayna snapped on a pair of exam gloves and pressed the end of her stethoscope to the dog's chest, listening for equal breath sounds. Axle sounded good, and his vitals were good, too. He was alert, and of course panting, likely still full of adrenaline. His temperature was elevated, which was to be expected since he'd suffered a trauma.

She had no clue if the bullet had ripped through the animal's chest, tearing into vital organs or not. And since they'd not found an exit wound, there was a good chance the bullet was lodged inside him still.

Andrea finished the IV and hung the bag. "What do you want to do first?"

"He's stable, so—" She blinked and stared down at Axle. Rayna's first instinct was to sedate him and perform surgery, but she didn't want to jump to any conclusions. She needed to stay level-headed. Calm. Decisive. "Okay, let's clip and clean the area. Need to get a better look at the wound before we do anything else."

Andrea moved, getting the clippers, and handed them to Rayna. After turning the device on, Rayna began shaving Axle's thick fur. "Andrea, no pain meds yet, right?"

"Not yet."

Rayna blinked. "Right. Two of hydromorphone IV."

"Yes, Doctor."

Once Andrea had administered the pain meds via intravenous, Rayna leaned over him and inspected the wound. The flesh was lacerated, but there appeared to be no penetrating entrance wound. Thank heavens! "Get me some lidocaine, please." Yes, the pain meds Axle now had on board had relaxed him considerably, but before she probed the tender area, she wanted to numb him there directly.

Gina returned with a needle, and Rayna took it from her. "Hold his head please. He should be fine, but just in case, I don't want him to snap or have to muzzle him."

Gina nodded and moved into position to hold the dog. When the tech was ready, Rayna injected a small amount of lidocaine around the wound.

Axle lay still the whole time, barely moved a muscle. Rayna set the needle aside and bent toward his ear. "Good boy." She pressed her nose to the top of his head. "Such a good boy. You hold still for me, okay?"

Rayna straightened and slowly examined the wound. She traced the deep groove of the laceration, and then pressed gently. Amazing. There was no entrance wound from the bullet, just a flesh wound. A deep one, but still, no entrance. "From what I can see, we've got a flesh wound only." She tipped her head in the other direction. "Patrick, pull that light closer for me?" He did, and Rayna looked closer. "Yes, flesh wound only. He's going to be fine. Get me a suture kit."

"Thank God!" Andrea shook her head and smiled.

Relief blasted through Rayna, and she wiped her forehead with the back of her hand. Without allowing herself a moment to think past the task in front of her, she grabbed the surgical instruments and then with the help of her staff, got to work on taking care of Axle's wound.

Only when she was done would she allow herself to think about why Derek wasn't there with his dog.

And based on that, what her next action would be.

Chapter 28

Agitation and impatience flowed through Derek's veins as he checked his text messages again. He'd been stuck in the ER for far too long and hadn't heard a damn thing from Jeff. They needed to discharge him already.

Yes, there was a bullet wound—technically two wounds, an entrance and an exit—in the side of his neck, a mere few inches to the left of his throat. Which meant he'd be fine. Truly. The damn thing didn't hit anything important, and no vital arteries.

Nothing major was bleeding. So, far as he was concerned, he was good to go. Frankly, he needed to get the fuck out of there so he could find out if Axle was okay too. If Jeff would only text him back, then maybe he'd feel better chilling a little longer and letting the doc stitch him up. If that's what they wanted to do.

Doc...

Derek's head fell back against the pillow. Christ, he missed her. Had Jeff brought Axle to Rayna to be taken care of like Derek had told him to do? He hoped so.

Rayna would take the best care of Axle, and because Axle knew her, he'd be a better patient, too. But either way, Derek knew that she would do everything within her power to ensure his partner was okay. Fucking hell, why hadn't his best friend checked in yet?

In the back of his mind, Derek knew that Axle was okay. He had to be. There was a lot of blood, which had scared the shit out of Derek, but judging by how Axle was acting, the injury was likely minor.

Then again, there was a lot to be said for adrenaline. Hell, Derek had known he'd been shot, but he hadn't felt it. Not until the situation had come to an end and Jeff offered to take Axle to get seen.

No one was dead. Not even the perpetrator. Which was good, because now the asshole would pay for his crime and spend some time behind bars. According to what one of the other officers told Derek, the dude was well familiar with Arizona jails. Apparently, the guy had a warrant for his arrest, which was why he'd run when he saw Derek in the first place.

Derek cleared his throat and stared at the curtain blocking his view from the rest of the people in the ER. Shame though, Derek would've liked to land a few punches on the dude's face, but it was too late for that now.

Shit, it was too late for a lot of things.

Like him and Rayna.

* * * *

Rayna pulled off her gloves, tossing them in the trash, and then walked down the short hallway leading to the lobby of her clinic. Coming to the opening, she scanned the seating area and found Jeff kicked back, feet crossed at the ankle.

Good grief, in uniform, with all his gear on, the guy looked like he was a well-honed machine, all calm, cool, and collected. Probably bossy for sure, but a far cry from the "goofy asshole" Tish liked to refer to him as. Not that Rayna ever agreed with Tish's assessment of the man. Still, he definitely appeared different in uniform, that much Rayna could tell.

Drawing in a breath, she twisted her hands in front of her and dragged her teeth over her bottom lip. She was stalling, distracting herself with mindless thoughts, while another part of her stayed suspended, caught somewhere in a web of utter and total fear. Forcing herself into action, she moved to the edge of the counter. "Where is he?"

Jeff got to his feet. "Banner Desert. He's g—"

That was all she needed to hear. Without another thought, Rayna pivoted and took off for her office. She heard Jeff yelling her name, but she ignored him, grabbed her purse and ran out the back door of the clinic and to her car.

It was nearly four p.m., and rush hour traffic had already begun. But Rayna wasn't about to let that slow her down, or stop her. She cut through a variety of neighborhoods, inching around the traffic in order to get to the hospital as fast as she could. The drive only took her twenty minutes, but it felt more like an hour.

After she pulled in and found a place to park, Rayna turned off the engine and sat in her car. With her hands locked onto her steering wheel, she stared straight ahead, wondering what the heck she was going to say to him.

What if he didn't want to see her?

What if...he hated her now?

Rayna leaned forward and pressed her forehead to the steering wheel. She couldn't bear it if Derek hated her. "A ton of education, but I'm still an idiot!"

She squeezed her eyes shut, trying to force the tears back. Rayna had worked so hard for her dreams, and she'd accomplished them all. However, the dream she'd never allowed herself to entertain, or even acknowledge existed, was one of a man who'd love her from head to toe and down to her soul.

Derek was that man.

Rayna straightened and wiped her eyes. Now she wanted that dream. More than she'd ever wanted anything in her life. And when she had a dream, nothing stood in her way from achieving it.

If he didn't want to see her, she'd just have to find a way to make him see the situation how she saw it. If Derek hated her, then she'd have to make him love her again. Simple as that—though she knew it wouldn't be easy.

Opening her car door, Rayna stepped out and walked into the ER entrance. She approached the admitting window. "Hello—" She waited for the young woman at the counter to look up at her. Rayna smiled. "I need to see Derek Hansen? Officer Hansen. He was brought in a short time ago, I believe."

"One second." The woman typed on her computer and then glanced back up at Rayna. "Are you his wife? We tried to reach you when he first arrived, but it seems your phone number is no longer valid."

Rayna jerked her chin back, unsure how to handle how that question made her feel. Plus, the fact that the woman had to be talking about Stephanie brought on a whole lot of feelings she couldn't sort through. Oh dear. "No, uh, no. I'm his...um, I'm just a friend."

"Ah, sorry, I just assumed."

Rayna drew in a deep breath. "Is he okay? Am I able to go see him?"

"I'm sorry, since you're not his spouse or a relative, I can't let you back there or give you any information. But you can have a seat, if you like, and I'll let you know if I get authorization to let non-family members back there."

Since you're not his spouse...

Good grief, that cut deep.

Razor-sharp heartache filled her chest, and it was all she could do not to clutch at her shirt. Rayna wanted to be the one listed in his file as his emergency contact, and she wanted to be able to say, yes, of course I'm his wife. For Pete's sake, that would be the best thing in the world!

Feeling like she was on autopilot, Rayna nodded and backed away from the window, finding a seat in the corner. There was no way to know if he was critically injured, and the thoughts racing through her mind did nothing but inspire more fear.

Was he stable? Was he fighting for his life? Rayna bit her bottom lip. What if... God what if he died? No! God no! That *was not* happening. Bending forward, she buried her face in her hands. Not knowing what was actually happening was going to drive her mad. The only thing Rayna did know was that she couldn't leave. She'd have to just find a way to cope until someone, anyone, filled her in.

"Girlfriend, are you *always* this dramatic? For realsies, I thought Derek said you were the epitome of calm, cool, collected, and all that jazz."

Rayna couldn't help but smile at the smart-aleck comments Jeff had just made. Of course, getting her to smile was probably his intent all along. Obviously he'd left her clinic after she did and was now here to save her from her voluntary pit of despair. Bless his heart, the man was an angel, and Tish was crazy for not seeing that.

Dropping her hands, she glanced up at him and blew out a harsh breath. "No, I'm never this dramatic. Derek was right, I *am* the epitome of calm, cool, and collected. Not sure about all the jazz, but I think this warrants just a teensy bit of hysteria. Don't you?"

Jeff frowned and tilted his head to the side. "Psshaw, whatever. Maybe if he were dying, but it's just a flesh wound."

Huh? Rayna stared up at him trying to understand how on earth they were clearly not having the same conversation. "I'm talking about Derek, not the dog, Jeff."

He nodded and pursed his lips. "Mmhmm. Yeah, look, don't say I said so, but once upon a time, those two terms were interchangeable. For realsies." He winked. "Anyway, in this case, I was *actually* talking about Derek, *not* the dog. Which, by the way, nice work on the stitches. Seeing as though you ran off all half-hysterical female, I left Axle in the care of your staff. Easier for me to now tend to you."

"Uh, thanks?" She shook her head, trying to sift through all that had just come out of Jeff's mouth. How on earth did he think he was going to tend to her? Ugh, Rayna wasn't sure she had the emotional capacity to go on the journey of deciphering that particular riddle. "Flesh wound?"

Jeff shrugged. "Okay, it's a little more than a flesh wound. But nothing major was hit as the bullet passed in and then out of his neck. Clean exit."

Rayna jumped to her feet and grabbed Jeff's shirt. *"His neck?"*

"Rayna, breathe, okay?" He rubbed her arms. "I already said he's fine."

She shook her head, fear still burning hot in her gut. "No, no you didn't."

Jeff frowned. "I didn't? Huh. Well, let's go see him."

He started to step away, and Rayna tugged on his arm, stopping him. "I can't. I'm not family."

He frowned at her. Again. "Girlfriend, you're his girlfriend. That's family in my book."

This time, Rayna let him lead her toward the check-in window. "Okay, but I bet they won't care what your book says."

He glanced over his shoulder at her. "Shh. I got this."

"Okay." Rayna shrugged and figured it was either going to work and she'd see Derek, or she'd have to wait. Either way, she still wasn't leaving. So Jeff could work any sort of magic he thought he had. Okay, yes, maybe he was a tad bossy like Tish thought.

"Hi there, sweetheart. I'm Officer Jeff Pearl."

Rayna could see from his profile that he'd pasted on a devilish "I know I'm good-looking" smile, and she rolled her eyes. Jeff was too much, but that was why she liked him.

Not missing a beat, he went on. "We're here to see Officer Derek Hansen." He tugged Rayna forward, and then raised the hand he held hers with in the air. "This is Doctor Rayna Michaels. She's Officer Hansen's girlfriend. Can you buzz us in, please?"

The young woman's eyes were wide, but a smile tugged at the corner of her lips. "Of course, Officer. Doctor." She nodded at each of them. "I hadn't realized. Go right in. He's in exam room twelve."

"Thank you, darling." Jeff smiled.

"If you need anything else, feel free to let me know. I'll be here for the next few hours."

"Much appreciated. If I can think of any need I have, I'll be sure to let you know."

Good grief, really? This time it was Rayna's turn to tug on his hand. "Can we go in now, and maybe you flirt later?"

"I'm not flirting. I'm persuading in order to get what we need."

Rayna rolled her eyes and couldn't help but let out a small laugh. "Whatever, Romeo. Can we go?"

"Yes, Doctor Ginger...stealer of souls." He winked before he turned and led them through the now open door to the ER bay.

"Stealer of souls?" Rayna frowned. What a terrible thing to say. Why would Jeff say that? Did he think that she was some sort of crazy or mean person? Without warning Rayna bumped into the back of Jeff. "Geez, what's up? Why are you stopping?"

"My work is done here."

"Huh?"

He jerked his chin up. "We're at our destination."

Rayna looked up where he had indicated, to see the sign with the big number twelve on it. Wow. She glanced back to Jeff. She hadn't even had time to think about what she was going to say, or do, or...anything. He distracted her with his comments, and... Rayna threw her arms around his neck and hugged him. "Thank you."

"Anytime, hon. Now get in there and make this right."

"Yes, sir." She kissed his cheek and stepped away.

Standing in front of the closed curtain, she drew in a breath and slowly released it. After another moment, she pulled the fabric aside and caught Derek's gaze across the room.

Rayna's heart thundered in her chest.

His eyes were as wide as saucers as he looked back at her.

There were no words...not yet.

Instead, they simply stared at each other for what felt like forever. Seeing him again, although she'd have preferred it be under different circumstances, was something she never thought would happen.

Gratitude spilled through her, filling cracks Rayna had been living with for six weeks. Gratitude that he was alive, and that she might now have a chance to make things right. She'd take it—the opportunity—the one and only chance she might get.

And pray she could make something from it.

* * * *

"Holy shit, please tell me Axle is okay?" Terror sped through Derek, making his heart race. It'd taken him a minute or four to get his brain back online after seeing the love of his life standing before him, and then he realized the only reason she would be here was because something must be seriously wrong with his partner.

"Oh!" She raised her hands. "No, Axle is fine. He's totally fine. Just a flesh wound, and he's all stitched up."

Relief chased the terror away, and Derek let out a gush of air as his head fell back on the pillow. Fuck, he was tired. "Thank God. Jesus, thank you, Rayna. Seriously, Doc. Thank you."

"No need for thanks." She waved a hand at him and shook her head. Another moment passed, and she glanced down at her shoes, then back to his eyes. "Is it—" She crossed her arms. "Is it okay if I come in and talk to you for a minute?"

Derek raised his head off the pillow and took her in. As always, her natural beauty and the sincerity in her eyes made his heart melt in his chest. If the woman wanted to talk, then he'd give her that. Hell, Derek would give her anything. "Of course it's okay."

"Thanks." Stepping into the small space, she closed the curtain behind her and moved to the foot of his gurney. After drawing in a deep breath, she nodded. "Thanks."

Saying nothing more, she fidgeted, twisting her hands together, looking everywhere but at him, and biting her bottom lip. Derek closed his eyes—it was too hard to watch, to know, to want.

Unable to stand the silence anymore, he cleared his throat.

Her eyes darted to his.

Derek tilted his head to the side. "Ray—"

"Dere—" Instantly, her cheeks went red, and she looked down. "Sorry, g'head."

Sadness covered him in an ice-cold blanket. "No." He sighed. "Please, you obviously have something to say, so please. Just…just say it."

Whatever it was she was there to tell him, he really wished she'd spit it out. The past six weeks he'd longed to see her face, hear her voice, but now he knew it was the last thing he needed.

To want her so badly and be unable to have her, and now seeing her again? It was pure fucking torture, and she needed to put him out of his misery.

Unable to look at her anymore, he heard her draw in a deep breath. "I owe you a huge apology, Derek."

He flinched but forced himself to look at her once more. With a nod, he rested his head back on the pillow, all his air left his body as he prepped himself for whatever she would say next.

"I should not have treated you the way I did. You didn't deserve it."

"I lied to you. I should've told you about Megan."

"Well, technically you didn't lie." She shrugged. "But I wish you hadn't kept such an important part of your life from me."

"I wish I hadn't, either." Derek swallowed past the lump in his throat. Jesus Christ, this was hell. A special kind of hell made just for him.

"But I'd be lying if I said that I didn't understand why you did. I do."
She blew out a breath. "I mean, don't get me wrong, I hate that you thought
I wouldn't understand, or that I wouldn't want to be with you. That hurts,
because...it's not true."

A tear fell from the corner of one of her eyes, and Derek's heart clenched
as if it was locked in a vise.

She wiped the tear away. "I would understand, I *do* understand, and I
wouldn't have left you. I don't want to leave you now."

"Wha...?" Derek frowned, and stared at her...hard. As if he could
somehow telepathically hit a rewind button to be sure he'd heard her
correctly. However, that wasn't possible, and he needed to know. "I'm
sorry, what did you say?"

She sniffled, another tear fell, and she wiped it away. "I said, I don't
want to leave you, Derek. I don't want us to be over. I miss you." She
covered her face and sniffled again. "Shit! I don't want to cry anymore."

Derek's eyes went wide. "Did you just curse?"

"Yes!" She laughed through a sob. "I'm so frustrated." Dropping her
arms to her sides, she stomped a foot. "And for Pete's sake, are you okay?
You were shot and Axle was hurt. And this is horrible. And they wouldn't
let me in to see you. Derek, I was so scared!"

With a shake of his head, Derek opened his arms. "Come here, Doc."

Moving like someone lit a fire under her ass, Rayna ran over to the
side of the bed and before he had even a moment to take in her sweet tear-
streaked face, she was in his arms. Fuck, she felt good. As good as she
always had, but more so now because he'd missed her so badly.

With her face pressed to the uninjured side of his neck, she sobbed,
and in between sobs, she spoke. "I miss you. More than I've ever missed
anyone." More sobs. "I can't take waking up without you. I can't take not
seeing you or hearing your voice. Or feeling your arms around me."

Derek held her tighter. "You mean like they're around you now."

"Yeah, but they haven't been."

"But they are now."

"Right, but they haven't been." She sat up. "Why are you...oh." She
rolled her eyes.

He grinned and cupped her cheek in his palm. Teasing her was all he
could think to do, mostly because he still wasn't sure where this whole
conversation was going. He had a feeling where, but he wasn't sure. Not
yet anyway. "God, I miss you."

She closed her eyes and pressed her face against his hand, then turned
her head and kissed his palm. "I miss you, too."

Warm pleasure from the touch of her lips bled from his hand through his veins, warming all the places the sadness had made cold. But still... Derek wasn't sure what it meant. He needed her to be clear. "So, I hate to ask and ruin the moment, but...is this some sort of emotional goodbye?"

Her eyes went wide. "What? No! Oh my gosh, do you think I'd come here and cry like a basket case, throw myself into your arms, only to say goodbye?"

"Not exactly like that, no. I'm just trying to make sure I'm reading you right." He shrugged.

"Do I have to get down on my knees and beg?"

A grin tugged at his lips. "Beg for what exactly?"

"Ugh! You're incorrigible, Derek!" She laughed. "You're lucky you're hurt. Otherwise I'd be swatting your chest."

"Well? My chest isn't hurt, so give it your best shot." He grinned. "Answer the question, Ms. Sassy Pants."

Rayna smiled, but then her expression turned serious and her gaze roamed over this face. "I'm sorry I overreacted. I'm also sorry for how I reacted when you explained why you'd not told me about your daughter. Being so cold must've hurt you. I know it hurt me. And I don't want either of us to hurt. Not ever again." Tears filled her eyes again, but she blinked them away. "So, no, it's not a goodbye. I don't want to say goodbye, Derek. Ever."

Sliding his fingers around the back of her neck, he pulled her close, close enough that her lips hovered just a breath away from his. "I don't want to say goodbye either, Doc."

"I love you, Derek. So much it scares me." Rayna closed the small distance between them and pressed her lips to his.

Needing more, Derek threaded his fingers into her hair, then gripped the soft strands. With a moan, she tilted her head to the side and opened for him, welcoming his tongue into the warmth of her mouth, as she always did.

He kissed her back, desperate to show her with his kiss how much he felt for her—how much he wanted her. How much he was in love with her. Overwhelmed, as all of his feelings for her, combined with a lust-fueled need, slammed into his body, Derek broke the kiss and sat up.

He took her face in both hands and drank in her sweet features, her plump lips. Her beauty. "I love you, too, Doc. Don't be scared, baby. I've got you."

"Promise?"

Derek pressed his forehead to hers. "Affirmative, Doc. Affirmative."

Epilogue

Three months later...

Rayna sat on the grade school cafeteria benches with Derek to her left, and sitting to her right, phone raised high on record mode, was Stephanie, Derek's ex-wife, and her husband, Steven. It was the grade school's holiday concert.

Six months ago, if someone had come up to Rayna in her vet clinic and told her that this was where she would end up, that she'd be surrounded by kids she adored, an ex-spouse she'd come to be good friends with, and a man who loved her more than she could ever dream up, she'd have told them they were insane. Yet, here she was.

Hannah, Stephanie and Steven's daughter, had already sung with her class. The six-year-old was so darn adorable, Rayna wanted to squeeze her. Now it was Megan's turn to sing with her fifth grade class. They'd already sung "Jingle Bells," and now they were belting out a fantastic rendition of "Let It Snow."

Stephanie was recording on her phone. Derek was grinning, still in uniform with Axle lying quietly beside him on the tiled floor, also in uniform. Geez, that dog was awesome. All calm, cool, and cop-like when he was supposed to be.

Rayna smiled and looked back up at the stage and focused on Derek's daughter. Megan was precocious and witty and sweet...and so many more amazing things, Rayna couldn't think of enough words to describe them all. Not to say she didn't have her moments that Rayna imagined all ten-year-old girls had, but even those were pretty darn cool.

This was Rayna's life now. And it was awesome.

The fifth graders being the last act, one more song and the concert was over. Everyone stood as kids fanned out into the audience of parents and family members.

Hannah, smiling and missing a front tooth, came over first and headed right to her father. "Daddy! Did you see me?"

Steve picked up his little girl and spun her around. "Best first grader up there!"

"You're going to give that child a big head." Stephanie laughed then kissed Hannah's cheek. "Great job, honey."

There was a tap on Rayna's shoulder, and she turned to find Megan there, grin on her face and two friends on either side of her. She nudged one with her elbow. "Told you she was pretty."

Rayna smiled, and her face grew warm. Geez, this kid. She was just like her dad with the compliments. "That was sweet, Megan. Thank you." Rayna looked at both girls. "I'm Rayna. It's nice to meet you."

Megan grinned, and her friends giggled. "Lissa and Courtney, this is Doc Rayna. She's my dad's girlfriend."

"It's nice to meet you," the girls said in unison before they ran off.

"Bye!" Megan shook her head and rolled her eyes and then focused on Rayna. "Were you guys bored? Did it suck?"

"It most definitely did not suck." Rayna winked at Megan.

"You rocked the house, kiddo." Derek came over and kissed the top of Megan's head. "Where'd your friends go?"

Megan shrugged. "Probably to find their parents. Oh, Mommy! Did you get it on video?"

"I did, yes. Don't worry, I'll text it to you and your dad." Stephanie hugged Megan. "You want a copy, too, Rayna?"

Rayna's eyes went wide, and she gave Stephanie a grin. "Oh, definitely! I mean, grade school concerts are the *best* things to have on my phone when it's slow at the clinic. My staff loves to watch them."

Stephanie busted up laughing. "I bet they do."

"Are we going for pizza?" Megan slipped her hand inside Rayna's palm. "You're coming with us, right?"

Derek took Megan's other hand, bent over, and pressed a kiss to Rayna's temple.

"Of course, sweetheart. I wouldn't miss it. Not for anything." Rayna smiled. She couldn't help but smile, so much her cheeks hurt.

Because, yes, this *really was* her life. And it was better than awesome because it was filled with love, tons of it.

More love than Rayna ever could've wished for.

Meet the Author

Dorothy F. Shaw lives in Arizona where the weather is hot and the sunsets are always beautiful. She spends her days in the corporate world and her nights with her Mac on her lap. Between her ever-open heart, her bright red hair, and her many colorful tattoos, she truly lives and loves in Technicolor! Dorothy welcomes emails at: dorothyfshaw@gmail.com. Or find her online at Facebook.com/AuthorDorothyFShaw and twitter.com/DorothyFShaw Newsletter sign up: http://bit.ly/DFSeNews.

Acknowledgments

A big shout out and thank you to the following awesome men in law enforcement for their dedication and service to the community. And their help with info on my book. Officer Matthew Warbington, Sheriff's officer Andy Tramundanas, and finally my wonderful adopted Dad, retired Connecticut state trooper, Sergeant Robert Gawe.

Special thanks to Dr. Jaimie Schmidt, an awesome vet and owner of Life Care Animal Hospital, for his medical consultation.

Sidda Lee Rain…as always, love you dearly, my friend. I hope I always know you.

And last but not least, to my Facebook, Night Writers group. To those that wrote with me night after night, thank you. You rock!

Printed in the United States
by Baker & Taylor Publisher Services